Falling Forward

JENNIFER COHEN

DEDICATION

To my parents, all I am is because of you. No 'thank you' is grand enough to express my gratitude for the sacrifices and unconditional love you've both given me. Mom, it was your relentless encouragement that propelled me to write this story, further solidifying your lifelong philosophy that mothers are always right.

To my tribe of girls, who helped me find the things I lost. My smile, my hope, my courage. You girls are the real deal and I am batshit grateful for you all.

To my husband, for loving me the way that you do. I will forever be grateful for your unconditional support and endless patience. Living one million lifetimes as your wife would never be enough.

To my son, Lucas. Of all the things I achieve in this lifetime, my greatest accomplishment will always be you.

And for every woman embarrassed or ashamed by the circumstances of her life - you are never alone. We are all just a bit beautifully broken. And that is never something to be ashamed of.

EPIGRAPH

In order to love who you are, you cannot hate the experiences
that shaped you.

Andrea Dykst

Chapter One

pproximately three years to the day she eagerly delivered her marriage vows underneath a hydrangea-covered chuppah at a swanky Miami beachfront hotel, Jess found herself staring down a stack of freshly printed divorce papers that lie atop her kitchen table.

She wiped the sweat off her hands and onto the front of her pressed Theory slacks.

I can do this, Jess whispered to herself with as much feigned confidence as she could muster. Staring down at the crisp, thick manila envelope, she realized that once ripped open, there would be no turning back. With one simple tear, she'd rip open her life, leaving her more vulnerable than ever before.

There are two types of people in this world, Jess' Journalism professor told her freshman year television writing class. *We have the folks who run away from the fire, and those who run right in.*

For nearly her entire life, Jess Klein was a *run right in* type of person. She was never one to ignore a problem, avoid confrontation, or run away from a problem. So, when she found herself staring at the stack of papers and deciding to ignore them altogether, she felt completely out of sorts.

With just momentary deliberation, she walked away from the table, instead allowing the growl of her stomach to direct her to the fridge, even though she lost her appetite weeks ago. As her eyes pointlessly scanned the content inside, her mind raced.

How the hell is this happening? How did I get here?

Just as Jess racked her brain for some sense of understanding how the hell her life seemed to implode as of late, Tiffany - her petite Pomeranian - yelped by her feet.

Her sidekick since junior year of college, Jess couldn't help but wonder - *can dogs feel heartache, too?*

Jess bent down, placing a bone-shaped bowl filled with kibble atop a *My Grandmother Loves Me* placement. A gift from her mom last Hanukkah, Jess lost every argument in which she asked her not to send holiday and birthday gifts for the dog. Sarah was thoughtful and generous, but stubborn as hell.

As Tiffany scarfed down dinner, Jess reached into her nearby backpack, tossing yet another uneaten lunch in the garbage. *Mental note*, she told herself. *Quit making lunches that you never seem to eat.*

She knew she couldn't ignore the papers forever, especially as she caught a glimpse of the envelope from her corner of her eye.

Just *get this shit over with.*

Reaching for her cell sitting on top her granite kitchen counter, Jess knew who she wanted to call. From her first boyfriend in middle school with a mohawk and double ear piercings to the narcist she willingly married, Jess had a less than desirable track record for her choice in men. Yet her taste in girlfriends couldn't be more spot on. She surrounded herself with a girl gang who could recite her three in the morning Denny's order with ease. Women who, when asked to help bury a body, would willingly leave all judgment and rationale behind only to ask, "Where's the shovel?"

And after months of living with her deepest secret yet, tonight felt as good of a time as any to come clean to her best friend.

As she cradled the phone under her ear waiting for Stef to answer, Jess slowly walked into the nearby powder room, staring at her tired reflection in the mirror. Her eyes were puffier than she expected. Her normally round cheeks looked sunken in. Mentally, physically, and emotionally, she sure as hell didn't look like the twenty-six-year-old woman she was. Recent months of sadness and grief took their toll – she officially looked as exhausted as she felt.

How could I fail on such a monumental level? This is worse than years of broken New Year's resolutions to cut carbs. Or my failed promises to call my parents more often. This isn't like missing a deadline at work or being passed up for a promotion. No, this is some epic, life-altering level fuck-up. I made an eternal promise to love, honor and obey. And I managed to keep that promise for less than two years. My iPhone warranty will outlast my marriage, she thought. *How pathetic is that?*

"Hey!" Stef said with a lightness to her voice that failed to lighten Jess' mood. "Isn't it late by you? Everything okay?"

"Not exactly," Jess began. "Chris and I are getting divorced." The matter-of-fact tone she spat it out surprised even her.

"WHAT!" Stef yelled through the phone. Of the few things the two had in common, mincing words was never one of them. "When the hell did this happen? I just talked to you last week!"

"He moved out three months ago," Jess confessed. Her eyes fell from the mirror as she stared at her hand gripping the white porcelain sink.

"Three months ago!" Stef yelled so loudly that Jess had to pull the phone away from her ear. "Why are you only telling me now?"

"Embarrassment? Mortification? Admission of complete and utter failure?" Jess sarcastically asked as she shook her head. "More reasons than you can even imagine."

"I'm sorry, babe. It doesn't even matter. What happened?" The calm, loving way Stef spoke felt like a hug from afar. Despite thousands of miles between them, Jess suddenly felt safer. It felt good to feel loved again.

"Honestly," Jess began, "just the same shit I've been saying for years now. We just kept fighting. But lately it became non-stop, knockdown, drag out fighting. I tried my best to be supportive, I really did. You know how much I tried after his mom died the month before our wedding. You know how much I worked my ass off for that last promotion, figuring a bigger paycheck would put a cease fire on our fights about money. But it was never enough. The impromptu date nights I planned, letting him study uninterrupted for the bar exam, making couple friends when we moved to Atlanta… Stupid me, I thought if we surrounded ourselves with happily married, young couples, he'd somehow want to become a better husband. But it just seemed like nothing I did mattered. He never stopped being so… so… selfish."

Stef stayed quiet just long enough for Jess to wonder if she accidentally hung up. A full-figured and boisterous native Arizonian and Native American, Stef came into Jess' life unexpectedly during her freshman year of college at Arizona

State. Despite a laundry list of differences, their lives were forever changed in one fateful Spanish class when Stef decided to cheat off Jess' midterm exam and Jess decided to let her. The rest, as the two loved to say, was history.

Finally, her voice re-appeared. "Well, I knew he was always an ass, but I just assumed you guys would work your issues out. Was there a final straw that made you guys realize it was too far gone to recover?"

Jess braced herself, as admitting this aloud for the first time was going to sting. "He told me he no longer wanted to have a family."

"Huh?" Stef asked, puzzled. "But you've always wanted kids. For as long as I've known you, you had names picked out. Pinterest boards of nursery décor. You've always been so vocal about wanting a family, I just assumed you two were on the same page."

The grumbles in Jess' stomach returned, and this time she didn't resist. Fixing herself a nightcap of Frosted Mini-Wheats, she fought back tears trying to explain how the heck her marriage unraveled before her very eyes.

"He simply said he changed his mind. After his mom died, he said he no longer saw the point in starting a family if everyone just ends up dead in the end."

"Fuck, that's dark," Stef said.

As she shoveled a spoonful of cereal in her mouth, Jess allowed herself to replay that final conversation from three months prior. It still brought tears to her eyes just as it did back then.

"Tell me about it," she said. "But of course, things had been unraveling for a while, so this was just the final nail in our marital coffin. We were standing right where I am now – barefoot in the kitchen – arguing yet again. Except this time, apologies were meaningless. The damage was done."

Without knowing what to say, Stef offered up about the only thing a best friend really could in a moment like this. "You know I love you, babe. I'm always going to be here for you. Whatever this next chapter looks like, count me in."

Over their years of friendship, they'd been through it all. Stef holding Jess' hair back at four in the morning in a desolate Del Taco parking lot, closing down nightclubs until the sun came up in Las Vegas, and Friday nights spent in their sweatpants, binge-watching original episodes of Sex and the City as they slurped noodles their favorite local, greasy Chinese restaurant. Jess helped Stef survive breakups with boyfriends who turned out to be secretly married, she told her what to tell her parents when Stef failed half of her Sophomore year classes, and she consoled her friend during the unexpected and tragic deaths of some of Stef's closest friends and family. They even shared a twin-sized bed for three weeks when Stef visited Jess during a study abroad semester in London.

Jess set her empty bowl in the sink and smiled for the first time in what felt like months. Her life felt as if it was ripping apart at the seams, and while her life-long dream to start a family seemed to now be a distant memory, one thing was for sure. She still had love in her life. Lots of it, in fact.

"Listen," Jess said, "I just didn't want another night to go by without telling you. Plus, I had to get it out. I'm glad you know now, and I'm going to thank you in advance for all the tears I'll surely cry to you. Just be patient with me, okay?"

Trudging upstairs, Jess walked down the long hallway towards her master bedroom. She cursed that over-sized king bed but smiled when she saw Tiffany curled up on her pillow.

"That's what friends are for," Stef reassured her. "But I do need to ask you one serious question."

"Shoot."

"How are you going to celebrate your birthday next week?" Stef asked.

Oh god. Between Chris moving out and work being so crazy, Jess completely forgot that her birthday was around the corner. The idea of forcing herself to celebrate when all she wanted to do was crawl under the blankets sounded torturous. "I'm on the no plan, plan. That day can come and go for all I'm concerned," Jess said.

"We'll see about that," Stef muttered. "Go get some rest, babe. I love you."

***

Peering at the clock, Jess begrudgingly peeled herself out of bed as the sun peeked through her bedroom windows. Today she was facilitating her first executive media training – faced with the monumental task of captivating, and keeping, the attention of seven corporate executives who would rather be on a golf course than in a room listening to Jess explain the do's and don'ts of fielding burning questions from relentless Journalists. One of the youngest employees at her company by nearly two decades, Jess worked her ass off to earn the respect and authority of her superiors, and despite the stress and demands of her job, she loved every moment of it.

Thirty minutes later, standing in her tailored navy suit, Jess stared out the kitchen window as she waited for her coffee to brew. She took notice of the rundown landscaping out back. The previous owner of her house undoubtedly had a strong affinity towards Asian architecture and design, because despite the home being Southern contemporary, the backyard featured an authentic Zen garden, complete with two Koi ponds and more bonsai trees than Jess could count. The yard had become the bud of many neighborhood jokes, as it starkly contrasted the rest of the homes in their sleepy subdivision.

The smell of freshly brewed coffee reverberated through the kitchen as Jess retrieved her backpack from the kitchen table.

There's that stupid envelope again.

The sound of her heart beating compounded with the silence of her empty house was so loud it was deafening. She stood, motionless for a moment, as if a single movement might make the papers combust. Feeling the cold tile beneath her bare feet, Jess swiftly grabbed her coffee mug, slipped on her nearby nude heels, and kissed Tiffany goodbye. On a day like today, any distraction - even if in the form of work - was wholeheartedly welcome.

***

Spring sprung early in Atlanta and Jess felt the warm, thick air wreak havoc on her frizzy hair as it left a layer of dew on her olive skin. As she walked into her bustling office building, each click of her sky-high heels made her temples pulsate. Lately, ten-hour days drafting press releases, gathering plans for the next round of layoffs and completing her fiscal year operating budget were her new normal. Even the humidity inside the building felt suffocating as she made her way towards her cubicle on the third floor.

Before dropping her bag, Lea - Jess' *work-wife* as colleagues dubbed her around the office – stared impatiently at the clock hanging above Jess' desk. "They're waiting for you in there," she said, cocking her head of thick, jet black hair towards the boardroom.

Teammates since Jess joined the company's marketing department about a year ago, the duo so often partnered on projects that they easily and quickly developed a friendship outside the office. Croatian-born and raised in Italy, Lea spoke English with a perfect American accent. Attending art school at Savannah College of Art and Design was far from home, but Lea embraced the American lifestyle with such vigor that she never could bring herself to return to Europe. It wasn't long before the girls became the yin to one another's yang, despite their polar opposite reputations. Jess was the no-nonsense, boisterous New Yorker and Lea was known as the reserved, subdued European.

'Just get to know her,' Jess found herself telling colleagues when asked how on earth she managed to befriend the girl who many had never heard speak out loud. 'I promise you, she's not as bitchy as her face would otherwise indicate.'

"We better get in there," Lea urged, beelining it for the conference room. With a stack of freshly printed handouts, her laptop, and large coffee in hand, Jess followed Lea into the oversized room saved for high-profile events such as these. Lea passed around Jess' material while they waited for the company's senior executives to flood in, and before long, all eyes were on Jess. Taking place in front of her audience, with all eyes on her, she felt completely in her element.

After seven, non-stop hours, Jess was exhausted yet satisfied.

"Everyone," Kellye, Jess' boss stood up to say, "I just want to take a moment and thank Jess today for her efforts. I hope you all found this session as informative and interesting as I did and I'm thrilled to know that when – not if – we face a crisis as an organization, we'll be better equipped to handle ourselves. Jess, thank you again. Tremendous job today." Just as Kellye concluded, a round of applause erupted. That was all the praise Jess needed.

Well that went well, she told herself.

Mark Westerly, the CEO of Recollect, had developed a reputation for his brash personality and harsh criticism. When he stood, everyone in the room held their breath. "I just wanted to echo Kelley's sentiment wholeheartedly," he said. "Fantastic job today, Jess."

Kelley beamed a smile Jess' way as everyone poured out of the room.

Staying behind like the loyal and helpful friend she was, Lea offered, "Can I run out and grab you some dinner? I've seen you choke down nothing but a protein bar all day."

"No, thank you though," Jess responded. "It's late, go home. I just need to finish packing up and I'll be right behind you."

After leaving the boardroom as pristine as she found it, Jess retreated to her cubicle to type up notes on the session's key takeaways. One email led to another and before long, the overhead lights automatically shut off. That was usually her signal to pack up.

How many nights have I been the last to leave, Jess wondered as she shoved her laptop inside her bag and beelined for the front door? With an office of nearly five hundred employees, she managed to be the last car in the deserted parking lot more nights than she could count. Jess opened the car door and felt the stale, warm air hit her in the face.

Tomorrow, park under the shade, she vowed.

With a quick turn of the ignition, she drove to the gym before her mind could convince her body to hit the gas pedal and drive home. A quick run followed by a brief yet satisfying weightlifting session gifted her with a temporary endorphin rush she so desperately needed. The grumbling from her belly signaled it was time for dinner, but she wasn't hungry.

Have I eaten anything besides that protein bar today?

It had been three months since Chris moved out and despite her best efforts to embrace her *new normal* with open arms, she was still struggling with how to pick up the pieces of her broken life.

It's all just a bit ironic, isn't it? Here I am, driving to my four-bedroom house made for a family, in my midsize sedan with ample room for two car seats, and yet I'm all alone.

Forty-five agonizing minutes later, Jess drove up her oversized driveway and pulled into the garage, strategically avoiding the piles of junk that lay all over.

He promised to organize this mess, she thought.

Surveying the contents of the two-car garage, it was amazing how much crap they accumulated in the short time she and

Chris lived there. Empty paint cans, piles of used sandpaper, and unused tools hung from the *Pinterest-fail* of a pegboard she built as a surprise for him when they moved in. Jess hip-checked the car door shut and carefully stepped around the piles of clutter. She walked barefoot into her travertine-laden kitchen to be met by her loyal companion.

"Hey, little love," she said, bending down to give Tiffany some much-deserved belly rubs. Despite hiring a dog walker to come twice a day, Jess felt overwhelming guilt leaving the little pup alone. As she dropped her backpack on the table, her eyes met the tan envelope yet again.

This is it, she told herself. *Enough is enough. Do it quick, like a band-aid.*

And just like that, Jess decisively reached for the envelope, taking it into her small, shaky hands as she swiftly pulled back the sealed tab. It took every ounce of willpower she had not to start sobbing. There their names appeared, in Arial, black font. Chris had a colleague at his firm draft the papers, which he chose to cowardly leave on the kitchen table while Jess was at work. No note, no phone call. No discussion or attempt to work it out. If she knew her still-husband at all, he likely shed not a single tear as he willingly left behind the life they were building.

That's just who he is now, she told herself.

A narcissistic, self-centered and immature twenty-something who made the fatal mistake of marrying his high school sweetheart before he took the time to figure out who he was or what he wanted out of life. Rather than give couples counseling a try or give a valiant attempt at wooing back his wife, it was completely in character for Chris to choose the path of least resistance.

I'm going to vomit, Jess thought as her knees felt weak. *I know we were far from perfect,* she considered as she placed her palms on the glass top table. The physical act of standing suddenly felt too much.

Is this really how it's going to end? Only months ago, while eating a plate of chicken parmesan, he tells me he doesn't want a family. He moved out before I could even mutter the word separation. How on earth are you supposed to work on your marriage if you're living separate lives? And now? Now we're just going to walk away. Leave the last five years behind and I'm supposed to magically pick up the pieces and just keep on keeping on?

Sure, she had her whole life ahead of her. At twenty-six with a career on the upswing and loving friends and family by her side, Jess knew deep down she'd be able to rebuild if she absolutely had to.

But do I want to start over? Her chest felt heavy at the thought of what an overwhelming task that would be. *Most of my friends are just now getting married and I'm already getting divorced? Divorce felt like a nasty little word that only middle-aged parents whispered. I'm too young to be a divorcee!*

The past few years were anything but easy on them, and Jess knew it. After Chris's mom lost her long and painful battle with breast cancer, something inside of him fundamentally changed. Her gregarious husband was gone and instead, the new Chris was recluse, often choosing to play video games and smoke weed in his man cave rather than have a simple conversation with his wife. Jess spent so many nights crying herself to sleep that she forgot what a dry pillowcase felt like.

It's the oddest feeling to be married, yet to feel so alone. It wasn't always like this, she told herself. When they started dating, Chris acted as though Jess hung the moon. Whether he believed she was the only woman in the world or not, he surely made her feel that way. And when they got engaged at twenty-one and their parents all thought they were nuts; she was convinced they'd be happy forever. Because up until then, they had been.

But after their nuptials, the pressures of law school, and figuring out their finances as broke, recent college grads all felt too much. And then his mother died. And the resentment he had towards life in general, in tandem with the overwhelming grief he felt, proved too much of a burden to bear.

Within what felt like moments, but transpired over an entire year, Jess watched Chris disengage. In their marriage, in his friendships, in life in general. To Jess, it felt like he simply gave up.

As she tucked the papers away, resolving to call an attorney of her own before putting pen to paper, she heard a beep from her backpack. Jess reached into the side pocket, wondering what work emergency was happening this late into the evening. Instead, she was pleasantly surprised –shocked, rather – by what she saw. A single text from Stef appeared:

You better not be reading this at the office. But if you are, get all your work in now, because your old ass is turning twenty-seven next week and friends don't let friends age without being there to make fun of them for it. I land at 5 o'clock on Wednesday – I expect you to pick me up. I love you. PS – stock up on some tequila. And wine.

Chapter Two

"I'm so happy you're here," Jess exclaimed as the girls exited Atlanta's bustling arrivals terminal late Wednesday afternoon. Jess would've never dreamt to ask her friend to fly across the country just to come give her a hug, but she was sure glad she didn't have to.

That's what true friends do, don't they? Jess thought to herself. *They just show up.* It felt nice to have someone in her life just show up.

"Me too!" Stef said, hoisting her purple suitcase into the trunk. "Not sure what you had planned for us today, but I'd love to take a shower and change out of these gross clothes before we go anywhere."

With curves in all the right places, Stef mastered the art of dressing her voluptuous physique. She knew precisely which cuts of fabric accentuated her shape and could always be counted on for a download of all the latest makeup trends and must-have beauty products.

She does realize I'm wearing sweatpants and haven't washed my hair since

Sunday, Jess thought.

"Sure," Jess agreed. "I don't care what we do, it's just nice to be together." The two hadn't seen one another in two years and the loving distraction from life lately was precisely what Jess needed.

Forty-five minutes later they arrived at Jess' house and together dragged in both of Stef's baggage.

"You do realize you're just here for the weekend?" Jess asked as she heaved one of the bags inside. Instantaneously, it felt comforting to have another warm body in the house besides her own.

"Looking good ain't easy," Stef huffed as she dragged her other suitcase to the top of the long flight of stairs.

"Last door on the left," Jess said behind her.

"Geez, this place is huge! You never told me you guys bought a mini-mansion," Stef exclaimed, plopping herself on the guest bed. "Are you planning to stay here? I mean, now that Chris moved out."

"No," Jess said, joining her on the bed. "I'm sure we'll sell it, it's just that he and I haven't talked about it – or anything – really. For the last few months, it's been a bit of radio silence. I'll deal with all that drama after you leave. No depressing d-word talk this weekend!"

Jess knew she couldn't avoid the topic much longer. Until the very evening when she spotted the stack of divorce papers awaiting her signature, she secretly held out hope that their separation was temporary. In the far corners of her mind, she hoped Chris moving into a temporary apartment would give him the space to realize he didn't want to lose her. That he couldn't imagine a life without her. She imagined him sitting on a stale couch, eating greasy takeout straight from the carton. He'd wipe his hands against his ripped Gap boxers, look around at the emptiness around him, and realize what his wife meant to him. He'd call her with the desperate tone she'd heard in countless Romcoms.

Yet thoughts of Chris and their unraveling marriage would wait. Whenever Stef was around, the forecast was inevitably full of laughter and memory making. The rarely used guestroom felt warm and inviting, despite the house feeling so devoid of love. Fresh tulips sat on the mirrored nightstand, while the white duvet smelled of fresh lavender.

"I know you wanted to shower, but why don't you come downstairs for a bit?" Jess placed her hand on Stef's knee. "I have a bottle of that rose you're going to love in the fridge. Let's go sit and have a proper catch-up."

The backyard was beautifully serene. Stef settled into one of the oversized lounge chairs next to the nearby koi pond. The sound of trickling water was complimented by nearby birds chirping from above. Jess settled into the chair beside her, staring up the bright sky.

"Well," Stef wasted no time. "How are you feeling?"

The million-dollar question.

Professionally, she was finally doing what she was meant to do. And better than that, she was finally being recognized for it. Work didn't just pay the bills, it invigorated her. The endorphin rush after nailing a high-profile presentation felt nearly addictive. Settling into a new city, her peers quickly became friends. Life in New York felt like a distant memory, and Atlanta now felt like home. Yet outside the office, she was an entirely different person. All of the clichés rang true. Food had no taste. She struggled to find joy in daily life. Her clothes hung concerningly loose around her petite frame. She continued running five days a week for no other reason than for the endorphin rush and serotonin boost. Sleeping more than a few consecutive hours felt impossible, and being home felt more painful than ever. The loneliness was palpable.

Idle time proved to be her biggest enemy, particularly whenever she imagined the new life waiting for her.

Will I ever find love again? Will I ever become a mother? What if I never find love again? As she sat across from the friend who undoubtably knew her best, Jess couldn't keep quiet any longer. *You can say it. Tell her that everything feels like it's falling apart. Tell her how sad you are. How scared you are.* Feelings of embarrassment wafted over her as a thick afternoon breeze passed through, sending the tall pines swaying. Jess buried her bare feet in a blanket nearby.

"Where are the fish in these ponds?" Stef asked, scanning the yard. "And are those bonsai trees? This backyard is really weird."

It is really weird, Jess admitted to herself.

"I've been better," Jess deadpanned. "He's my family. Was my family. We spent so many years together, and now it feels like I'm starting over again. Thirty is around the corner and I feel more lost than ever." Admitting it aloud made Jess' eyes water.

"Excuse me," Stef interrupted, holding her palm in the air. "Quit aging yourself. You're not even twenty-seven until tomorrow."

"Fair," Jess let the wine hit her lips. "But you get what I'm saying. I've been with the same guy since I was twenty-one years old. I'm starting to wonder if I can't work it out with the man who knows me better than anyone, maybe I won't be able to work it out with anyone." The idea of growing old alone sent anxiety pulsating through her veins.

"Well that's just nonsense." Stef popped a cube of cheese in her mouth. "There's nothing wrong with letting yourself grieve, but don't start thinking that just because it didn't work with one asshole is any indication that it won't work with anyone else. I hate to share this late breaking news, but you do realize he's not the last man on earth?" She cracked a smile that Jess didn't return.

"I do, but it's still scary. The last time I was single, online dating didn't even exist. How the hell am I going to meet someone now? You're going to have to show me the ropes. It's all so overwhelming." Jess twirled the blanket's gray fabric around her fingertips.

Stef cocked her head to the side as she refilled their glasses. "Dating without swiping right? Please, do tell me about the olden days."

"Hilarious. You know what I mean. I guess we all just met at bars. No websites, no apps. Just got old fashioned drunken conversation. It's utterly bizarre to be this young yet feel so ancient in this new era of dating. I'm like a grandmother now."

"Everyone should have a grandma as hot as you." Stef smirked.

"It's just not what I wanted for myself." Jess put her head in her palm and left it there. An optimist by nature, she didn't recognize the woman speaking in her head. "One of the worst parts is that when I'm not busy feeling sorry for myself, I'm feeling so angry. I supported him through everything, Stef.

Private law school, multiple bar exams, moving on a whim whenever he decided he was 'tired' of where we were." She pressed her thumbs into her temples. "I was a damn good daughter in law, too. And you know the thanks I got for that?" The question wasn't rhetorical. "My asshole of a father-in-law called me last week. At first, I ignorantly thought, *how nice. How thoughtful of him to check on me.* Nope. He called asking me to give back the necklace that he gave me for my birthday last year. Said he thought it would be better suited to stay in his family. Whatever the fuck that means."

"Well that's an easy one." Stef sat tall. "I think it's pretty obvious what you should do."

Jess furrowed her brow.

"Sell it." She took a casual swig of her wine.

"OMG Stef, I couldn't!"

"Why not?"

Why couldn't I, Jess wondered? *Technically it is mine.*

"Well, I guess I *could,*" Jess' voice trailed off as she considered the possibility.

"Just humor me. Let's just go to the jewelry store and see what you can get for it. Tomorrow's your birthday – a little extra cash never hurt!"

"Ugh," Jess groaned. "Don't remind me." Any other year she wholeheartedly loved celebrating her special day. This year, she prayed it would simply disappear.

"Listen," Stef said, placing Jess' wine glass on the table and taking her hands in hers. "I totally get that life sucks right now, and I get that you're feeling like you've just been kicked in the ass. But this weekend is all about toasting to you. It's your birthday and friends do not let friends sit around feeling this sorry for themselves. I have no idea how this is all going to play out, but what I can promise you is that everything will be okay." Taking her glass and raising it high in the air, Stef made a toast. "To my best friend. Another year older, and hopefully a hell of a lot wiser!"

"I don't know about the wiser part," Jess muttered. "But I'll cheers to this nightmare ending. And a new year of life with a clean slate." She popped a grape in her mouth and felt its juice explode.

***

"Given the size of the stone and the weight of the platinum, I'm comfortable offering you one thousand dollars for the necklace," Lucy from Jacob's Jeweler told the girls that afternoon.

"I don't know," Jess said, looking at Stef. The anxiety rose like bile in the back of her throat. "Should I really sell it? Maybe I just give it back? I don't want to be a total ass hat about this."

"An asshat just like Chris?" Stef deadpanned; hip cocked out to the side. "You don't owe him or his family anything. It's your necklace to do with what you want. And if you ask me, I say sell that shit."

Despite her best efforts to appear otherwise, Lucy was eavesdropping in the most obvious fashion. When Jess locked eyes with her, the middle-aged Asian woman jumped in her skin. Frazzled, she muttered, "Let me give you ladies a few minutes," as she quickly scurried away.

"Why do I feel so guilty for doing this?" Jess whispered. "I know things aren't great right now, but I still love him, babe. What if he hates me for selling it when he finds out?"

"I didn't want to have to do this," Stef leaned against the glass display, locking eyes with Jess. "But let's remember that your future ex-husband has been no prize over the years. What about the time after you guys moved to Atlanta and brought your car in to tint the windows? You were at the shop alone and called him to pick you up. He called you selfish for calling in the middle of the NFL draft and hung up on you. When you tried calling him back, he sent your ass straight to voicemail."

Oh god. Jess closed her eyes and felt transported back to that day. She smelled the scent of burnt coffee and motor oil as she cried in the auto body's waiting room.

"What's your point?" She hated how defensive she sounded.

"All I'm saying," Stef said, "Is that you shouldn't feel guilty for doing something for yourself for once. It's been years of his rules. His family's rules. They called the shots and you just went with the flow." She used air quotes for emphasis. "You're a strong woman but for some reason, this man is your kryptonite. I say let today's decision be the first of many for the *you. The new you!*"

Jess stood in silence, feeling Lucy's eyes on her from across the showroom. She shifted the weight between her feet, feeling torn. Flooded with memories of arguments, feelings of disregard, and tears shed, she knew her best friend had a valid point.

The new me, she recited in her mind. *I like the sound of that.*

"Lucy!" Jess yelled out, waving the anxiously awaiting saleswoman down. "We're ready."

Stef's eyes went wide.

As Lucy approached the counter, Jess blurted, "Will the thousand be in the form of a check or cash?" She laid the necklace back onto the black felt mat in front of her. "I'd like to sell this."

***

"I'll take a spicy, skinny margarita, please," Jess felt herself shouting to their server. The bustling neighborhood taqueria was unusually packed with the local after-work crowd looking to escape the day over a few glasses of tequila and baskets of overly salted tortilla chips. Jess' mouth watered as she anticipated the cool, spicy liquid about to hit her lips.

"And I'll do a Cadillac margarita, Patron floater," Stef called out without so much as glancing at the menu. "Actually, fuck it. Let's make it two floaters. I'm on vacation!" She handed her menu to the server and laid her arms on the table in front of her.

Only once the task of ordering cocktails was complete and their server was long gone, Jess leaned in, cautiously asking the question she held off asking since her friend's arrival. "So, babe, how's your mom doing?"

It was only one year ago that Stef moved to Oklahoma to care for her mother after she was unexpectedly diagnosed with lung cancer. "These things sometimes happen," the doctor explained, even if her mother had never lit a single cigarette. Stef rarely spoke of her decision to leave life in Arizona behind, but Jess imagined how difficult the choice had been. The life of any party, Stef lived a fast and furious life in Scottsdale.

Between an endless supply of friends and a packed Tinder inbox, her social calendar was always jam packed. Trading it all in within a matter of minutes to live on an Indian reservation in rural Oklahoma didn't seem like an easy pill to swallow. Going one step further, Stef quit her job as a college admissions counselor and traded in happy hours and first dates to become a caretaker for her dying mother.

"She's hanging in." The heavy tone felt so strange coming from her. "No real changes, which I guess is good. I guess." Her eyes darted down towards the chip basket as Jess searched her face for the first sign of emotion. There was a justifiable sadness in her eyes, but Stef had a way of shutting down topics of conversation that were too painful to discuss. Jess had the wherewithal to respect her friend's wishes.

"Enough about me," Stef said. "I came out here for *you*. What are we doing for your big day tomorrow? Bottle service at a club? Matching tattoos? Shopping spree with the crisp thousand bucks burning a hole in your purse?"

Jess shook her head. The ideas might be incredulous for some, but there wasn't the tiniest sliver of sarcasm in Stef's voice. "You do realize we're not in college anymore, right?"

"Oh, I'm aware. My tits now look like empty coin purses and if I eat anything spicy after 8 p.m., I end up with a base case of acid reflux. You don't need to remind me we're not twenty-one anymore. But I am your best friend, and part of my job is to pull you out of this funk you're in." Stef dipped her chip in the warm bowl of queso now sitting before them. "Listen, I get that Chris is a lawyer now, and one day, despite being a total asshole, I'm sure he'll be very successful. But no amount of money will ever buy you happiness. And that's the reason you stayed with him this whole time, isn't it? The idea of what the high life married to a hotshot lawyer would be like?"

Without hesitation, Jess retorted. "Of course not! The entirety of our relationship he was either in school, studying for the bar exam, or working with zero paycheck. I was never enamored by some fancy lifestyle. I genuinely – and probably quite foolishly - thought we'd last. I know it's hard to imagine since I so often bitched to you about him, but we did have good times together. He was a generous guy - always bringing home flowers and showering me with gifts."

"But those are materialistic things," Stef was completely unimpressed. "Besides, aren't husbands supposed to do those types of things for their wives anyway?"

"I mean, sure," Jess crossed her arms in front of her. *Stop being defensive,* she told herself. "But it wasn't all bad, otherwise I never would've married him."

Just as their conversation took a slightly contentious turn, two platters of sizzling fajitas appeared.

"All I'm saying," Stef continued, assembling her fajita, "Is that you deserve a man with both feet in. Not a guy threatening you with the word 'divorce' whenever a fight breaks out, because fights *will happen*. He tossed that shit around like confetti, without ever considering how it began to chip away at your confidence – in yourself and the relationship."

She's got a point, Jess considered. *Why did I stay? Could I ever have walked away without feeling, with certainty, that I gave our marriage everything I could? If I had left, it would've felt like quitting. Like giving up on the most sacred pact I've ever made.*

Jess struggled with failure, but she struggled with the notion of quitting even more. Sophomore year of college she accidentally signed up for an Elvis Appreciation Class and when she showed up on the first day to tell her professor about the registration error, he seemed so genuinely enthusiastic about her being there that she stayed for the rest of the semester. The fear of offending the sweet old man was enough to keep her from dropping the completely irrelevant class. When she ripped the crotch of her running tights during the first mile of her first half marathon, she pushed onward, lady bits exposed, for the next twelve miles. Mortified and rather cold, she refused to succumb to defeat. She hated to fail, but she refused to quit.

It's who I am, she told herself.

An unusual sadness appeared in Stef's voice yet again. "I know you've considered leaving him over the years but were too scared to start over. And I know you're terrified to fail at something for the first time in your life, but it happens. It happens to every one of us. Maybe not in the form of divorce, but trust me, we all fail."

"I know," Jess resigned.

I'm signing divorce papers tomorrow, Jess reminded herself. The thought made bile rise in her throat. After all their years together, their entire relationship would come swiftly to an end with a few signatures of a ballpoint pen.

"Listen," she told Stef as she dabbed the inner corner of her eye with her dinner napkin. "You did not fly all the way out here to wallow in this with me. Can we just drop all the Chris talk for tonight? We'll have enough of it tomorrow at the attorney's office, and I'd rather not spend the rest of the night crying."

***

With full bellies and a nice buzz, the girls entered Jess' kitchen, immediately noticing an arrangement of gerbera daisies placed on the island.

Those weren't here earlier, Jess thought.

A tiny, white envelope propped against the clear vase and Jess' stomach sank at the sheer sight of it. There was only one person other than herself with a key to their house.

Why did he leave these? She looked at Stef in shock as she reached for the envelope.

"Read it out loud," Stef said, breathing over her shoulder.

Dear Jess. Happy Birthday. I hope you have a great day. Love, Me.

"Is he serious?" Jess yelled, slamming the card on the counter. "First of all, this message is about as stale as his personality. Secondly, why the hell is he coming into the house when we both agreed he'd call first?"

Suddenly it felt like a million degrees, and the faint scent of the daises made her feel sick. In one fail swoop, she tossed the fresh flowers, vase, card and all, into the garbage can.

She also made a mental note. *Choose a new favorite flower.*

"Okay," Stef yelled from behind Jess, clapping her hands together. "Change your outfit. We're going OUT!"

With no will to argue, Jess obliged, heading upstairs to change. A night out would probably do them both good. She styled her newly dyed brown locks in a high ponytail, completing her look with a bright red lipstick buried at the bottom of her vanity drawer.

Chris would've hated everything about this, she told herself as she smoothed out her ponytail. For years he made her promise to continue dying her hair platinum blonde. *Dark colors just wash you out,* he'd tell her. He also told her a boob job after forty was *a must* and she should never wear bright lipstick. *That's for hookers,* he'd say.

It sure feels good to do what I want to do.

Pleased with the reflection staring back at her, she and Stef left for a girl's night out.

At one of Atlanta's hottest nightclubs – a recommendation from Lea, a self-professed nightclub aficionado – the duo danced off the copious amounts of chips and margaritas and drank away the day's heavy conversations. After too many shots, they returned to the dance floor with a distorted yet admirable sense of confidence. *Give Me Everything* by Pitbull blared so loudly that Jess could hardly hear her thoughts, which was nice, for a change. The girls twirled around and around, sipping vodka sodas out of tiny plastic cups until the bright white lights came on at two o'clock in the morning. Somewhere shortly thereafter, Jess propped herself against a car out back, holding Stef's hair as she spewed steak fajitas all over the abandoned parking lot.

Some things never change, Jess thought to herself. *It's nice to know that even when it feels like life is falling apart, there are some things that I can always count on. Like the love and support of your best friend.*

"It's okay," Jess slurred, still holding Stef's hair away from her face. "I'm here. I've got you."

***

Fewer things are more depressing for a recently separated woman than waking up alone in a king-sized bed. Unless that is, you're waking up alone, on your birthday, to meet with a divorce attorney.

Along for moral support, Stef sat patiently next to Jess as they waited for the attorney to greet them in the lobby.

"He seriously couldn't have met with you any other day?" Stef asked as she sipped stale coffee from a Styrofoam cup. She hadn't brushed her hair and decided, in very uncharacteristic fashion, to wear jeans and a sweatshirt, forsaking fashion for comfort as she nursed a massive hangover.

"Unfortunately, not," Jess whispered. "This was the only day he had open – thanks to a last-minute cancellation. Otherwise, I would've had to wait months just to meet this guy. And lord knows I can't drag this out any longer."

Maybe it won't be as bad as I think it will, Jess told herself. "Besides, what are you trying to say? This isn't what you had in mind to celebrate my birthday?"

Despite feeling hungover and rather sad, it did bring Jess tremendous comfort having Stef by her side for this hellish ordeal. The idea of coming to sign divorce papers all alone, on her birthday, sounded too pathetic for her wildest imagination.

After a brief introduction, Jeff, the middle-aged attorney, brought the girls into an oversized boardroom and offered to top off their stale coffee. Pleasantries ended quickly and Jess' felt her mouth dry up as she listened to Jeff utter phrases such as "Down payment. She supported him through law school. Paid for two bar exams. No additional marital assets. No children."

Likely a professional hazard, he stated things so flatly that it left Jess wondering if he realized he was talking about her actual life or if somehow, she was suddenly acting as an extra in an episode of Law and Order.

This is it; it's happening. Tears silently cascaded down her face and despite her best attempts to *pull it together*, the tears continued to fall, making an audible landing on the shiny mahogany table beneath her.

I'm going to have to sell the house. Shit, I'm going to have to find somewhere else to live. Can I even afford to buy another house? Should I rent? Do I move home to New York or stay in Atlanta? But my job is here, my friends are here. Where is Chris going to go? Why do I care?

The thoughts became too much to handle, and for the first time since the night he left, Jess let herself truly become unhinged.

She dropped her head into her hands and, without care for the others around her, allowed herself to sink deeply into her feelings.

"Errr. I think we're going to need some tissues in here," Stef spoke out. While Jeff sprang into action, Stef rolled her chair in close, putting an arm around her friend. "It's okay, babe. It's going to be okay."

"Did you even put on deodorant?" Jess asked, pushing away from her friend. She let out a much-needed laugh and signaled to Jeff, who appeared to be completely unaffected by the emotional outburst, that she was ready to proceed. The next hour continued at what felt like a glacial pace. Each signature, each memory recounted, felt like self-inflicted torture. The final proverbial nail in the coffin came when Jeff's assistant entered the boardroom.

"Sorry to interrupt, folks, but I'm going to need to collect payment for today's appointment."

Way to kick a lady when she's down, Jess thought. Rationally she knew her legal services wouldn't be free, but was this the right moment to come in asking for money?

I guess there really is no right time, she told herself.

"Alright," Jess said with a tight breath. "What's my total?" Suddenly realizing she'd be officially on her own, with only herself to count on, made her acutely aware of every dollar she spent from here on out.

"Today's balance is $575," the assistant said. "We take cash or check."

Gritting her teeth, Jess reached into her handbag and took nearly half of her newfound thousand dollars she made yesterday, sliding it across the shiny table while simultaneously pushing out her chair.

"Well," Jess spoke, "Thank you. Unless you need anything else from me, I'm going to head out and try to salvage the day."

"We're all set," Jeff said with an outstretched arm. "Happy Birthday to you, dear. Once we finalize the paperwork, we'll get everything submitted for you."

An uncontested divorce in the state of Georgia, as Jeff informed her, could be finalized in thirty-one days. Thirty-one days. In less time than it takes for the DMV to mail out a driver's license, her divorce would be official.

After obligatory handshakes, the ladies wasted no time hightailing it for the bank of glass elevators. Once the doors closed, Stef flashed a sneaky smile. "Okay birthday girl, enough of the sadness for today. Let's go do something fun!"

Jess rolled her eyes. "I think I've had enough fun for today," as she pushed G and let the elevator take them down to the garage.

"I'm serious!" Stef yelled with slightly feigned excitement.

The only thing Jess felt like doing was crawling underneath her covers and reappearing once this whole nightmare was over.

"Honestly all I want to do is relax. What do you think about a little spa day? Massages and facials sound heavenly right about now. Think you can handle a low-key day, Ms. Life of the Party?" Jess prayed for Stef's agreeability.

"Considering I can't remember the last time another hand beside my own touched my naked body, that sounds wonderful to me. I'll look up places right now!" Stef exclaimed, reaching in her purse to retrieve her phone.

***

"*Madela,* Happy Birthday!" Jess' mom sang to her later that day.

Still riding the waves of bliss and relaxation from their day of pampering, Jess' heart warmed at the sound of her mother's voice.

"I know it's already the afternoon," Sarah continued, "but I was saving this call because you know your dad and I always call you at the exact time you were born. Half-past four o'clock in the evening, twenty-seven years ago, my life changed forever. My body changed forever too, but that's not really your fault now is it? Let's just be thankful you didn't inherit these hips of mine!"

"Thanks, mom," Jess rolled her eyes as a slight smile spread across her face. "That's very sweet of you to say. Dad hasn't called just yet, but I'm sure he's giving you a two-minute grace period."

Despite their divorce when Jess was a mere two years old, the duo continued to impress her over the years, nailing the whole *co-parenting* thing long before it was a trendy buzzword. They still called each other on their birthdays and Jewish holidays, seizing every opportunity to share a laugh or a dance – including the evening of her college graduation dinner - in a busy restaurant with no dance floor and plenty of confused onlookers.

"How did it go at the attorney's office?" her mom asked. "I know it's a bit of a downer to bring this up, but life isn't always unicorns and rainbows now is it? Did you sign all of the papers? Is everything finalized?"

"It went as well as could be expected," Jess told her as she signed the receipt at the spa's front desk. Stef patiently held the large, floor to ceiling glass door open as she waited. "Everything is signed, and now we wait for it to be finalized through the courts. When you and Dad got divorced, how did you feel? I can't help but just feel..." she searched for the right words. "Empty?"

"Hang on," her mom said, her voice muffled. "My pot is boiling over. Gosh how come I can't ever seem to even boil water right?! Ouch! Oh no!" Jess didn't need to see her mother's kitchen to imagine the mess currently taking place.

"Mom, are you okay? What's happening over there?" Jess asked as she now stood on the street, searching left and right for Stef, who had wandered into a nearby clothing boutique. Their spa appointments were conveniently situated in Buckhead, on a quaint side street flanked with local boutiques in every direction. They planned to linger afterward and do some window shopping.

"I dropped the phone! If you're talking, I can't hear you! Hold on!" Sarah yelled. "Okay. Crisis somewhat averted!" She said triumphantly. "I'm back, but that damn pot overflowed all over the floor. Then I dropped the phone and I think I've cracked the screen now. Do I just take it into that all-white store at the mall? Every time I walk by it's just so crowded. Do you think if I call and speak to the manager, they'll send me an envelope so I can just mail it in? You know my disdain for going to the mall, darling. And waiting. Your mother hates to wait."

"No, Mom. Unfortunately, you'll need to bring it in. I pay for a warranty, so you're covered. But why aren't you using those headphones I sent you? They're meant so you can talk on the phone but be completely handsfree." Jess felt frustration kick in, as her mother tended to act rather flippantly when it came to subjects such as these. She did her best to take care of her mom in little ways, from covering small bills that added up over time to sending thoughtful and practical gifts just because she thought they'd make her mother's life easier. When she felt the efforts were disregarded, it made her blood come to a slow boil.

"Sorry, now what were you asking me, dear?" Sarah asked, still distracted as she mopped up the spilled water.

"Never mind, mom, I'll talk to you tomorrow. Love you." Jess hung up before her mom could argue that she was listening, even though both knew she wasn't.

Within seconds of hanging up, Jess' phone buzzed.

"Hey dad," she said with a smile.

"Has mom called you yet?" he asked, without skipping a beat.

"Yes dad, she did."

"Oh good, I waited a few minutes to let her get through. Happy Birthday, sweet pea! How did it go today?" he asked with genuine concern. Adam always had a soft spot in his heart for his only daughter. He's the reason she loved being outdoors, taking photographs, and overusing the words *I love you.*

"Oh, it was fine," Jess said as she reached for an absurdly overpriced, yet stunning ivory silk chemise. "You know, as far as divorces go."

Despite the heaviness she felt in her heart, Jess resolved to focus on the things she could control — her attitude being one of them. She had a lot of time to think over these last few months, and one thought that resonated was, *did I just ignore all the signs?* After years of living in a state of *waiting for the other shoe to drop*, she tried to stop romanticizing her failed marriage and realize she was mostly walking on eggshells - as to not unknowingly piss Chris off to the point where he'd then throw his arms in the air and yell out *Fuck this, I want a divorce!* That happened far too many times than she'd be willing to admit aloud.

"Well dear," her dad continued. "You're with your best friend and the night is young. Go out and enjoy yourselves. Think of today as the first day of the rest of your life. I love you!"

"I love you too, Dad," Jess said with a comforting exhale. As she hung up and considered her dad's words, she realized she could easily wallow in sadness — or she could make today the start of the rest of her life. The choice, for the first time in a very long time, was all hers.

"I'll take it," she told the cashier as she placed the silk blouse on the counter. "It's my birthday, if I don't treat myself today, then when?"

***

"I'm so sorry I can't take you to the airport," Jess told Stef the following morning as they sipped piping hot coffee in their pajamas. "If I didn't have to go back to the airport later today to fly out myself, you know I would."

The sounds of birds chirping, and the spring morning air provided the perfect backdrop for the final moments of their cherished time together.

"I know, don't even worry," Stef reassured her, burying her bare feet underneath the blanket. "What a bummer work is making you fly out on a Sunday!"

Truth be told, Jess had been looking forward to this trip. Not only would it make for great face time with the executives, but she was hosting a media event that if her projections were correct, would garner a ton of coverage for her company and as a byproduct, praise and accolades for her.

"It's only a few days," she said as she shrugged her shoulders. "It'll be fine."

From over the top of her bone-white China mug, Stef's eyes locked on Jess. "Promise me one thing when you get back?"

"What's that?" Jess asked, wrapping her hands around the warm mug.

"Promise me you'll go talk to someone."

Jess' eyes squinted and her brow wrinkled. "Talk to someone? About what?"

Stef sat up straight, indicating that the words about to come out of her mouth contained something of significance. Jess' ears perked up. "You may be able to pull that innocent attitude with your parents, or your new friends here, but you're not fooling me. I know you. *The real you.* And I know you're sad. Shit, I'm sad myself. It's not easy going through the things we're going through. I just don't want you doing this alone."

Jess felt the moisture in her eyes. Sure, her divorce was painful. The new life ahead scared the ever-living crap out of her. But her best friend, the woman sitting next to her, was fighting her own battle.

Losing a parent - no matter how old you are - must be one of the most painful losses imaginable, Jess considered. And Stef was in the throes of it. Yet even while she grieved her own loss, Stef was more concerned about Jess' emotional state. *Have I been acting that sad?*

Jess stretched her arms open wide and softly spoke, "I promise, babe. I will."

Stef melted into her embrace and they sat, perfectly still - for what felt like a long time - until the birds stopped chirping and the breeze stopped blowing.

Chapter Three

Saying goodbye to Stef stung like the time when a bee
landed on Jess' bikini top, wiggled itself inside, and stung
her right on the breast while vacationing in Puerto Rico.
Jess continued missing her friend even after a brief yet
distracting business trip to Salt Lake City. And she wished even
more that her dear friend lived closer once she unwillingly
found herself back in her big, empty house.

Never one to fall back on a promise, Jess followed through on
her commitment to Stef and scheduled an appointment with a
local therapist.

The rain poured down that Saturday afternoon as she arrived
for her first session. Dr. Green's name had been tucked away
for over a year, turns out, after she convinced Chris to see
someone after his mother's death. After many heated arguments
and much resistance, he obliged, showing commitment to their
marriage and his mental health by going to Dr. Green. Once.

As she let herself into the small waiting room at the end of the
hall, Jess noticed the laminated sign "Please be seated" hanging

on the ivory-colored wall. Doing as instructed, she reached for a Women's Health Magazine and took a seat on the empty sofa. After a few moments, her mind began to wander. *Did Chris only come here because I forced him to? Did he open about his darkest thoughts? What did he say about me? About our marriage?*

A white-haired woman in a matching lavender pantsuit appeared. "Jessica? The doctor will see you now."

Jess stood, following the woman into a room at the end of a long corridor. As she took a seat in the quaint office, she couldn't help but notice how it reminded her of the damp basements she grew up playing in New York. Definitely not what she expected from a psychologist charging by the hour. The stale odor of coffee and tobacco filled the air as she gazed around, noticing hundreds of running medals adorning the walls. 5ks, 10ks, half and full marathons. *This shrink is quite the athlete.* She imagined him to walk in, tall, fit, and lean.

Her thoughts quickly interrupted as the brass door handle turned. Unlike the image she had in her mind, Dr. Green sported a full head of grey hair, wore a slightly wrinkled suit and Prada loafers long overdue for a shine. He appeared to be in his seventies and shot her an easy smile as he walked across the room.

"Well hello there." His voice was gentle voice and comforting in an otherwise anxiety-filled moment.

Jess wiggled to stand from the sunken-in couch. "Nice to meet you," she said with an outstretched hand. She feigned a smile although her pulse raced. *Calm down,* she told herself. *It's just therapy. Why am I so nervous? He's here to help you.*

"Please," he said, motioning for her to sit, as he smoothed out the front of his white button-down shirt.

"So, tell me," he asked, "You were referred to my office?"

"You could say that, yes," Jess said. "Chris Steinberg, a former patient of yours."

"Ah, yes! What a nice guy. So, tell me, what can I help you with?" Green asked, cocking his head to one side. She already slightly hated him for paying her ex – whose name sent the hairs on the back of her neck up – a compliment. *Nice? I don't think so.* His words cut her silent thoughts off. "This is about your journey, dear. Start wherever you'd like."

"My journey…" she began, watching him cross his legs and settle back into his chair. "Well, let's see. A few years ago, I married my best friend. We were young. But we dated for a good amount of years. We were engaged for the "right" amount of time. We were planning to start a family…" She stopped herself as her throat tightened.

"Okay," his brow slightly furrowed. "That all sounds wonderfully promising. What happened?"

The simple question made her laugh out loud. *What happened? If I knew the answer to that, I wouldn't be here, would I?*

"Well, for starters, he grew to become a raging narcissist." She said flatly.

"If it's alright with you," Dr. Green interjected, "let's avoid labels for now. Why don't you tell me what he did specifically?"

That's fair, she thought. She hated him for it, but the logic was hard to argue.

"A few months before we were set to get married, his mother died rather suddenly. And something in him forever changed. He wasn't the man I fell in love with years before. Everything about him changed. Which I guess is to be expected. But we made lifelong plans and promises. And then, what felt like completely out of nowhere, he changed his mind about everything."

"Everything is a broad statement," Dr. Green interjected. "How exactly did he change his mind?" He watched Jess over the top of his wire-framed bifocals.

"For starters, he decided he no longer wanted to have children. He told me that a year into our marriage. He became completely introverted – with his friends, family, and with me. He took up smoking pot and lost his desire to do much of anything but wallow in his sea of sadness." Jess felt her hands ball into small fists. Her sadness was rapidly turning into anger. "And the worst part of all is that when things got tough, he just *quit*. He refused to fight for me, for our marriage, for any of it."

It was the first time she truly admitted – out loud - what she was so hurt about. *He just quit on us. He quit on me.*

Dr. Green sat silently for a few moments as Jess took a few deep breaths. He looked at her with compassion and finally spoke, "Let's focus less on him and more on you, shall we? Help me understand what it is that brought you here today. I assume you two are divorcing. Is it coping with the embarrassment of being divorced so soon? Explain to me what you're grieving about." He never broke eye contact.

"Well," she began. "That's a complicated answer."

"That's fine," he reassured her. "We have time." He crossed his legs in the other direction and patiently allowed her to collect her thoughts. As she did, he reached for the coffee mug on his desk. *#1 Grandfather* in gold, script lettering.

I wonder if my dad will ever get to drink from one of those cheesy mugs, she wondered.

"Yes, I'm embarrassed. Most of my friends are just now getting engaged, and I'm getting divorced. I'm only twenty-seven years old, and divorce feels like something reserved for old people. But also, I'm…" she searched for the right word to articulate how she felt. "I think I'm… resentful. I chose to stay married to someone who made me feel like I was all alone. And despite my best efforts, it didn't work. I feel like I failed. How do you fight to stay married to someone who doesn't want to be with you anymore?" she asked.

"You can't," He said over the top of his mug.

Like a volcano past eruption, emotions began to flow so easily that they surprised even her. "I don't know why I stayed and fought for so long. I feel a bit lost as if I could use some sort of compass to guide me. My parents, although they're two of the most loving people I know, they themselves have no idea what a successful, healthy relationship looks like."

"I take it your parents are also divorced, then?"

"Yes, they split when I was two. I honestly never thought much about it. They're not perfect, but whose parents are? They love me unconditionally and I love them. They've always chosen to support me in all I do." She paused. "Well, except for getting engaged as young as I did."

"They didn't approve?" he pushed.

"No," she began. "Neither of them liked my ex… or his family. My in-laws were always a bit 'higher than thou,' if you know the type. Chris favored his family and minced no words about it. It was always his way or the highway, and my parents resented him for that. I think they also felt as though we were too young to get married. Too immature."

Just as Green looked as though he was about to respond, an alarm sounded, indicating their session was over.

That flew by, she thought.

"Thank you for coming in, Jessica," Dr. Green said, leaning forward. "It's my sincere hope you come back to continue this conversation. I'm here to help you navigate this time of change. But I promise you one thing, whether it's with me or not, just know that you will be okay. A smart, young, driven girl like yourself…. Something tells me you're going to be better than okay." His reassurance eased her mind and based solely upon the feeling calmness she felt; she knew she'd be back. Throughout the session, she noticed him scribbling on a small, yellow post-it. He stood and put the paper in her hand.

As she stood and accepted the piece of paper, she thanked him for his time.

Her steps felt a little lighter that day. Later that evening, she reached her hand into the pocket of her sweatshirt, retrieving the note Dr. Green gave her.

A Promise to Myself, it was titled. *I will have faith in the future. I won't be too scared or prideful to admit I've failed. I am committed to moving on towards the life that's waiting for me. I will take that first step, even if I can't quite see the whole staircase.*

She smiled, sticking the yellow paper to her vanity mirror that night before bed. *Perhaps,* she wondered, *if I spend less time fighting my feelings, and more time simply allowing myself to be open to them, the less powerful they'll become.*

***

"Hey boo," her dad cheerfully responded to Jess' call that Sunday evening. Normally not one for lengthy phone calls, since Chris left, her dad called far more often to check-in and Jess didn't mind one bit. "How was your weekend? Did you do anything fun?"

She was washing her bowl after another dinner of Honey Nut Cheerios while struggling to drum up anything *fun* to share. "I saw a therapist yesterday," she deadpanned.

A first-generation American with conservative European parents, Jess' dad knew nothing of therapists or *sharing feelings*. Despite showering his only child with love at every chance he got, he didn't grow up hearing the words 'I love you' nor did he hear the phrase 'I'm proud of you.' He was raised in the belief that children should be seen and not heard. Men didn't cry. They worked. They provided. And should a man ever *feel* anything, he should suppress those thoughts and simply *get over it*.

"A therapist, huh?" he seemed genuinely interested. "Well, how did that go?"

She considered the hour spent with Dr. Green and smiled. "It went really well. I think I'll keep seeing him. Let him help me sort out some of the feelings I'm having about this whole divorce situation."

"Well, I'm happy you're talking it out, but I do think there's plenty you can do to get your mind off of everything," he said. "I was looking on the internet, and I know you love stand-up comedy. A great comedian is performing over at the Punchline tonight. You should go! My treat!"

It that some sort of unspoken rule? Jess wondered. Was *my treat* printed in bold letters somewhere in an official copy of the *Jewish Parents Handbook?* Her mother, also a fan of the term, loved calling to say *Madela, why don't you go buy yourself something to cheer you up. My treat!* It was a sweet gesture, especially given how much Jess loved visiting the local comedy club. Punchline was an institution in Atlanta – hosting all the best from Eddie Murphy to Jay Leno and just about everyone in between. Sure, she appreciated the gesture, but accepting gifts from her parents at this age didn't feel right anymore.

"Dad, I appreciate you trying to get me out of the house, but there's no way on earth I'm going out, on a Sunday night, alone, to a comedy club."

"I'm just saying, Sweetheart. I think putting yourself out there will do you some good. Get some fresh air. Idle minds are a dangerous thing, you know."

"Thanks, Dad, I'll consider it," Jess fibbed.

"One last thing," he said. "I want you to know… just because you aren't married anymore doesn't mean your chance to have a baby is over. You do know nowadays that women don't even need us men to start a family."

Oh, holy hell. Jess braced herself for what was to come. "What are you talking about?"

"Well they have these banks on the internet," he continued. "You know, where you can flip through a catalog. All sorts of men who get paid for donating their sperm! I've heard some are doctors and scientists and such. That could be pretty cool, don't you think?"

"Okay, bye Dad!" Without hesitation, she hung up. Her divorce was not yet final and talk of sperm banks and single motherhood all felt entirely too premature. If she couldn't stomach the idea of venturing out to a comedy club alone, she had little to no faith in her ability to flip through a random sperm catalogue in search of a father to her unborn child.

Start small, she told herself. Heeding her dad's advice, Jess changed out of her pajamas and into her most socially acceptable sweatpants - void of any holes or unexplained stains – and drove to her favorite frozen yogurt shop. Ten dollars' worth of frozen yogurt later, she ate it alone in her car, as a single tear hit the steering wheel.

***

The Monday afternoon sun shined bright through her windshield and Jess cursed herself for buying a black car with black leather interior. Thankfully traffic was relatively light as she meandered the local streets to her primary care physician's office. A rule follower through and through, she never missed an annual physical, even though, today especially, she was already dreading the canned mental health questions her physician would surely ask.

How are you feeling? How are you sleeping? Any changes in your life that I should be aware of?

All of which she'd feel compelled to divulge not only was she going through a painful divorce, but she hadn't remembered sleeping through the night in months.

Parking in the adjacent garage, she walked through the building and rode the elevator up to the third floor. Down the dark, narrow corridor, she stopped at the last door on the left. Sally, the near-retirement aged receptionist, greeted her with a smile.

Peering up from her oversized bi-focal glasses, Sally cheerfully shouted a few audibles higher than necessary, "Hiya! Do you have an appointment, dear? Please sign in and fill these forms out. Bring them back to me when you're done, doll!"

The women exchanged polite smiles as Jess balanced her purse alongside Sally's clipboard as she took a seat on the wingback chair in the far corner of the waiting room. The mauve wall color matched the outdated pink décor, along with a bowl of fake peonies adorning the coffee table, accompanied by a stack of WebMD magazines. On the clipboard, most of the form fields were standard. Age, weight, height, and address. About halfway down the form, a field stopped Jess dead in her tracks.

Emergency Contact.

It hit her like a ton of bricks. Those two simple words had the uncanny ability to send her into a complete downward emotional tailspin. *I suppose I could list my dad. Although he lives in Boston. And my mom? She lives in Miami. Her voicemail has been full since I set it up for her two years ago. What if I were to fall in the middle of the night on my way to the bathroom? What if I slipped and cracked my head open on the porcelain tub? No one would know. No one could help.*

Irrational thoughts churned through her mind faster than she could process. If it's true that a tree can fall in a forest and not be heard, surely, she could fall in the bathroom and never be found.

She could see the headlines now: *Young, divorced woman suffers head trauma after cracking her head open on her bathtub. Dies alone. Her Pomeranian turned over to animal services. No further details at this time.*

Without realizing it, she was emotionally unraveling in the quiet waiting room. Her worries quickly interrupted by a young physician standing at the doorway. A tall woman in her mid-thirties appeared in light green scrubs.

"Jessica Klein? I'm ready for you."

***

"Loneliness can take a serious toll on your well-being," the doctor told Jess as she handed over a box of tissues. "It's completely normal to feel this way as you go through a divorce. I'm going to write you a prescription for an antidepressant to help you cope with the feelings you're experiencing."

Sitting on the exam table with her ass stuck to the thin layer of tissue paper underneath her, Jess felt vulnerable in more ways than one. *Why is she so quick to prescribe me something?* A patient of the practice for the past year without a single symptom of depression, Jess meant to respond with confidence, but it instead came out sounding like a desperate plea, "But you know me. I'm not a depressed person. I'm just sad. There's a difference, isn't there?"

"There is and there isn't," her doctor responded. "At the least, this will help you manage the sadness."

Jess was bewildered. *I've never taken medication before. Happy pills are not going to make this pain magically go away. And if they do, what the hell is that teaching me? Shouldn't I be feeling the pain so I can learn from it?*

Her physical continued, checking off all the standard protocol including her blood pressure, pulse, and the all-dreaded pap smear. At the conclusion, Jess was handed her a small slip of paper. "Just take this, Jess. Trust me, it'll help."

She left the appointment feeling more conflicted than before. Sure, she may have shed a few tears while completing the standard intake form, but she wasn't depressed. Of all things she had to be uncertain of, this was not one of them.

How could anyone in my shoes not feel lonely and afraid?

When the life you live comes to an end, how on earth are you supposed to, without skipping a beat, pretend everything is fine.

Will it ever be fine? She wasn't convinced. But one thing she was certain of is that while she needed *something*, magic happy pills were not the answer.

As she left the office building late that afternoon, she tore the prescription to shreds, tossing the scraps into the trash bin at the base of the parking garage.

How does anyone expect me to overcome the feelings of despair and sadness, truly moving past them, if I can't feel them at all?

Chapter Four

“ “Any reason you're still wearing your wedding ring?” Lea casually asked, sliding a box of coffee across the boardroom table as they waited for the rest of the team to flood in for their weekly marketing meeting.

"Umm..." Jess mumbled as she looked down and instinctively twirled the sparkly ring around her finger. Until this moment, she hadn't realized she was still wearing it.

No one at the office, other than Lea, knew of Jess' divorce. Just as she'd rather shove bamboo shoots underneath her fingernails before admitting failure on a project, she surely didn't feel comfortable admitting to business colleagues that her marriage failed.

“I guess I'm just not ready for the rumor mill to swirl or the great inquisition to begin,” she admitted, re-arranging the tray of mini muffins and chocolate croissants before her. Just as Lea opened her mouth to refute Jess' comment, a handful of coworkers filled the boardroom and an unspoken pause was put into effect.

These weekly staff meetings came from a proposal Jess made upon first joining the team. Her idea stemmed from the notion that best practice sharing could increase collaboration and boost morale. But today, somewhere between 'Where are we with the latest press release' and 'Jess, do you have any thoughts on the menu for next week's customer event in Nashville?' Jess had nearly zero fucks to give.

Instead, she silently replayed Lea's question over and over again.

It's been months… Why the heck am I still wearing my wedding ring? Her engagement ring contained a two-carat diamond passed down from Chris's grandparents, which sat in a platinum setting that he purchased on his own. It sat on her ring finger stacked atop a diamond eternity band he gave her on their first wedding anniversary. Each time Jess needed comfort she twirled the set of rings with her left thumb. Simply feeling them there brought her a sense of peace, even now.

They're just jewelry, she told herself. *Maybe it's finally time to take them off.* Thoughts of people asking her where they went, or worse, people whispering behind her back, consumed her. Suddenly, she felt her heart beating so strongly, it drowned out her ruminating thoughts. *Did someone just turn the heat on?* She felt hot. She thought about answering questions and explaining why, after such a short amount of time, she was already divorced. She felt sick. Pushing back her chair and promptly jumping to her feet, Jess murmured a quiet "excuse me" and sped to the women's room.

Hovering over the toilet in four-inch heels and her new *this will make me feel better even if I can't afford it* Theory shift dress, she felt the hot vomit rise into the back of her throat. As her head hung closer towards the toilet, she heaved until there was nothing left.

This divorce feels like a wild ride, Jess thought. *It's like I'm stuck on the Cyclone in Coney Island, trapped in my seat until the very end.* I know it's going to be terrifying, and I already feel like I'm going to throw up. But I can't get off. *All I can do is brace myself and hold on tight, praying for it to end.*

After a deep breath and a few moments to collect herself, she splashed cool water on her face and put one high-heeled foot in front of the other. She had a business meeting to attend and a career to manage. This roller coaster of emotions, however painful, however, gut-wrenching, was her ride to take.

***

It's time to sell the house, she considered while walking Tiffany later that week. Not only was the house a reminder of the life she no longer had, but it was a bitch to maintain. Providing a few thousand square feet more than she needed, Jess was also growing tired of driving an hour each way to and from the city.

Let's not forget the minor detail that I never wanted that damn place, to begin with, she recalled.

One evening, nearly two years ago, shortly after they moved from New York to Atlanta, Jess arrived home from work to receive news she never imagined.

"Jess," he nearly yelled in her face as she came through the door that evening. "I found the perfect house." Well past eight o'clock, she hadn't eaten all day, and her feet ached from running from a nine-hour string of back to back meetings. Chris hadn't just caught her off guard, he caught her at the depths of exhaustion. "Don't be mad," he forewarned her. "But I submitted an offer."

As she stood at the doorway, bending down to slip off her black pumps, she looked up in disbelief. He had to be joking.

"You can't be serious?" She said, standing barefoot, frozen in the doorway. Her empty lunch bag still in hand, she took deep yoga breaths while consciously squeezing her eyes shut. *Count to ten,* she told herself.

"I'm serious, Jess. It's beautiful," he sounded confident. "You'll love it. I saw it listed yesterday and drove by during lunch. It has everything we need. So, I called the listing agent while I was in the driveway and submitted a verbal offer. Just trust me, I promise."

"I'm sorry," she shook her head as her voice escalated a few notches. "You haven't even seen this place, and you offered to *buy it?* Chris, we weren't even seriously looking for a house! Why on earth would you do this?"

This was the man Chris had become. Over the past few years, he had grown into the epitome of selfishness, exhibiting nearly every sign of a narcissist, according to her afternoon Google searches at the office.

To anyone who didn't know him well, he seemed like an up and coming, highly confident young lawyer in the making. But Jess knew better. His cool exterior was merely a facade for the monsters of self-doubt lurking inside. Coupled with his blatant lack of emotional empathy, he rarely considered how his words, actions, and decisions made her feel. Finding it too humiliating to accept blame, Chris rarely apologized for the things he said or did. In fact, Jess could count on one hand the number of times he owned up to the hurtful things he said over their years together.

Right there, standing frozen, Jess stared intently at the look on his face. Did he look…. proud?

I want to stay in the city, Jess pleaded with him. She never wanted to live the life of a sleepy suburban wife, and while she was angry with him for putting her in this position – she was angrier at herself for allowing him to. But no level of anger, resentment or disappointment that she showed mattered. Chris had a one-track mind – with a ruthless dedication to his own agenda and his alone.

Now a twenty-seven-year-old spinster, ala Bridget Jones, Jess craved a house more suitable to her new normal. *Don't all single people live in swanky high-rise buildings above trendy coffee shops and blow dry bars?*

As the months rolled on, Jess knew it was time. She was ready to move out and move on. Once sold, they agreed to split whatever profit remained, and with her annual bonus quickly around the corner, Jess knew she'd be able to afford a modestly priced condo closer towards the city.

Determined to find something hip and youthful, Jess picked up the phone and dialed Raquel. A friend she met at the gym, Raquel's genetics never got the memo that it was unfair to be that hilarious and that beautiful. Thanks to their mutual admiration for takeout sushi and bottles of red wine, the girls often found themselves laughing in unison over Cabernet and rainbow rolls.

"I'm ready," Jess blurted out the second Raquel answered.

"Who is this?" Raquel asked.

"Oh, sorry," Jess said. "This is Jess. I thought you had my number saved." Her voice trailed off in embarrassment.

"I'm totally fucking with you," Raquel erupted in laughter. "I know it's you! What's up? You're ready for what?"

"Well," Jess began. "The last time you and I spoke, you told me to tell you when I'm ready to get rid of this house and make a move into the city."

"That's right!" Raquel said. "And? You're ready to pull the trigger?"

Jess paced around the kitchen. "I'm ready. When can we go look?"

The decision to sell their house was a no brainer. She hated everything about it - how big it was, how dated it was, she even hated the smug neighbors. The youngest by at least two decades, each time Jess walked by in the cul-de-sac, she felt judged. They'd whisper from their driveways as they waited for the children to come home from school. Jess and Chris never fit in, and she knew it. *I need to get out of here,* she'd tell herself every time she passed them by.

The neighborhood also reminded her of the life she never had. While she hated the house itself, the idea of selling it stirred up unexpected emotions. Once gone, all signs of Chris and the life they shared would become a distant memory. No longer could she look at the bench in the backyard and remember the time he suggested that it become the 'first day of school' bench where they'd snap photos of their toothless little ones each year. She couldn't stand in the shower and remember how he'd wash her hair while the steamy water beaded off their bodies. As painful as it was to turn the page and leave the house of memories behind, she knew it was time. Selling was the first step.

"I'm free tomorrow. Pick you up at five o'clock?" Raquel asked.

"Sounds great." After watching things fall apart for this long, Jess was finally ready to see somethings fall into place.

***

"I had no idea how many streets in Atlanta started with the word Peachtree," Jess observed as she and Raquel arrived at the last stop of the day. Going into this, Jess envisioned a sexy, new high rise with trendy amenities such as on-site dry cleaning and a rooftop pool. But after a few hours and about ten showings, she surprised herself. A unit in a mid-rise condo situated in the community of Sandy Springs stole her heart. The family-friendly suburb had the peaceful charm of neighboring towns like Brookhaven and Buckhead, but without the Michelin rated restaurants and ritzy cocktail lounges. Not only did it offer a bit of respite from bustling city life, but it enabled Jess to have a much more reasonable commute to the office. Spending more time exploring the city, working out, or making dinners at home sounded far more appealing than spending countless hours commuting as she had until now.

As she walked through the wrought-iron doors of the main entrance, a sweet woman sat at the welcome desk.

"Good afternoon ladies," she said warmly with a thick Southern drawl. "How can I help you?"

"We're here to see the vacant unit on the fifth floor – I have the realtor key." Raquel retrieved the key from her purse. "May we let ourselves upstairs?"

"Well, let me welcome you to the Senato Condo Building! My name's Wanda and I'm the concierge. Just sign in on this here piece of paper and then you're free to go see the unit. Please do check out all of the building's amenities and let me know if there's anything I can do for you during your visit with us today."

As the girls walked down the expansive hallway, Jess noted cute wreaths adorning nearly every door they passed. She saw doormats with the words *Welcome Home* and thought to herself, *I think I can really see myself living here.*

They rode the elevator up to the fifth floor and stopped when they reached unit 5202. Using the master key, Raquel opened the front door and before Jess took a single step inside, she was captivated by how light, bright and airy the space felt.

From inside, she loved the way natural light poured in through the countless windows and how the hand-scraped hardwood floors looked like they'd been there for decades even though the building was just built. The unit had two bedrooms, each with their own on-suite bathroom. The master bath boasted a double vanity, walk-in shower and jetted tub. The walk-in closet was large enough for her wardrobe and then some, and as she walked from room to room, Jess felt as though she could finally breathe.

The building was a quick drive to just about everything including her favorite boutiques and go-to restaurants, yet far enough from the city that she could enjoy scenic views and avoid Atlanta's notorious traffic. As she stood in the empty living room, a sense of peace and calm came over her.

Joining Raquel in the kitchen, Jess took a mental inventory of the plethora of cabinet space. The appliances, as with everything else in the space, were brand new and top of the line. Despite not cooking in what felt like an eternity, suddenly Jess was ready to host a dinner party. As Raquel ran her hand over the cool, white marble countertop, she smiled. "I can totally see you living here."

Jess closed her eyes. She imagined coming home after a

weeklong business trip and drawing herself a bubble bath in the jetted tub. She pictured Sunday mornings cuddled in bed with Tiffany, watching reruns of Sex and the City as the tall trees swayed outside her window. It was easy to imagine the space filled with friends and family, having dinner parties where wine and conversation flowed into the wee hours of the morning.

Just like that, Jess made one of the easiest decisions to date.

"I want it," she told Raquel with an ear to ear grin. Turning towards the wall of windows, Jess looked out over the lush greenery and felt like she just came home. "Let's get the paperwork started."

***

Step one, find a condo you love. Step two, call your ex-husband to tell him it's time to sell the house.

While no time felt like "the right time," Jess decided to wait until the hectic work week was over to call Chris. Unsurprisingly, her call went directly to voicemail. It had been so long since the two spoke, and he was now notorious for refusing to take her calls.

Hey there, it's me. I was hoping to talk to you. I know you've told me to take the time I need with the house, but I wanted to let you know it's time. I'm ready to put it on the market, and I have a friend who offered to list it for us. Give me a call back so we can discuss a listing price and the next steps. Thanks.

Even though they were no longer together, the act of leaving Chris a cold voicemail felt sacrilegious. At one point in time, he had been her best friend. Her husband. Now it felt like a foreign experience hearing his name before the beep.

During their separation, she'd let herself slip the occasional "I love you" into her voice messages, but the sentiment was never returned and eventually she vowed to stop being his doormat.

That night, as she climbed in bed and reached for the book lying on her nightstand, her phone beeped.

"Hey, Jess. I got your voicemail. I've been ready to sell the house, just wanted to give you a little time. Let your friend tell us what's fair market value and just unload it. I'm fine to split the profit if there is one at all. Thx."

He listened to her voicemail and replied via email. *Did he have to be this heartless? And since when did he become so busy that he can't be bothered to spell out 'thank you'?*

It infuriated her that he just never seemed to care. The next morning, she called Raquel, and the two swiftly decided on a listing price.

"If you want to sell quickly," Raquel told her, "I'd suggest we price a tad bit lower than fair market value. This way we'll ensure you get multiple offers in a short period."

A novice to real estate, Jess obliged, proceeding to spend her entire Sunday scrubbing the massive house top to bottom, ensuring it was ready for prime time viewing and an open house, if need be.

By Wednesday, multiple offers rolled in. Before Jess could buy moving boxes, the house was under contract. And while the only thing worse than sinking their entire, albeit small, savings into the house was losing it all when they sold it. Owning it for around a year left no opportunity to build equity, although Jess felt a sense of relief to soon be done with the house – and Chris – for good. The stained carpets, 90s decor, and barren Koi ponds would soon be someone else's responsibility.

"The house sold," she told her mom later that night during one of their routine phone dates.

"Holy crap, that's a record. What? Only three days on the market? Well, that's good news, Hunny!" Judging by the silence she met, Sarah realized that perhaps Jess didn't share her same jovial sentiment. "It's good news, isn't it?"

Against buying the house from the very beginning, Jess was oddly sad to sell it. Despite having no desire to leave their last rental within the city limits, Jess embraced suburban life the best she could. But the nagging question she couldn't get out of her mind was, *If I didn't want the house when we bought it, why the hell didn't I stand up for myself back then?*

"Dear? Did I lose you?" her mother asked.

"No, no mom. I'm here. Yes, it is good news," Jess said with a tinge of reluctance. "I definitely won't miss these stained, dingy carpets and the sea of travertine tile. I won't miss trying to bake holiday cookies in these tiny double ovens," Jess continued, staring at the 1980s appliances in her dilapidated kitchen.

"I never did understand how he convinced you to buy such a big, run-down house," her mother said. "Sure, it was in foreclosure and you kids got it for a bargain, but still. At the time, I thought maybe that meant he was ready to start a family. I mean, what else would you do with all those extra bedrooms? But then that didn't happen, and I just thought he was an idiot for dragging you out to the country for no good reason."

Her mother was right, they did get the house for a steal. Due to the fire-sale price, and the recent life insurance policy left by Chris's mother, it was within their means to buy despite her near entry-level salary and his unpaid internship. Yet they still had a mountain of his law school loans to contend with, and each time Jess broached the subject of creating a household budget, Chris was either too tired or too stoned to discuss it.

"The house wasn't too difficult for us to buy," Jess said. "But what's proven to be more difficult is the upkeep. Do you know how much a landscaper quoted me to maintain the backyard? Last week he told me one of our trees was hanging over into our neighbor's yard. It's going to cost almost a grand to cut it down! I'll be relieved to have this place in the past and be living in an easier to manage place and space of my own."

But the question still nagged at Jess. *Why didn't I stand up for what I wanted?* For a young woman who had no qualms about asserting herself to men decades her senior in the boardroom, she struggled to stand tall when standing beside her husband. It was as if her voice became weaker as his grew louder.

The death of his mother left Chris forever a changed man. His mother had all intentions of attending her eldest son's wedding, having a gown custom made for the occasion. She helped Jess plan the upcoming nuptials from a distance and while the two didn't always see eye to eye, Jess loved her future mother-in-law for raising her husband. Her death came as a sudden loss.

She knew her marriage was deeply flawed, yet somehow, over the past few months, she hoped they'd persevere. *I refuse to fail at this,* she'd tell herself. *I will not end up like my parents. It's just a rough patch,* she'd lie. *Everyone struggles during their first year of marriage. Law school is stressful. He just lost his mother.*

She had more excuses than a pregnant nun. And they had all run their course.

Chapter Five

"I read a statistic online that childless couples face a forty percent higher divorce rate than those with children," Jess told Dr. Green during their latest session. He met her statement with an inquisitive look.

"And?" he asked.

"And I was wondering if maybe Chris and I got divorced because we never started a family? What if we got pregnant right away like I thought we would?" Jess' question made her feel vulnerable, but she'd been toying with the question ever since she came across the statistic in the first place.

Dr. Green peered at her over his #1 Grandfather mug. "Did having a child prevent your parents from getting divorced?" he asked.

She sat in silence. "I was only two at the time, I'm not sure I'd be the best judge of that."

"Let me ask you this," he pressed. "What is the worst thing about the divorce thus far?"

Well, that's easy. Divorce has felt like a death. She wasn't simply grieving the loss of her husband. She grieved the loss of a second family. Chris's dad, his baby brother, countless aunts, uncles, cousins, and his spitfire eighty-year-old grandmother. The very same family who graciously accepted her all those years ago now shunned her completely once news of the split broke.

"I think the shittiest part of getting divorced at this age is the stigma of it all. There's a stigma – I believe anyway – to being divorced this early on in life. None of my friends can truly understand, because most of them aren't even married yet. I can't even fathom dating right now, because I feel like introducing myself on a first date as 'Hi, I'm Jess. I'm a twenty-seven-year-old divorcee' would turn guys off from the start. So, I'd say the worst part is feeling like I just epically fucked up my life and while I want to learn from it all, I don't even know where to begin."

Jess leaned back into the sofa. For the first time since sitting on his couch, she took a deep breath and simply let it all go. The vulnerability, the admission of failure and embarrassment, the desire to learn from this somewhat tragic situation... all of it.

This feels good.

Call it a professional hazard, but Dr. Green had thus far always given his most valiant attempt at withholding visual emotion. He never laughed, rarely seemed to judge, and mostly looked as though he was intently listening to every word she spoke. Which she appreciated, but in moments such as these, she wished he'd display the slightest bit of emotion to indicate – on some human level – that she was on the right track.

Just as she waited in silence, a faint smile appeared across his face. "I think that's very wise of you. Wanting to learn from this all. Tell me more about this social stigma you mentioned."

"For starters, it's well known that gossip spreads in Jewish families as fast as a drunken sorority girl's legs at Arizona State. Being unfriended by my eighty-year-old former Grandma-in-Law on Facebook last week was a recent record low," she said. "I just hate feeling like anyone thinks this was all my fault. I didn't put my marriage on the back burner. I didn't completely disengage. Granted I have no benchmark of what a successful marriage looks like, but I'm pretty certain that marriages are not made of husbands who purchase homes on their lunch breaks or of wives who feel they have to mute their own voices just so their husbands' could be heard."

"You're correct there," Dr. Green took a breath as the alarm rang.

Do these sessions go by faster each time?

For someone initially hesitant to accept therapy, Jess now looked forward to their time together. She left feeling more accepting of herself, and almost always more enlightened.

"That's our time today," he said, slapping his hands against the top of his knees. "Consider this," he told her as he looked right into her eyes, "Sometimes we're faced with some tough decisions. Including how much we're willing to sacrifice in order to find out who we really are."

Who I really am? It's been so long since I haven't been a girlfriend, fiancé, and then wife… Even if I knew who I was then, I surely am no longer her.

"Well," Jess said as she stood to leave. "I can't say I know who I am at this very moment, but I sure do look forward to finding out."

With a quick smile, she left to tackle the day ahead.

***

Alrighty, Jess said aloud to her empty house later that evening. With the closing of both her current house and new condo both happening next week, procrastination was no longer an option.

She entered the larger-than-life walk-in, gazing at the rows upon rows of clothing.

When the heck did I buy this denim jumpsuit? More importantly, why did I buy a denim jumpsuit?

She took notice how simply holding some pieces elicited an emotional response. The Diane von Furstenberg wrap dress she wore to his law school graduation. The Herve Leger dress she wore on the last date night they had before he moved out. The barely worn bikinis she purchased for their scheduled vacation to Cabo San Lucas this winter. Each reminding her of the good memories she somehow lost hold of while wallowing in a sea of sadness.

I know our love was real. Their trips to Napa, sipping wine and soaking in the serene mountain views. Seeing Greg Giraldo perform live at the Comedy Cellar during their years living in New York City. Years of laughter and joy had quickly become overshadowed by vicious arguments and building blocks of resentment.

As Jess stood in her closet like a deer in headlights, she felt the urge to scream.

How lucky was he?

He was able to toss his clothes in a few suitcases, throw a couple of pieces of furniture in the back of a friend's pickup truck and just leave. She, on the other hand, was left to pack up their leftover life.

How the hell did I get stuck with this shit task?

After methodically hanging the remainder of her clothes in the final wardrobe box, Jess set aside a pair of boyfriend jeans and a loose t-shirt for moving day. She stood, brushing her hair away from her face, realizing that she subconsciously saved the hardest room for last. The long hallway was silent, and as she gently slid her hand across the wrought iron railing, the reality of Jess' unmet dreams wafted over her. As she reached the last door on the left, she slowly turned the brushed nickel doorknob and came face to face with the room she'd avoided since the day *divorce* was said.

It looks so empty, she thought. A few old sweaters and spare pillows spewed about, with a stack of dusty law textbooks stacked in the corner. The room had just a few physical belongings, yet the air felt almost too thick to breathe. Jess lowered to her knees and carefully placed the musty textbooks in a box, followed by some spare pillows, and eventually taping it shut. She grabbed a nearby marker and scribbled "GOODWILL" on the top.

Her eyes scanned the small but cozy room, noticing how the light-flooded through the two windows and illuminated the pale blue paint color on the walls. This room, of all the spaces in their house, was the hardest to sit in. It had been nearly four months exactly since Jess entered. It still hurt as it did then. She stood, walking toward the doorway, and just before turning out the lights, took one last look around. With tears streaming down her cheeks, she felt the dampness of the neckline of her favorite oversized, faded 1980s t-shirt. This would have been her baby's nursery.

***

Jess was consciously rediscovering her relationship with sleep – meaning she was finally getting some – and weekends now became a time when she could rest and take a break from the weekday work pressures. Her sleepy slumber hadn't fully worn off this early Sunday morning before she woke to the sound of her phone ringing. Rubbing her eyes, she blindly reached for it, wedging the cold phone between her pillow and her ear. Before she could muster a mumbled *hello*, a cheerful voice bellowed at her.

"Get up! It's a sunny day and we're going for a run."

"Who is this?" Jess muttered.

"Funny, wise-ass," Lea retorted. "Get up and put some clothes on. I'll meet you at the river in 20 minutes."

Before Jess could argue, Lea was gone.

A running trail buried within Atlanta's city limits was the place Jess and her girlfriends always referred to as *the river,* because it was tucked alongside the Chattahoochee River, winding for miles underneath shady, Georgia pines. It was the perfect respite from everyday life and Jess' *happy place.* Whether she was walking, with Tiffany begrudgingly trailing behind her, or running at breakneck speed alone or with friends, Jess felt the runners high every single time she laced up her sneakers and hit the dirt trail. The beauty of running, she considered, is that there's no special equipment needed. Other than a solid pair of sneakers, all she needed was a dependable sports bra to ensure she didn't end up with two black eyes by the time she finished.

Jess arrived at the trailhead twenty minutes later, tucking her car key into the small zippered pouch of her waistband. Spotting Lea as she bent over to stretch and tie her sneakers, Jess snuck up behind her to playfully give her ass a pinch.

"What the…?" Lea turned, hands balled into fists, ready to knock someone out.

"Don't punch!" Jess laughed with her arms held high.

Lea shot back a slight smirk. "Why must you always seize the most inopportune times to violate me?" she playfully asked.

"I'm thinking we take the first entrance up and wind through the back," Jess suggested. "You up for seven today?"

"Seven as in seven *miles?*" Lea already sounded exhausted.

Before Lea could continue her complaints, Jess took off, leaving her friend with two options. Follow or get left behind.

***

With a red face and tight lungs, Jess felt like a million bucks at the end of the run. *That's the beauty of this,* she thought. *No matter how impossible it feels while I'm out there, no matter how shallow my breath becomes or how much my legs ache, I can do hard things.*

"I'm starving," Lea groaned, leaning against a nearby light pole to catch her breath once they returned to the parking lot. "Can we go eat before I get hangry?"

Jess lifted her arm above her head taking a quick whiff. "I've got to shower! Are you up for going back to my house? I'll hope

73

in a quick shower and then we can figure something out. I have snacks at home, in case you're wondering."

Lea conceded and within ten minutes, Jess was kicking off her sneakers at the door. "Okay, help yourself to anything in the kitchen. I'll be right back."

Jess took the stairs two at a time and hurried through a quick shower. Reappearing downstairs in a pair of sweats with her hair wrapped in a towel, holding a Tylenol bottle in the palm of her hand. "Look what Chris left behind," she said, giving it a rattle.

"Tylenol?" Lea looked rightfully confused.

"Look inside!"

"Is this pot?" Lea asked with such innocence.

Feeling a bit like a giddy teenager, Jess thought the idea of smoking a joint together sounded sort of fun. Something she hadn't done since college, she envisioned them throwing on a movie, eating salty snacks, and laughing until they nearly peed their pants. At least that was how she recalled her pot-smoking days back when.

"Sure is!" reaffixing her towel turban atop her head.

"Are you asking me if I want to smoke pot? What am I, twenty years old?" Lea's serious tone and straight face made Jess momentarily panic.

Shit. Did I overstep?

"I'm kidding! What are you waiting for? Go get papers and a lighter."

Jess eagerly rummaged - albeit unsuccessfully - through every cabinet to find rolling papers and a lighter. Finally, in the back of the kitchen junk drawer, she triumphantly held a bright red,

Bic lighter in the air. Jess picked out the dusty green bud from the bottom of the Tylenol bottle, lighter in hand.

"I haven't done in this over ten years," Lea confessed. "You're going to have to go first."

"I'm no pro myself!" Jess admitted. "But I do realize we have a glaringly obvious problem. We have nothing to smoke this in..."

The girls looked at each other with blank expressions. Determined to problem-solve her way out of this, Jess sprung to her feet.

"Hang on, I'm pretty sure I have a little cigarette-looking thing around here somewhere," Taking the stairs two at a time, Jess reached her bedroom and dropped to her knees beside her bed. She retrieved a giant, clear Rubbermaid plastic storage container, taking a brief walk down memory lane as she emptied the contents of the bin. Wooden, painted sorority letters, postcards from her semester abroad, and a small, engraved box with Greek letters etched into the maple grain. She surveyed the contents of the bin but was left empty-handed. *Where the hell did it go?*

"Okay, so don't judge," Jess told Lea as she returned to the kitchen and pulled the fruit stand towards them. With a granny smith apple in hand, Jess took a paring knife and went to work.

"What's happening?" Lea asked. "We're stopping for a snack?"

"No, no," Jess waved her hand in the air, with the paring knife coming alarmingly close to Lea's face. "I don't have anything else for us to use. But we did this once when my roommate bet me to see if we could make pot taste like apple." Lea looked on. "She was wrong," Jess continued. "But it worked functionally, anyhow. You just cut like this, make a hole here, and bam!" She continued the surgical procedure until the apple had two large connecting holes. "Pass me the pot," she said, nodding her head.

Within moments, their apple prototype was ready to go. With the lighter in one hand and apple in the other, Jess took a long inhale, filling her lungs with smoke until she coughed a thick cloud of smoke into the air.

Twenty minutes later, the bud was gone, a pizza was nearly demolished, and a bottle of wine half drunk.

"Holy shit, I forgot how good this stuff is," Lea slurred, slouching into the sofa with marinara sauce pooling into the corners of her mouth. "I don't even care that I'm still in these stinky running clothes! This pizza is delicious!"

When was the last time I ate pizza, Jess wondered? *Jesus, this is incredible!* She folded her slice like any respectable New Yorker and reached for the remote control.

"Pretty Woman!" Lea yelled out, nearly sending her glass of wine all over the couch. "Stop! This is my all-time favorite movie. I've probably seen it at least fifty times," she declared.

"My grandma, mom, and I were mugged coming out of this movie at the theater," Jess said, gnawing at her pizza crust.

"Seriously?" Lea turned to look at her.

"Afraid so," Jess told her. "The movie ended late – maybe ten o'clock – and the parking lot was dark and empty. We all got in, and before my grandma could close her door, some guy in a ski mask jumped across her lap and grabbed her purse – and my mom's. He ran off before we even processed what the heck had happened."

"Jesus Christ," Lea whispered over the top of her wine glass. "How old were you?"

"Around eight, I think?"

"Off-topic, but your mom thought it was a good idea to take an eight-year-old to see a movie about a prostitute?"

Jess had never thought of that minor yet significant detail before. She laughed so hard a bit of wine came out of her nose. "That's Sarah for ya!"

After the rest of the pizza pie vanished, the girls snuggled up on the oversized sofa. With a belly full of melted mozzarella cheese and tannic Cabernet, Jess smiled. Tomorrow she could worry about selling the house. About proceeds, about down payments, about moving and about all the other worries taking up valuable emotional real estate in her mind. For tonight, all she wanted was to be alongside her friend, enjoying the present moment.

Overcome by love and happiness - and a wee bit of cannabis - she felt a new emotion waft over her. Something unrecognizable.

She felt content.

***

You do not have time to fall apart in there, Jess told herself as she walked into the closing attorney's office in the bustling suburb of Alpharetta that afternoon.

Knowing it would be the first-time seeing Chris in months, the idea of keeping herself composed and civil while emotions flooded her seemed like a monumental, if not impossible, task.

You can do this, she repeated to herself as she entered the conference room.

There he was, sitting rather stoically, in an oversized brown leather chair fidgeting with his tie. *Is that a new suit,* she wondered? She had chosen a pair of Banana Republic slacks which now hung so loosely it looked as though she pooped her pants, yet Chris appeared in a freshly tailored suit. The sheer sight of him took her breath away.

He doesn't look like my husband, anymore, she thought as she took the last open seat at the table, unfortunately directly across from him. She so badly wanted to be confident and look him boldly in the eyes, but she couldn't. Her heart ached and her hands shook. Her eyes darted around the room, avoiding all eye contact, eventually landing on her lap.

Isn't it just the craziest thing, how someone who only a few months ago was your husband now feels like a total stranger?

Even if she never loved that house, it still hurt to sell it. It was the first home she ever purchased. It was the place she envisioned bringing home her children. She remembered the day after they received the keys, when Chris led her by the hand into their new backyard. He sat her on a small bench behind a mature magnolia tree and pulled her onto his lap.

"I was thinking this is where our kids would take their first day of school photos," he casually told her. "My mom always took pictures of my brother and I and then she'd frame them around the house. What do you think?" He stared into her dark brown eyes and for a split second, Jess wondered if he was crying.

It was memories like these that made her realize she did love him. At one point, anyhow. It was so difficult to believe that less than a year after that day, they were sitting across from one another at an attorney's office, selling that very house. No photos were ever taken, no less framed. No children ever had.

Tears welled in her eyes as glanced around, wondering if anyone noticed. The attorney sitting to her right discretely handed her a tissue.

You were fine just an hour ago, she told herself. *You're fine. Do NOT let him see you cry.* Yet it felt as though her hopes and dreams were crumbling down upon her. She discreetly wiped a single tear with the back of her hand, happy to see Chris was so preoccupied on his phone to not notice.

"Let us begin, everyone," the attorney announced.

The new buyers couldn't have been more than thirty years old. They represented everything Jess wanted. They were young, happy, and seemingly in love. She noticed how they held hands under the table. With each signature, they exchanged big grins and looked lovingly into each other's eyes. The husband kissed his wife's hand every so often as bile rose in Jess's throat.

It was Jess' turn to sign.

Take the pen, she told herself as she felt her right arm go weak. *Take a pen!* The attorney patiently held out his Mont Blanc ballpoint pen as all eyes turned toward her. Embarrassed, she finally took it, sheepishly hanging her head low. Sitting in stillness, Jess took a few deep breaths, she waited until she felt composed enough to continue. *This is it. A few signatures and this chapter of life is officially closed. The house is gone. The life you had is no longer yours.*

Acutely aware of her overt display of emotion, Chris leaned across the table, whispering, "Please, Jess. You're embarrassing us right now. Collect yourself."

Screw you, she thought, no longer capable of suppressing her feelings to placate him. It was time she spoke her voice, even if it shook.

"I'll take as long as I need, thank you very much," she said rather loudly, making zero effort to return his whisper. She was suddenly able to look him in the eyes, and it sent chills down her spine that she felt nothing but disdain.

Her eyes met the gaze of the new buyers, and a new wave of emotions came over her. *Look at them, all happy. Just wait, you two. Just wait until promises go unfilled. Wait until curse words bounce off the walls, doors are slammed, and silence fills your house.* Her feelings of jealousy and bitterness repulsed her.

"Thanks, everyone," the attorney said, pushing his chair back. "Final papers should arrive in the mail to all parties within the next two weeks. All that's left to do is hand over the keys and we're all set."

After sliding them across the table, Jess stood, unintentionally locking eyes with him. In less time than it took her to blink, she pivoted on her heels and marched out with all the false confidence she could muster. Not only would a conversation between them likely end with her in tears, but frankly, she didn't even have a minute to spare. She had precisely thirty minutes to make it to the closing of her condo.

Rushing towards the door, she preemptively grabbed her keys and picked up her pace, praying she'd make it to her car before Chris could follow her out.

She quickly slipped the car in reverse, as he tried waving her down. Whatever he had to say no longer mattered. Today was a day for new beginnings.

Purchasing her new condo, all on her own, felt like the first step towards a new future. Did she have the answers to know what was to come? Certainly not. The future was still full of unknowns and the condo certainly would not miraculously solve all of life's problems, but as the song by Scene Aesthetic goes, there is beauty in the breakdown.

She just needed to look for it.

Chapter Six

*U**npacking is for the birds,* Jess told herself, sitting Indian style on the kitchen floor of her new house. No doubt, she *loved* the new space, but what a pain in the ass it was fitting the contents of her larger-than-life suburban home into her now modestly sized city condo.

I think four wine decanters might be slightly excessive. Where am I putting these things? And why did I manage to keep all these unused gifts from our wedding registry? Overwhelmed and feeling slightly defeated, Jess was thankful when her phone rang.

"Hi Dad," she said, struggling to stand, legs asleep from two hours of sitting cross-legged on the wood floor. "Just unpacking over here. How's it going?"

"Just calling to check on you, sweetheart. How's the new house coming along? I'm sorry I couldn't be there to help you move, although if I calculate all the times I helped you move over the years, I'd say my tab is paid."

Jess recalled her dad arriving just two days shy of graduation to help her pack up the tiny studio apartment she called home during her time at Arizona State. 'Are you sure you're all packed?' he asked. 'Dad come on, of course I am,' she lied. By the time he arrived, horrified to see she hadn't packed a single box, he vowed that would be the last time he helped her with a move.

They ended up packing her Ford Mustang with suitcases, shipping the rest, and making a cross-country road trip her college graduation celebration.

"Oh, it's going." Carrying a load of freshly washed towels into her master bath. Her college days felt like a lifetime ago. "Just trying to unpack as fast as I can to get all the boxes out. You know how much I hate clutter!"

Jess' reason for the rapid unpacking was twofold. One, she was anxious to make room for the new furniture that was about to arrive in the coming days and two, she was about to head out of town for two weeks on the heels of some recent news at the office.

"Oh, Dad, I forgot to tell you. I got a promotion!"

"Well that's not surprising. I'm so proud of you! You've been busting your butt, haven't you?"

The first on both sides of her family to attend college, and the first of her immediate family have a steady career in corporate America, Jess' parents beamed with pride when talking of her accomplishments, only fueling her desire to work harder. Her dad, a first-generation American, was raised by two Eastern European parents who Jess never knew to express the slightest emotion. They delivered tough love when raising their son, and at the age of seventeen, gave him one option for his career – to join the family textile business. Staying true to his commitment, Adam worked alongside his parents until the final days before they passed away decades later. Truth be told, her dad worked harder than any man Jess had ever known.

"I have! My boss and the execs took notice. They gave me an advance on my holiday bonus, a new title, and a fifteen percent pay increase. Which, of course, made it a heck of a lot easier to buy this new place. Well, that and these amazing Georgia real estate prices. Could you imagine what a two-bedroom apartment would go for back in New York?" She asked the question hypothetically, knowing full well it would be leaps and bounds out of her range, even on her new salary.

Serendipitously, the Pottery Barn Outlet was a mere twenty-minute drive, and although Jess undoubtedly went overboard, the new furniture and décor she recently bought made her chic and modern condo feel like a warm and inviting home. Every inch of the space - from the thinly-lined silver-framed family photos to the bright and bold abstract art now hanging in the living room – all emoted peace and happiness.

"Listen, Dad, sorry to cut you off, but the fridge is empty and I'm starving. I'm going to run out and grab a quick for dinner so I can finish unpacking before bed. Thanks for calling to check on me. I love you."

"I love you too, sweetheart. I'm proud of you."

Hearing that never gets old.

Jess' stomach rumbled on the drive to Whole Foods Market. While standing at her beloved salad bar contemplating which arugula salad to add to her biodegradable container, a distractedly handsome guy caught her eye.

Based on the green, leafy contents of his compostable to-go

package, he too shared her habit of healthy eating. Standing well over six feet, the handsome stranger wore a tailored gray suit, sported a full head of thick, perfectly styled blonde hair, golden skin, and a square jawline.

He noticed Jess as they both reached for the same pair of metal salad tongs, at which point he displayed a bright, white smile.

"Please," he said, handing them over. "You first."

Jess smirked. "Thank you," Accepting them without argument.

Am I flirting? The sensation felt so foreign she barely recognized it.

She nervously beelined for the checkout line, wishing she added more chickpeas to her salad. He got behind her, and as they waited, he stepped in closer.

"I know this is a little strange," he began. "But my name is Greg. And I'd love to get your number if you're interested. I'd like to take you out for dinner sometime. You know – the type served on an actual plate." He flashed his pearly whites yet again, holding out his phone.

"Sure," she smiled with a confidence that surprised her. They swapped numbers, and by the very next night, Jess had a first date on the books.

***

"Your journey – start wherever you'd like," Dr. Green told her as he crossed his legs and sipped his coffee the following week.

Jess now looked forward to her sessions so much more than she initially imagined.

Why such a stigma around talking to someone, she often wondered.

Being able to air out her innermost thoughts, concerns, insecurities, and fears to someone who had no biases, no real *skin in the game*, felt freeing. It didn't hurt that Dr. Green was such a genuinely sweet man, either.

"Well, I met someone!" she told him.

His eyebrows raised, a first considering he rarely showed any reaction when Jess spoke.

"Surprising, I know," she said.

"This is exciting. Tell me more." She loved how he propped his elbows on his knees and leaned forward, ensuring to not miss a single word.

"Well, life has been hectic. I was unpacking and desperately needed a break. I went to the grocery store and by total happenstance, met a guy while making a salad."

"Well, sounds like you already have one thing in common," he noted.

You never realize how important having things in common are, Jess considered *until you don't share any commonalities at all.*

It felt slightly ironic that it took a budding romance to begin for Jess to reflect.

"We didn't always feel like strangers – Chris and I," Jess began – turning the tables from discussing her new love interest to her ex. To her surprise, he was where she wanted to start in today's session. "When we met, we were both young and impressionable. We went to college, ruthlessly pursued our careers, and felt like we were going to take over the world together. We'd make plans – move out of Florida to somewhere more… youthful? We'd have a family of our own and raise them with the Jewish traditions we loved as kids. We loved traveling together. Having weekly dates over fajitas and margaritas. I learned to cook because he loved homecooked meals. It wasn't until the end that we stopped having anything in common at all."

The simple act of recounting their relationship pulled on her heartstrings. Being this angry for this long allowed very little freedom to roam down memory lane. She remembered the night he surprised her with a proposal. Their Grecian honeymoon, sipping chilled wine while watching Santorini sunsets in their bathrobes. Purchasing season tickets to the Miami Heat during the team's glory days.

We had some good times, she remembered.

"When did things change?" Dr. Green asked.

That was easy, Jess thought. "When his mother passed away, something inside him changed forever. Which was hard to see as his wife, and impossible to relate to – as I thankfully have both of my parents. Suddenly he became so recluse, and despite my best efforts, I couldn't get through to him. We had nothing to relate to. Nothing to talk about. He honestly seemed bored of me, bored with everyone."

"Well, it's interesting that a chance encounter with a gentleman at the grocery store has you reflecting on all of this," Dr. Green commented. "Are you excited to date again? Meeting someone new – especially for the first time since the divorce – is significant. How are you feeling?"

Truth be told, she was excited. "I'm ready. I don't like being alone. Evenings feel lonely, weekends are so isolating. It's one of the reasons I try not to spend much time alone. I'd rather be out with friends. Exercising. Heck, I'd rather be traveling for business, than to lay alone in bed at night reminded that the life I had is gone. I think dating again will be scary – uncharted territory – but I'm ready."

"Really ready," she repeated, sinking into the sofa.

***

Her first date with Greg was met with a belly full of butterflies. He impressed Jess by choosing one of her favorite local restaurants, whose claim to fame is a menu of farm-to-table entrees all under 500 calories.

She wore a newly purchased dress for the occasion – a plum-colored, slightly above the knee dress with one shoulder – that felt special, but not like she was trying *too hard*. He stood outside, waiting for her when she arrived promptly at eight o'clock. She spotted his strong jawline from nearly clear across the parking lot. He was taller than she remembered.

"It's amazing to see you again," he said, leaning in for a hug. "You look beautiful." Escorting her inside, with his hand resting between her shoulder blades, the simple touch sent electric energy through her.

When was the last time a man, other than Chris, touched me? She couldn't recall.

The young hostess sat them at a secluded booth in the far corner of the dining room, placing laminated menus before them. Greg politely waved them away.

What the heck is he doing? Did he eat before our date? Curiosity must've gotten the best of her because he could tell she was confused by nothing more than the expression on her face.

"I had a late lunch," he justified, settling into his seat.

But I didn't, Jess thought to herself. It being their first date and all, Jess felt hesitant to speak up – *but why? This is a potentially bright red flag waving in your face, are you just going to ignore it? The guy asked you to dinner but he's not going to allow you to eat. Say something!*

Yet like she had done many times before, Jess stayed quiet. Making sad eyes at the hostess as she walked away, menus tucked underneath her arm, Jess was left with a hot date and an empty belly.

This feeling of silencing myself feels all too familiar.

"Tell me about yourself," he asked just as Katie, their server approached.

"What can I get started for you two?" she asked.

Without skipping a beat, Greg spoke. "We'll take a bottle of the 2014 Duckhorn Cabernet. That's all. Thank you."

He spoke with such conviction that Jess became quickly mesmerized. *I happen to love that wine,* she thought. *But he didn't know that.*

Despite taking a backseat to all decision making on their first date, Jess surprisingly enjoyed herself. The bottle of Duckhorn turned into two and as the bright overhead lights came on, she realized they closed the restaurant down.

"I should call you an Uber," he told Jess as he reached into his pocket to retrieve his phone.

"Thank you," she said, noticing she was slightly slurring. Eight hours since her last meal, she spent the last three hours listening to Greg and his endless supply of stories. By day, he sold insurance at a boutique agency in Atlanta and by night, he rebuilt and sold high-end luxury cars to a niche market of investors around the world. When he wasn't working, which wasn't often, he loved to fish, hunt, run marathons and do extreme mountain biking treks around the world. He beat Chris' non-existent hobbies by a landslide, although Jess realized there was no longer a reason to keep score. If nothing else, her night with the mysteriously unhungry man left her intrigued. It had been so long since she dated anyone other than Chris that she felt like an entirely new person this time around.

"Your uber should be here in five minutes. Let me walk you out."

He helped her up, which was harder to manage than she expected. A slight haze appeared as she blinked to refocus. *I've been overserved!*

"Thank you so much, I had an amazing time tonight." Her smile, while genuine, was likely purple from three glasses of wine. As they reached the front entrance, she wondered whether he'd kiss her goodnight. She wanted him to.

"This was great," he said grinning at her. Towering at least a foot over her petite frame, he gently bent down and kissed her cheek. The sensation of his five o'clock shadow rubbing against her face sent quivers down her spine. "I'd love to take you out again. That is if you'll let me."

She wrapped her arms around his broad shoulders, rising onto her tiptoes to look him straight in his clear blue eyes that reminded her of the buildings she'd once seen in Mykonos. "I'd love that."

Chapter Seven

It had been nearly a decade since Jess dated and boy was it exciting. She willingly trotted around town with Greg – everything from long trail runs that set her legs on fire to the cult-like SEC football games he loved to watch with her at local sports bars. It felt good having a man to do things with. It was fun to have *fun* again. He impressed her with his beautiful house, where they'd stare up at the stars until the wee hours of the morning in his meticulously landscaped backyard. Cuddled up under blankets, she loved the feeling of his big, warm body wrapped around hers. Their early morning workouts, fun-filled days and late nights between the sheets left Jess feeling on cloud nine.

I can't believe this is happening, Jess thought, laying naked in his bed one Saturday morning.

Greg was handsome – in the obvious sort of way. Likely the most good-looking man she'd ever dated, she loved how girls stared when they were out. More successful than most men his age, Jess was turned on by his success. Her VW Passat and two-bedroom condo paled in comparison to the life he built for himself, but he never made it feel like a competition. In fact, it surprised her just how much she liked how it felt to be out and about on Greg's arm.

Being with him made her feel desired, wanted. Granted, he was just a few years her senior, but the way he seemed to have it all together reminded her that not too that long ago, she and Chris were arguing over whether or not she deserved a new pair of Lululemon workout leggings.

During their first few weeks together, Jess learned that he was originally from Overland Park, Kansas, but spent his childhood summers with family fishing and hunting in Alaska, which explained his rough and tough yet somehow squeaky clean persona that managed to stop women – herself included – in their tracks.

Getting to know Greg seized her attention as nothing had in a long while. Weekend mornings spent sipping freshly brewed Columbian coffee on his back patio, listening to him speak lovingly about his mother who overcame a long battle with anorexia, the tight bond he had with his father – a three-time cancer survivor - and his desire to start a family of his own. He prioritized his career and fitness regimen over dating thus far, and from his shortlist of prior dating stories, it didn't seem like he saw many women for a second date after closing the door of their Ubers on Sunday mornings.

It felt like music to Jess' ears, as she sat, legs crossed with his baggy t-shirt pulled over her knees, hanging on his every word. Captivated by his confidence, strength, and how she felt in his arms, Jess felt sexy and desired.

His testosterone-laden approach to affection sent the small hairs on the back of her neck to standing, and the way he wrapped his strong hands around the small of her waist each time he pulled her in for a kiss made her weak in the knees. Suddenly her nights spent binge-watching Bravo were traded for evenings spent wrapped around him.

As summer ended, they spent nearly every waking moment together. And it felt amazing to simply be wanted again.

***

It was a cool Sunday morning when Jess met Lea, Raquel, and Megan for brunch. By the time Jess arrived, the girls had already snagged a corner table on the back patio, strategically underneath one of the outdoor heaters.

She felt slight pangs of guilt for her recent disappearance. Ever since Greg came along, Jess knowingly blew off runs, brunches, and happy hours – trading girls' night out for couple's night in. She knew, like sharks during shark week, it would be a feeding frenzy once she sat down at that table.

"What's with the glasses?" Lea asked as she spread honey butter on a warm biscuit. General Muir was hands down their favorite brunch spot, mostly due to the memorable pastry basket exploding with warm croissants, buttery biscuits, crusty scones, and gooey cinnamon rolls. Sometimes Jess wondered if Lea came earlier than the rest of them to call dibs on the biscuits before anyone else had the chance. It was once a month that Jess allowed herself the gluttonous indulgence of eating said pastries, which she rarely regretted – outside the time she polished off the entire basket alone and had to drive home with her pants unbuttoned.

"Seriously though. Why are you all incognito?" Raquel asked as she took a sip from her coffee mug.

Just as Jess was about to stutter her way through an ambiguous, pre-rehearsed response, their server arrived with a round of mimosas that Raquel no doubt ordered.

"What do you mean?" Jess asked in her most nonchalant response. "We're outside. I always wear sunglasses when I'm outside."

Her oversized glasses tucked underneath the Yankees baseball cap pulled low over her eyes made her look as if she'd been running from a TMZ reporter. No one, unless you're a celebrity, needs to look so inconspicuous for brunch.

"What's all over your cheeks? They're beet red!" Megan said as she leaned in from across the table.

"Yeah, what's wrong with your face?" Lea said, squinting to get a better look at whatever Jess was trying to conceal.

With an audible exhale, Jess stripped away the armor, knowing her relentless group of girlfriends would not stop until they got the answers they wanted. As she laid the hat and glasses in front of her, she sat – with a rash-filled face and slightly blood-shot eyes.

"What the hell happened to you? It looks like you got into a fight with a rose bush," Megan shouted. The rest of the restaurant turned to see what all the commotion was about.

Of all Jess' friends, Megan was the most striking. With golden blonde hair that hung well below her collar bones and long, toned legs that seemingly went on forever, she had the type of physique that captured the attention of both men and women wherever she went. Beyond aesthetics, Jess loved her magnetic personality. When they met the year prior – at the same gym as Raquel – Jess found herself drawn to the tall, bubbly girl who always smiled her way. Before long, the two were grabbing coffees after their workouts and running at the river when they weren't slinging weights at the gym.

"Shhh," Raquel hushed as she reached for her mimosa. "People are staring!"

If this were a high school yearbook and superlatives were being dished out, Megan would win for Most Likely to Become an Actress, while Raquel would win for Most Southern. Her propensity towards all things proper, in combination with her desire to please everyone around her, rounded out the other girl's larger than life personalities. Lea would likely win for Most Likely to Travel to All Seven Continents, given her love of seeing and exploring the far corners of the world.

"If you guys think this rash is bad," Jess said as she leaned back in her chair. "You should see the hickey on my inner thigh!"

"Okay that's it," Megan exclaimed, sending bits of almond croissant across the table. "You can't leave us hanging. What the heck is going on?"

"You guys," Jess began with a level of glee that surprised even herself. "The night I moved into my condo... you know, the night none of you bitches would come over and help me." She made eye contact with each girlfriend for dramatics. "Anyway, that night I grabbed a quick dinner and while I was standing at the salad bar, this crazy hot guy just starts chatting with me. At first, I thought maybe someone was standing behind me that he was talking to, but nope – it was me. He asked me out, and I said yes."

"You said yes?" Now Lea was screaming. "So, help us understand this. You went out – an entire week ago – with a new guy and are just telling us about this now? How the hell have you kept this secret?"

She's right, Jess thought. *I did keep this a secret.*

But that was by design. The reality was, Jess wasn't sure what to think of the whole thing. Initially, she was so shocked such a good-looking guy asked her out during a chance encounter at the grocery store that she wasn't sure what to really say about it. She contemplated calling one of the girls to help her find a first date outfit but decided that might multiply her jitters. If she kept this to herself and the date was an epic failure, she'd save herself the embarrassment of talking about it. And after spending so many months – likely now a year – talking about the most intimate details of her marriage, it felt nice to keep something to herself for once. Yet now with time in the books, Jess was bursting at the seams to tell her friends all about this mystery, kale-loving man.

"He's just... sexy as hell," she began. "He drives a new BMW M5 and sells insurance – I think a combo of health, home, and life – but I'm not entirely sure. All I know is it's a huge relief that he's settled into his career. I mean he owns his house, knows how to work a BBQ, and has three German Shepard's. He's like a real man's man."

"He's nothing like Chris, is what you're saying?" Leave it to Lea to cut right to the chase.

"He's nothing like that guy whose name we won't mention," Jess continued. "Last night he cooked me dinner."

"We're going to need every detail," Raquel demanded as she dove into her smoked salmon bagel and cream cheese, without breaking eye contact with Jess.

"Well, his house is so charming. It's a two-story bungalow – I think he might've built the addition upstairs – but it's surprisingly nice for a bachelor pad. Huge backyard with a fire pit and outdoor speakers. After we ate, we brought a bottle of wine outside and listened to music and talked until midnight." Jess felt her cheeks hurt from all the smiling.

"And then," she continued, "we came inside. I had every intention of leaving, but he kissed me. And oh my god, was it sublime. Next thing I knew, we're making out on his couch – rolling around on top of each other like teenagers."

Megan smacked the table with the palm of her hand. "Yes!" she screamed without giving a single shit who watched. "Finally! I'm so happy for you. This is exactly what you've been needing."

"Well, thanks," Jess said. "But thanks to his five o'clock shadow, I'm now left with this ridiculous rash all over my face. I look like I wrestled with a rose bush."

"It's been so long for me," Lea said over her glass, "I'd take a good wrestle with a rosebush any day!"

***

One morning after digging herself out of a sky-high inbox, Jess reached for her cell before her first meeting of the day.

Do you know what today is? She text Greg, throwing smile and wink emojis for good measure.

Good morning, gorgeous. No clue. Tell me.

Taco Tuesday! There's a fantastic place near my office – meet me after work for happy hour?

Her stomach flipped at the notion of staring into his eyes over a spicy mango margarita. Yet when his reply came through, it fell significantly short of matching her enthusiasm.

Eh, I don't love going out for dinner during the week… but if you really want to go, I'm in. Let me know where to meet you. Have a great day!

Well, Jess thought. *He didn't say no, so I suppose that's good. But what the heck does he have against a Tuesday date night? I go to his house during the week for dinner… what's the difference?*

Her stomach sank slightly, feeling the tiniest bit deflated by his response, but she tried stayed positive and excited for the night ahead.

After a string of meetings, conference calls, and press release writing, she abandoned the office at 5 o'clock on the dot and anxiously raced to meet Greg.

***

"Hey guys," their server greeted them. "What can I get y'all to drink?"

"I'm good with water," Greg replied. "And whatever the lady wants."

Jess watched him with a slightly horrified expression. "Seriously? You're not even going to order a drink with me? They make the spicy mango puree from scratch. It's heavenly!"

"No," he said flatly. "If you knew how many calories were in a margarita, you'd think twice about getting one, too. Trust me."

There was an icy tone to his voice she hadn't heard before.

I guarantee you it won't, she thought. For Jess and her friends, margaritas were practically a dedicated food group.

"Well fine," she conceded. "At least have some of this guacamole with me. Their chips are seasoned with some sort of lime chili." She pushed the small wicker basket towards him and watched as a frown spread across his face.

"I don't eat carbs after breakfast," he replied, arms crossed in front of him. "It bloats me."

Jess peered across the table, observing Greg's odd behavior as she placed a perfectly seasoned chip in her mouth. As she tasted the saltiness of the chili lime and the crunch of the corn tortilla, she recounted the past month since their fateful meet-cute at the Whole Foods salad bar. It suddenly hit her like a ton of bricks.

I've never really seen this guy eat.

Technically, she had. He BBQed at his house a few times, but she recalled what he ate each time. *Salad. He always ate a salad.* Occasionally he'd top the salad with a few slices of the steak, or an unseasoned chicken breast, but a small salad was always center stage. And not one of those Chinese Chicken Salads Jess often ordered at the mall food court – the one with the wonton noodles and sesame dressing. His salads were dry as the Sahara – lettuce and meat. Plain and simple. And disgusting.

Maybe that's why his abs look the way they do, she considered, as she watched him sip his water. *Is he seriously going to eat a side salad with a glass of lemon water?*

For the entire five years Jess and Chris were together, they had a *no-matter-what* Friday night tradition. Regardless of which city they lived in, regardless of what shitty circumstance was happening at the time – from stressful law school exams, to the death of her beloved Grandmother, to the tragic passing of his mother – their Friday nights were reserved for a pitcher of margaritas, copious amounts of chips and salsa, and a sizzling plate of steak fajitas – just the two of them. *No matter what.*

They'd make a game of alternating who chose the restaurant, typically finding insurmountable joy in surprising one another with somewhere new – from a hole in the wall to the occasionally fancy Mexican fusion hot spot. A few hours and lots of tequila later, they'd climb in bed and rub each other's overstuffed bellies, laughing and swearing that they'd stop at one basket of chips the following week.

Having Chris as her de facto benchmark made dating difficult. Every comment, every behavior, every touch… were all compared to him.

Greg's bizarre behavior irked Jess because she truly didn't understand where it came from. For a guy who worked out as much and as hard as he did, when the hell was, he eating? In over a month of dating, she surely couldn't figure it out.

Food is such a big part of who I am, she considered as they sat in silence together. She loved trying new restaurants. Cooking new recipes. Sharing meals.

Can I see myself with someone who won't enjoy this with me?

The red flag she witnessed on their very first dinner-free date waved strongly in the wind, but she ignored it. Scared at what she might discover, Jess kept her rose-colored glasses on, picking and choosing what she wanted to see. Consumed by a few too many business trips, squeezing in workouts with Raquel and Megan, and seemingly just life lately, time flew by.

Suddenly, the week of Thanksgiving approached.

Her first holiday as a divorcee, Jess was more than ready to trade in exhausting days at the office and her newly conflicted feelings about Greg for a long weekend soaking up the South Florida sunshine with her family.

***

Thanksgiving was Jess' favorite holiday. The intoxicating smells of her Grandmother's sweet potato casserole topped with perfectly toasted marshmallows and slow-roasted turkey brought back the fondest childhood memories. Women largely outnumbered men in their family, and more than a dozen female cousins – Jess included – always assumed the role of cooking their entire meal, so long as music blared, and coffee flowed freely.

Years ago, Jess cultivated her own annual tradition of waking up before her family so she could start the holiday with a run. A big believer in getting the blood flowing and metabolism firing, she always looked forward to working up an appetite on the one day a year she refused to count a single calorie. Rather than obsess over how much butter was baked into the potato casserole or calculate how many miles it would take to work off the pecan pie brownies that inevitably would follow, she chose to start right and stay right on this glutinous day.

For the last ten years, Aimee – Jess' eldest cousin – hosted the family for Thanksgiving. Filling her small home with rented tables and chairs to ensure all thirty family members had a place to sit. Dinner began in the late afternoon, leisurely extending until late in the evening – when leftovers would be reheated, a movie would play, and sounds of children playing filled her home.

Despite her best efforts over their years together, Jess was never able to convince Chris to join her at Aimee's annual dinner. From their courtship to engagement, and married life thereafter, Chris stubbornly and selfishly insisted on spending all holidays with his family. For the first few years, Jess offered to alternate homes – even suggesting they visit both families since they were only a twenty-minute drive from one another – yet he consistently refused.

"You go enjoy time with your family," he'd tell her when dropping her off at Aimee's without so much as offering to come inside.

"You realize we're married now," she told him on their first Thanksgiving as husband and wife. The way in which he managed to completely dismiss her family embarrassed her while simultaneously making her feel like complete shit. Just knowing he lacked all desire to spend time with those who mattered most to her felt like the ultimate slap in the face.

This year Jess had no excuses to make to her family, no justifying his absence, and no looking at her cell throughout dinner wondering if or when her husband would text her. She was finally free.

She laced up her running shoes, popped in her new earbuds and let her little legs carry her for a gloriously peaceful three-mile run. The thick, humid Florida air curled her hair, infiltrated her lungs and labored her breath. Running over the years had become her time of solace, of reflection and truest form of self-love. It was her uninterrupted time to be completely alone. By the time she returned to Aimee's peaceful neighborhood, her lungs felt heavy and her heart content.

Jess slipped off her shoes and quietly brewed a pot of coffee to fuel their marathon-long day of cooking. As she chugged a glass of cold water in silence, smelling the freshly brewed coffee percolate, she waited with excitement for the kitchen to be filled with love, laughter, and new memories.

***

"It feels so good to be here," Jess said aloud to no one as she stirred the gravy at the stovetop a short hour later. Aimee was rather engrossed in tearing the ends off green beans at the sink.

"Hey cookie?" Aimee called out without taking her eyes off the colander of beans. "Do you remember when I took you to your first concert?"

"How could I forget?" Jess replied, adding another tablespoon of butter, along with a hefty pinch of salt and pepper to the pot. "Janet's World Tour! Mom and Dad didn't know you were taking me, and you showed up at my door in your new Ford Mustang. I thought you were literally the coolest person on the entire planet."

"Ugh, I can't believe I missed that!" their cousin Michelle yelled from her knees as she dug out the bag of marshmallows from the back of the pantry.

"You missed it," Jess chimed in, "Because you were four years old."

The girls giggled. They were close – all of them - in a sisterly type of way. They shared just about every intimate detail of their lives with one another and always managed to display unconditional love despite their uncanny ability to argue just as passionately as real sisters do.

Around the time Jess and Chris began dating, Aimee gave birth to the first of her two daughters. To Jess and the rest of the cousins, Aimee's girls may as well have been their true nieces. Jess helped Aimee pick out baby names, willingly read *What to Expect When You're Expecting* to her belly bump, and offered unlimited babysitting services, despite not knowing the first thing about caring for a newborn.

"Don't forget to stir out all the lumps," Aimee instructed as she peered over Jess' shoulder. Across the kitchen, Jess' mom joined the girls, perching herself up on a nearby barstool at the black granite countertop.

"It's so lovely having you girls together," Sarah began. "Especially since the harder you work in there, the less I have to do over here!"

For as long as Jess could remember, her mom was a Velveeta mac and cheese type of mom. She much preferred the convenience of ordering from the neighborhood Chinese restaurant and made no apologies for it. When it came to baking, the one and only time Sarah attempted to make a cake it came out of the oven boiling. Her hilarious attempt marked her retirement in the world of baking and introduction to the phrase 'let's order in.'

The sound of their youngest cousin Ashley shuffling downstairs made everyone's heads turn.

"Good morning, lazy lady," Jess called out. Of all the girls, Ashley was known for her inexplicable ability to sleep through just about anything. Last year, on this day, she managed to sleep straight through a hurricane that rolled through South Florida with a vengeance.

"Oh, shut it," Ashley mumbled. "Someone, for the love of God, pass me a cup of coffee."

"Here you go, Darling," Sarah said, handing a mug to her niece. "The pot is full, help yourself."

That's how they were, this family. And it made Jess miss living nearby. It felt freeing – not being preoccupied with thoughts and worries about where Chris was or why he refused to join her and her family.

Yet she knew life in Atlanta was the smart decision. South Florida's job market was weak at best, and the hot, humid summers were enough to make her appreciate the life she was building – where a weekend with her family was thankfully only a short flight away.

As Jess looked around the crowded kitchen, she couldn't help but notice the beautifully unspoken rhythm amongst them as the girls stirred, sautéed, baked and broiled.

"Hunny," Jess' mom called out to her, "your phone is vibrating. Shall I check it?"

"No mom, that's okay," Jess wiped her hands on the dishtowel draped over her shoulder. She hadn't spoken to Greg since the day she left Atlanta – just one day after their last dinner-free date. When she saw his text message appear, it actually caught her by surprise.

Hey there! I just wanted to say hi. I hope you're having a blast with the family.

I am! Just about to whip up my family's notorious bourbon pecan pie brownies. How's your trip?

Oh man! Brownies?! He wrote. I hope you're going for a run afterward!

Jess stopped to re-read his message three times before bringing herself to reply. *That's odd,* she thought as she felt her eyes squint and her brow furrow. *And a little bit rude.* Sure, she had already gotten a run in, but what's it to him? *Who is this guy to tell me to run off my dessert?*

Already ran this morning!

Sweet. Me too. How far did you go?

Three miles around the lake. This South Florida humidity is brutal!

Is this turning into a competition, she wondered? *Why am I feeling the need to justify my workout to this guy?*

Oh. It's frigid here, around twenty degrees when I got up this morning. My mom and I only went for a ten miler, but she promised we'd go back for another ten before dinner. Gotta earn that dinner, baby!

"Why are you making that face?" Sarah asked, casually resting her chin on Jess' shoulder. "Who are you talking to?"

Jess slipped her phone face-down on the counter and walked away. "No one, Mom. It's nothing important."

As Aimee took the turkey out of the oven and Jess got to work on the brownies, her mom, Ashley, and Michelle set the tables that filled the tiny living room. The women moved in effortless synchronicity, and judging from the smiles spread across their faces, they loved every minute of it.

***

"God, I should not have eaten that third brownie," Jess groaned as she rubbed her full belly. Always one to practice self-control, something about Thanksgiving left Jess' innate ability to keep her mouth shut by the wayside.

"You always eat the third brownie, Darling," her mother responded. The two curled up on the sofa, watching in delight as the men in the family were left to contend with the mess in the kitchen. Once Aimee, Michelle, and Ashley announced their walk around the neighborhood, Sarah seized the opportunity to spend some uninterrupted time with her daughter.

"So. tell me, Madela, how are you doing?"

"I'm good, Mom," Jess offered without expansion.

"I'm afraid I'm going to need a bit more context other than *you're good*, dear," she prodded.

Jess knew how this conversation would go. With Jewish mothers, there simply was no detail left behind. *Oversharing* didn't exist. To Sarah, the more information, the better. She raised Jess to embrace her emotions and hide nothing.

Jess shifted on the couch, bracing herself for the heavy conversation that would inevitably follow.

"Things are good, Mom. I mean, the divorce was difficult – but I've been staying busy. Thankfully I've made some great girlfriends in Atlanta, and you know all about the promotion and how great work has been. It's definitely keeping me on my toes, but I know that's a good thing." Jess wholeheartedly believed everything she said. She felt immensely grateful for the evolving friendships she made. She wasn't entirely sure how lonely she'd be without the support of Lea, Raquel, and Megan – but she was thankful she didn't have to imagine it. And even though work was exhausting many days, she was thankful her hard work was recognized, and despite being the youngest and least experienced, she built a reputation at her company which she knew was no easy feat.

"I'm happy to hear you're staying busy, darling," Sarah added. "I know after your Dad and I divorced, I dove headfirst into my career – but that was because I had a two-year-old daughter to raise."

"No offense, Mom, but you weren't raising me alone. Dad was always there." Jess felt herself get slightly defensive any time her mother insinuated that she was a single, woe-is-me, mother. The fact was her dad showed up – *always in all ways.*

"You're right," her mother conceded. "Your father is a great man, always has been. Well, speaking of men… I know it hasn't been terribly long, but you're young and you don't have a little one at home to raise. May I ask – have you started dating yet?"

Jess had contemplated mentioning Greg during this trip… Truth be told, she was beginning to question whether he was the guy for her or not. And more so than that, was she even ready to meet someone? She didn't feel open – at least not in the deep, emotional type of way. In fact, she still hadn't shared with Greg her divorce. Every time she asked herself why, she couldn't come up with a clear answer other than simply not being fully ready.

"Well, there is someone. We met just after I moved into my condo. At Whole Foods, of all places."

Sarah sat up straight. "Continue." An oversharer by nature,

Sarah loved discussing all things love and lust related with her daughter, despite Jess' pleas to make her stop. As a woman twice divorced and once widowed, Jess' mom knew all too well the high and lows that came with make-ups and break-ups.

Yet, Jess felt herself hold back. *What if I go on and on about how great I think this guy will be, and it doesn't work out. Again. What if this relationship fails, too?*

It felt overwhelming, truly, to meet another man. To put herself 'out there' and let herself become vulnerable, without any guarantee things would work out.

But what is guaranteed in life?

"Well, what do you want to know?" Jess asked. "He's a few years older than I am. He's from Kansas but now lives in Atlanta, has a successful career, a great house, and we've been having a lot of fun until recently."

It's nice, being together like this, Jess thought to herself. The two women saw each other only a few times a year and through decades of ups and downs, Jess was never entirely sure how their visits would go. Sometimes they'd laugh until their bellies hurt, cuddled up in bed watching When Harry Met Sally for the fiftieth time, while other trips ended prematurely, with Jess booking herself on an earlier flight home just to escape the tension between them.

But this trip felt different.

"Well," her mom began. "I just love that you're open to meeting new people. I think you spent long enough trying to make something work that was destined to fail if I'm being honest."

"Ouch Mom, that hurts."

"Listen, dear, I don't mean to hurt your feelings here, but we knew this marriage was laced with problems from the beginning. Chris was always a bit of an asshole if you remember. When he asked your father for permission to marry you and your dad said no, but he did it anyway? Come on. He lost my respect that day."

This was news to Jess.

"Dad said no?!"

"He sure did," Sarah continued. "You two were so young. You were just beginning your career and he was just starting law school. You didn't have two dimes to rub together – that's no way to start a life together. Plus, Chris was always picking fights about the dumbest things and insisting you drop everything to cater to him and his family. Dad and I saw through his bullshit from day one."

It felt as though someone came by and dumped an ice-cold bucket of water on her head. Shocked, Jess continued to prod.

"I don't understand why you never told me this before."

Sarah's baby blue eyes scanned the room, breaking contact with her daughter. When they returned, they were tear-filled.

"Because," she said. "I never wanted you to end up like me."

***

"Jesus Christ!" Ashley said, exasperated, as the ladies returned from their post-feast walk around the neighborhood. Her white t-shirt soaked all the way through, and a bright pink sports bra peeked out from underneath. Sarah inconspicuously and quickly wiped a lone tear from her cheek.

"I swear!" Ashley continued. "I don't know how you guys live down here! I'm not sure if I'm just wet from the shower this morning or if that's really how humid it is outside."

A spitfire, twenty-something prosecutor making a name for herself in New York City, Ashley was just the firecracker every family needed. Her presence managed to shake up family events and bring a level of lightheartedness that made Jess appreciate family time beyond words. Last year, when the family celebrated New Year's Eve, Sarah had the cousins line up along Aimee's staircase to 'capture the moment'. Just as Mike, Aimee's husband, snapped the photo, Ashley drunkenly fell down the entire flight of stairs. Her sequin mini dress flung over her head, arms, and legs spread wide.

Those were the times Jess loved most - everyone being their raw, imperfectly hilarious selves. When laughter flooded the room and embarrassing moments were forever engrained. In moments like these, the loss and loneliness she still occasionally felt melted away and the only feeling left was pure, unadulterated love.

Chapter Eight

What the hell am I doing, Jess wondered as December snuck up and Greg was miraculously still around.

She wasn't sure *why* she was still seeing him. Was she just afraid of being lonely? Or did she relish in just how different he was compared to Chris? He loved taking her out into social settings and could always be counted on to try something new. The newness and excitement of her first single girl fling still felt relatively shiny and new. Having a workout partner to sweat with, to push her outside of her comfort zone, all while helping to expand her horizons exhilarated her. Yet the more their pseudo-relationship consumed her, the more she noticed herself muting her own voice just to appease him.

And it surely didn't make things easier that he continued to approach their relationship with gusto. He wasted little time introducing her to his closest friends and family. With every interaction, Jess learned more and more about the nuances of his personality – the life experiences that shaped him and the things that made his heart sing.

He doesn't even know where I live, Jess considered. Their first date happened months ago, and she had yet to invite him over– and oddly enough, he never asked for an invite. For months she managed to keep her divorce – and address - a mystery. She wasn't entirely sure if it was intentional or not – but there was undeniably something in her sub-conscious holding her back from opening up.

***

With the holidays in full swing, Greg was like a kid standing at the counter waiting for an ice cream cone. Anxiously awaiting the opportunity to tout Jess on his arm whenever the opportunity presented itself, he proudly and boldly introduced her as his new girlfriend.

Girlfriend. Every time she heard him say it aloud, despite her best efforts to embrace the innocent enough moniker, her skin crawled ever so slightly. She liked the lightheartedness that came with dating. Titles and formalities felt a little... too soon?

One night, as he lay naked underneath his crisp linen sheet, propped up on his golden hued arm, blonde curls cascading messily over his forehead, he looked Jess in the eyes.

"Come to my office Christmas party," he smiled, brushing a stray hair out of her face.

She stared into his crystal-clear eyes and partially because she had nothing else going on that Saturday night and partially because she found his baby blues impossible to refuse, she willingly accepted his invite, ignoring the pit forming in her stomach.

***

"This holiday party is at Chops, in Buckhead," Jess yelled out to Lea from the inside of the dressing room the following day.

While she slightly dreaded the idea of spinning around a room on Greg's arm, being introduced by the measly little title that made bile rise in her throat, the idea of a free meal at one her favorite steakhouses excited her. The notion of dining on tender filet mignon as she sipped a bold Napa Cabernet sounded delicious, even if she'd be the only one doing the eating.

"You think he'll let you eat his steak if he doesn't want it?" Lea joked.

Greg's oddities were often the topic of conversation at their brunches, and all her girlfriends concurred. This guy has some serious issues. But in this precise moment, Jess was less concerned with conducting a psych evaluation and more interested in the black lace cocktail dress she just slipped on.

"Damn!" Lea yelled from the accessories counter. "That thing is hugging you in all the right places."

Once Jess caught her reflection in the mirror, she was sold. Thankfully, her holiday bonus made the purchase a no-brainer. A reflection of how much she poured herself into work this past year, her bonus was in fact so generous that she planned to head over to Neiman Marcus after this to purchase a pair of sky-high black patent leather Louboutin's to match. *Yolo,* she whispered to herself as she smoothed the front of the skin-tight sheath.

"Hey," Jess turned towards Lea. "What are you doing with your bonus?" The question was rhetorical. Lea would likely slip it into savings. She was practical and pragmatic, notorious for adhering to a rather stale corporate wardrobe consisting of black slacks, a few of the same white button-down shirts, and simple leather flats. Basic stud earrings. She was a minimalist before it became a *thing*, well before Netflix produced a documentary about how living with less allows you to live more.

"I think I'll just save it," Lea told her. It's what she did with every bonus she'd ever received, Jess knew with certainty.

I'm glad one of us has some willpower, Jess told herself as she stared in the mirror one last time. When was the last time she felt this confident? This sexy? Racking her memory, she couldn't recall. But it felt damn good, that was for certain.

Two stores and over a thousand dollars later, the girls grabbed cappuccinos at the quaint café adjacent to Nieman's before calling it quits.

"I hope no one asks me about this pseudo-relationship on Saturday," Jess blurted out.

"Well, what are you guys? I mean – is this a relationship or what?"

"Honestly, I enjoy his company. But I think this thing – whatever you want to call it – has an expiration date." Since Thanksgiving, the way she looked at Greg changed. And while sure, it was nice having someone to spend Friday and Saturday nights with, the more she found out about him, the less enamored she became.

And once Jess convinced herself of something, it was damn near impossible to change her mind.

***

"Be prepared for some inquisitive minds tonight, baby," Greg told her on their way to Chops that Saturday evening.

In the few days leading up to tonight, she secretly wished she could've turned back time to the night he laid naked before her and decline his invitation altogether. The sheer thought of answering the basic questions of strangers about their relationship made Jess' palms sweat. She began checking check emotionally, although it didn't seem as though Greg felt the same.

As they entered the stylish restaurant, more than fifty couples dressed in suits and cocktail dresses flooded the dimly lit room. To her relief, initial conversations flowed as freely and easily as the Cabernet. Standing alone at the bar awaiting a refill in her glass, Greg's boss - a middle-aged, balding man with a round belly and short stature took his place in line behind her.

"Well hello there! I'm Stan," he outstretched his hand for her to shake. "I hear you're the lucky lady our Greg has been dating. What do you think of our guy over here? He's great, ain't he?" Jess' eyes followed Stan's gesture, landing on Greg from across the crowded room. Regardless of how she felt about him, it was undeniable. He was the best-looking man in the room. He was likely the best-looking man in *any* room. He shot a bright smile to Jess.

"Nice to meet you, Stan," she said with a tight smile, shifting the weight between her feet as she offered up her free hand. "Yes, it's been great getting to know him." *Too bad he doesn't know a damn thing about me,* she considered.

"You know," Stan continued, gently resting his sweaty palm on Jess' forearm, "Greg talks incessantly about this beautiful new girlfriend of his. In the decade that he has worked for me, I've never heard him gush over someone like this. Meeting you tonight, I can see why!"

His cheeks were as red as the soles of her Louboutin's and a bead of sweat dripped down his unmanicured brow.

How the heck could he be so smitten? What does he even know about ME? Not just my margarita order, or my favorite hiking trail, but the real me. She stood there silent, contemplating how to get Stan's damp hand off her arm.

Jess' eyes once again shot across the room as Greg's eyes met hers. He smiled once again, raising a cocktail shrimp high in the air, cheering her with the crustacean.

At least he's eating something. Other thoughts flooded her mind, too. Much of their time together was spent with Greg talking and Jess listening. At first, she didn't mind as she was genuinely interested in the things he had to say. But as of late, she grew less interested and more concerned with the fact that he never seemed to notice.

Cocktail hour wrapped with the sound of the Greg's CEO over the speakers. He thanked everyone for a prosperous year and asked all guests to take their assigned seats. Attendees were served an elaborate feast of filet mignon and lobster tail, accompanied by crab macaroni and cheese, sautéed spinach, and a slew of other scrumptious side dishes Greg would undoubtably avoid.

Thank goodness I didn't wear double Spanx tonight, Jess told herself. Nothing sounded more painful than feeling the tight spandex constrict against her expanding belly. Each course was more delicious than the next, although Jess made herself a mental note to save room for her favorite dessert of all time – their famous molten lava chocolate cake.

When the oeey, gooey, dessert was placed before him, Greg slapped his six-pack with his oversized palm. "Who can eat all of this food? Am I right?" he asked the table, but no one replied, as everyone – Jess included, was too busy digging into the molten cake before them. Just as she lifted her first spoonful to her mouth, Greg grabbed high onto her inner thigh. "Make sure you don't eat too much tonight. I need you to have plenty of energy when we get home." She felt the scalding chocolate hit her tongue as he flashed a devilish smirk.

For the love of everything in this world, please stop pinching my thigh fat, she thought.

Around him Jess became someone she wasn't entirely sure she liked. Despite the weekly sessions with Dr. Green and the plethora of self-love she practiced, being around him left her feeling uncomfortable in her own skin. She suddenly second guessed herself, hesitating before making otherwise innate decisions.

Regrettably, she pushed away from the warm chocolate cake after just one bite. For tonight, it would be easier to miss out on devouring the dessert that remained rather than face Greg's judgmental stares while she feasted on the caloric-laden plate.

After the plates were cleared and glasses emptied, the party came to a close. At the doorway, Stan found Jess once again. Hugging her tightly, the pressure of his round belly made her wince. Leaning in, he whispered, "Be careful there, missy, you caught yourself a good one. Don't let him go!"

Concealing an obvious eye roll, Jess was saved by the call of the valet.

"I have a Black BMW M5 ready!" the young attendant yelled, waving a set of keys in the air.

As they sped away, Greg once again slipped his hand high between her legs, sending her heart into rapid speed. "Baby, please stay with me tonight?"

His oceanic eyes and bright white smile seemed to twinkle from the glare of the streetlights.

Sure, he drove her crazy, but his simple touch made her body pulsate. And with her mind clouded by copious amounts of wine, how could she resist?

***

Their sex was like none other. To her surprise, the fact that she wasn't in love with him somehow made it easier to be completely uninhibited with him. It intoxicated her the way in which his blonde hair tickled between her thighs and she craved the way he picked her up with ease, pressing her back against the wall as she wrapped her legs around him. She never slept as well as she did after hours of having sex with him.

Divorce bared many unwanted gifts, and if there was one Jess resented most, it was the newfound insomnia. In her entire twenty-seven years of life, she had never lived alone. Learning to sleep in a king-sized bed alone proved far more difficult than she ever anticipated. When Chris first moved out, she'd often stare at the ceiling, counting the minutes and wondering how long the feelings of loneliness would last. Sometimes she'd count for so long, the sun would peak through the windows, signaling another sleepless night.

Yet when wrapped in Greg's arms, Jess felt nearly comatose.

Next to him, sleep was easy and deep.

***

Just one week later, with a New Year around the corner, something utterly strange happened. Greg went an entire three days without contacting Jess.

He *always* called. He *always* text. But suddenly, nothing.

And another day passed. Still nothing. By day four, Jess was somewhat concerned, and mostly curious. Decidedly, she fired off a casual text message.

Hey! I haven't heard from you. How's it going?

Radio silence.

This is so unlike him, she thought. Another twelve hours passed, and she fired off text.

Hello? I haven't heard from you in almost a week. If I didn't know better, I'd guess you've been busy out on a hot date or something?

What the heck is going on, she wondered? *Where the hell was he?*

Suddenly, her phone beeped.

Hey. Work has been nuts. Lots going on. I wouldn't call it a hot date, but I did just finish dinner with Jamie. It was nice getting lost in conversation, so I didn't even glance at my phone. I hope you're having a great night. Talk tomorrow?

She re-read his message four times, each with greater precision than the previous time. Her blood pulsated in her veins and she felt her heart begin to race. Her reaction felt uncharacteristic.

She felt... hurt? Since the say the met, he never let a single day pass by without a call or text, and apparently, she became quite accustomed to it. Not only did his flippant response disappoint her, but it made her react rather irrationally.

Who the fuck is Jamie? And why wasn't I invited to this dinner?

She did what any rational girl would do in a heated moment such as this. She rapidly sent a text to a reliable girlfriend for advice.

Greg just told me he had an amazing date with some slut named Jamie. Not even sure how to respond. Do I bother? Do I ignore? Need help!

Less than 10 seconds later, Lea replied.

Are you kidding me? What a douche. Tell him you're happy he went to dinner - maybe this time he actually ate something! Screw him, Jess. From his unsolicited advice on what you should and shouldn't eat to his complete lack of interest in you and your life, I say cut your losses and just end it here and now.

She replayed the brief courtship in her mind. Sure, she didn't have both feet in. Like a smell in the fridge that you couldn't quite identify, there was an unknown reason why she couldn't make herself feel the feelings she wanted to. But that didn't make this situation hurt any less. It had been a long time since she was with anyone other than Chris. And for it to come to an end was something she hadn't prepared herself for.

Is he openly dating other women without telling me? If so, is he sleeping with them? What about Jamie? Is he sleeping with her, too? I'm such an idiot!

Once her tsunami of thoughts came to slow swirl, she crafted a response.

I don't know who the fuck Jamie is, but I hope your dinner was just wonderful. I assumed with how much we've been seeing each other that this was exclusive, but it sounds like I'm not enough for you to keep it in your pants. I hope Jamie likes water and side salads, dressing on.the.side. Good luck and don't bother calling me ever again.

She hit the send button with vigor, tossing her phone on the bed. It felt reckless and a bit over the top, but he had it coming. And after the hell she'd been through with Chris, she'd be damned if she let anyone walk all over her again.

Impressed with her newfound confidence, Jess marched into the kitchen and grabbed a bottle of wine off the rack. What better occasion to open a special bottle of Cakebread Cabernet than the day she finally stood up for herself? She used her favorite wine key to open the bottle, yelling *Cheers* to no one as she poured a full glass to the brim.

As it hit her lips, the wine tasted of dark cherries and sweet oak. She let the plush texture coat her mouth as she swirled the glass around on her marble countertop. The light reflecting through the goblet accentuated the perfect purple hue. She felt damn satisfied with herself. No longer willing to roll over and take shit from anyone, the days of remaining meek were long gone.

How dare he think he do this - without so much as an explanation? And casually slip it into conversation that he's seeing someone else? Jackass.

The brief feeling of empowerment was interrupted by the sound of an all-too-familiar beep. *No matter what he says, just remember – this is over*, she told herself as she walked back into her bedroom.

Please tell me this is a joke.

Do I sound like I'm joking, asshole?! This guy has some nerve! Emotions got the best of her as her arm flung in the air, sending wine *splashing onto* the white linen duvet cover.

No, Greg, I'm not joking. I hope you're happy with Jamie or whichever other girls you're seeing. I don't deserve this - from you or anyone. We're done.

Less than two minutes later, and while she searched for a rag to clean her mess, he replied.

Jess, I don't know what the fuck is going on with you. I've told you no less than twenty times that Jamie is my old college roommate. He's married and very much not my new girlfriend. I prefer the company of women, as I hope you'd know by now.

Her face fell as she processed the last few words of his message.

Oooooh crap. That's right. I do remember him telling me about his college roommate. He did have a name that I thought sounded better suited for a girl, didn't he?

Could she have been this off base? Why on earth did she assume he was guilty until proven innocent? She set her phone down as feelings of embarrassment wafted over her.

What am I doing, she asked herself? *What is wrong with me?*

As it turns out, jumping back into the dating game proved to be far more complicated than she anticipated it to be. Ill-equipped to handle her broad spectrum of varying emotions, Jess realized she was capable of many things, but dating right now was not one of them. Feeling needy yet standoffish and secure yet uncertain all felt widely uncomfortable. Unwilling to open herself up to give any relationship a proper chance, she knew what needed to be done.

Before she lost her courage, Jess crafted a straightforward and succinct text message:

Listen, I'm truly sorry for the outburst. Clearly, this isn't the right time for me. I wish you the best of luck and know you'll find a great girl – I'm just not her.

She knew that would be the last time they'd ever speak. In fact, she was at peace with it. Because despite her inexcusable meltdown over a misunderstood text message, Jess knew this was not where she was meant to be. And even though Greg was hot, and even though he was a warm body to lie next to, it wasn't enough – and it never was. Being alone going forward might present some ugly moments, but she knew that there was nothing more beautiful than a woman who realized she was worthwhile.

Chapter Nine

"I just got fired," Lea blurted out.

"Hang on," Jess yelled out, haphazardly pressing the buttons on her steering wheel. It was already eight o'clock in the morning and usually she'd be in the office. Due to an accident blocking four lanes on one of Atlanta's bustling highways, she was running unusually late. "Okay, sorry. I had to adjust the volume. Say that again. For a split second, it sounded like you said that you got fired."

"I *did* just get fired," Lea repeated. "I'm at the office and just walked out of the HR office. Kellye and John are laid off too. I have no idea if you're on the chopping block, but I wanted to call you ASAP and give you a heads up." Her voice lacked emotion, which wasn't completely atypical for her friend, although it did surprise Jess.

She had a million questions, but only a few words came out. "Fired? But why? Are you sure?"

Given her role as Recollect's corporate communications lead, the executive team typically involved her once significant business decisions were made. Not because they needed her to help *make* the decisions but because they needed her to help *communicate them.* Last year when a company crane fell on one of their employees in Jaipur, killing him instantly, Jess was left to contend with reporters asking for company statements in the middle of the night. Just a few months ago when the company completed a sizeable round of layoffs, displacing more than one hundred employees, Jess managed the entire communication process, down to drafting emails to impacted team members. She was rarely surprised by company news and preferred to keep it that way.

But this? This was completely unexpected.

"Oh, I'm sure. HR came by and seized my laptop as soon as my ass hit my chair this morning. Natalie said something about unfortunate cutbacks. That woman is the worst – she didn't even give me enough time to pack up my stuff. Would you grab the plant off my desk if they don't rush you out, too?"

Jess' head spun faster than her legs at a SoulCycle class. *Just like that? Her entire team just… gone?*

"This doesn't seem right," Jess mustered. "I'll be there in fifteen minutes, tops. Wait for me?"

"Too late," Lea replied. "I've already hit the parking lot. John seemed composed, but you may want to give Kellye a call. She seemed pretty distraught. The kids were just going off to college and she seemed as shocked as I was. Let's just talk later, my head is pounding."

And just like that, her friend was gone.

***

127

What the hell is going on. Her mind raced as she nearly sprinted through the Recollect's lobby a mere ten minutes later. Rushing past reception without exchanging the usual pleasantries, she sped past rows of co-workers in silence and head straight for John's office.

Far more successful than most thirty-five-year old's, John earned himself a much-deserved seat at the executive table for his reputation and track record of building and leading powerhouse teams of employees who got shit done. Jess particularly respected his honesty above all and his ability to lead with true integrity. He never asked someone who worked for him to do something that he himself wouldn't do. Even though she did not directly report to him, Jess had no qualms about marching straight into his office whenever she needed clarity, guidance, or simply an ally from the powers above.

As her heels clicked and clacked on the floor underneath her, Jess walked with a tremendous urgency, anxious to see him and figure out what the heck was happening. When she finally reached his oversized mahogany door, she knocked forcefully.

No answer.

She knocked again.

"Can I help you?" a female's voice appeared from behind, spinning around on her heels.

"Oh, hi, Natalie," she quickly responded. "I'm just looking for John." She stuck her hands in her trouser pockets to conceal the sweat that she felt poured off of them. Whenever someone from HR appeared, trouble usually followed. In fact, the middle-aged, soft-spoken human resources manager seemed to otherwise hibernate in her windowless office unless she was summoned to emerge.

"Ah, yes," Natalie motioned with her arms towards the hallway. "If you'll come with me, best we have this conversation in my office." Jess followed her down the dimly lit hallway.

Jesus Christ, Jess thought. *I cannot afford to get fired right now. Please don't let this be happening.*

When they reached Natalie's office, she motioned. "Sit, please," waving Jess towards the chair across from hers. She silently closed the door behind them.

Closing the door was never a good sign.

"So, there have been some changes to the team as of this morning. Changes that you may or may not be aware of." She stopped speaking and observed Jess' face, waiting for a reaction. When Jess didn't give her one, she continued. "Due to some business constraints, we've had to make some difficult decisions. As a result, the marketing department - less yourself – has dissolved. I realize you had close connections with your team and that this is likely a lot for you to absorb, however I have been given authority to reassure you that your job here is secure. Mark and the entire leadership team are very grateful to have you and the decision did not come lightly. In fact, the entire team was involved – and one of the main contributing factors for keeping you on were your determination, grit, and dedication. I've been empowered to reassure you that you will *not* be impacted by the recent changes."

Jess sat, stunned. *My whole team is gone. But they kept me.*

She knew should feel relief to still have her job, but it somehow felt like punishment. Ever since the separation and inevitable divorce, Jess logged more hours mainly because she needed financial independence – but also simply because she had the time. She no longer had anyone to come home to – and sometimes slurping lo mein noodles over her desk felt easier to bare than spending another night alone in her big, empty, house. Never was it her intention to *upstage* her team. *Am I responsible for this,* she wondered?

Suddenly, she felt sick.

"Listen," Natalie finally spoke again, filling the silence. "I know this is a lot of change, and likely hard from a professional and personal perspective, but take a few weeks to settle into the new normal around here. Let's you and I meet again next month to discuss how you're doing. In the meantime, we're counting on you to keep things moving in Marketing."

With that, Natalie stood, and Jess followed suit, walking silently back to her cubicle as she stared at the beige tile beneath her feet.

To say she felt shocked would be an understatement of grand proportion. John, Kellye, and Lea weren't just co-workers, they were friends. They were her respite from the insurmountable amount of turmoil she experienced at home.

Now I'm going to be expected to somehow produce the same amount of work as a team of four?

It seemed highly illogical. Her few years of post-college experience hardly qualified her for the arduous task. With no support system on the home front – financially or emotionally – Jess had very few options. She had to approach the challenge head on.

Over the next few weeks, she clocked so many hours that

ordering dinner to her cubicle from local Chinese and Italian restaurants became the norm. Befriending the delivery men proved to be advantageous, with complimentary garlic knots and wonton soups "slipped her way" with every order.

"I know it can't be easy on you, Jess, with your entire team no longer here. I see you're putting in the work. We're lucky to have someone like you," her CEO commented each time he walked by, seeing her head down, working all hours. Despite her resentment towards the company for letting her *entire* team go, Mark's validation became intoxicating. It fueled her addiction to continue pouring all of herself into her work.

She wasn't surprised at all once Lea, Kellye and John quickly landed on their feet, securing new jobs within a matter of weeks. But the void at the office still existed, and nothing felt the same since.

It was one evening two weeks later, as Jess carried out her new routine of burning the midnight oil, that she heard the clacking of keys from a keyboard a few cubicles away. Setting down her Styrofoam container of chicken lo mein, Jess got up partly to stretch her legs and partly to lay eyes on the person potentially as crazy as her.

Who else subjects themselves to working this late?

His name was Erik, according to the laminated nameplate hanging off his carpeted cubicle wall. Jess was only able to catch a glimpse of his side profile as he was so in the zone he didn't so much as look up when Jess walked by. He had broad shoulders and dressed in slacks and a tailored button down. His hair was perfectly styled, and his glasses made him look a bit like Clark Kent. After catching his name and returning to her cube, Jess executed an extensive trifecta search via Google,

Facebook, and LinkedIn. Within a matter of moments, she discovered that Erik was the company's finance manager for seven years. Eight years her senior, he appeared to be an Atlanta native and according to his Facebook status, as single as they came.

"Erik?" Jess' coworker responded to her inquiry the following day over lunch. Quinn, a middle-aged man who worked in Recollect's logistics department had a larger than life, flamboyant personality that Jess found entertaining beyond belief.

"Yeah, I know him. We started on the same day. Nice guy apparently, just super quiet. I thought he also batted for the other team, which made me foolishly think I had a chance, but it turns out he fancies the ladies."

Jess quickly uncovered that Erik was the office crush for the ladies and the gentleman alike.

Not surprising, given his strong jawline and perfectly coifed, light brown hair. He was sexy in a very understated, unassuming way. *And he seemed to know it.* Yet despite all his undeniable physical attributes, Erik earned the nickname *Sandpaper* around the office for possessing a personality one could only describe as dry as an actual piece of sandpaper.

"Dryer than dry," Quinn told Jess, placing an egg salad sandwich on his plastic tray. "Such a shame. That face. That bod. Yet that personality."

***

Around seven o'clock the next evening, with two press releases left to draft, Jess searched through her desk drawer for the Italian food menu.

132

Is it a lasagna or panini kind of night? She picked up the office phone and dialed the local eatery, and as she waited for Kate from Giovanni's to answer, the sound of footsteps approaching her cubicle startled her. She hung up the phone and spun around in her chair.

"So, you're my stalker?" The way he nonchalantly yet confidently asked made Jess' jaw drop.

"I'm just joking around! But I did notice you were looking at my LinkedIn profile yesterday, and while I know we'd never met before, I recognized you. You're the girl a row of cubes over who also burns the candle on both ends," he said with a smile. "I'm Erik." He offered an outstretched hand.

Through all her investigative work, she ignorantly never considered that Erik could – or would – be notified that she looked at his profile. As she awkwardly stood to shake his hand, she got the first glimpse of his golden skin and green eyes up close.

"Nice to meet you. I'm Jess," she said, unknowingly darting her eyes in nearly every direction but his. She also realized they were nearly eye level – and at five foot two inches, that was a rarity for her.

"Surely, you're not still working?" he asked, gazing over towards her monitor. "I'm about to wrap up myself. What do you say we both pack up and I walk you to your car?"

She knew she should say no. After all, two press releases and Kate from Giovanni's were waiting. But something about him left her interest peaked. His sweet, Southern accent sealed the deal.

"I was just about to pack up," she lied. She smiled at Erik when she felt a piece of rogue kale in between her teeth. Immediately panicked, she covertly used her tongue to try and dislodge the leftover salad without drawing much attention to herself.

"Great," he said. "Let me grab my things. I'll come back to pick you up in five."

Grab your shit and grab it fast! She told herself as she began haphazardly tossing her belongings into her laptop bag. As she glanced into the tiny mirror she pulled out of her purse, she realized the piece of kale was thankfully gone. Now she could focus on quickly smoothing her hair while applying a swipe of lip gloss. *This is about as good as it's going to get after eleven hours.* Just as she zipped her bag shut, Erik returned, hanging casually over her cubicle wall.

"Ready?" he asked in the coolest yet charismatic way.

Jess followed him out of the dark, quiet office and just before they reached the parking lot, he broke their temporary silence. "So just when I thought I met my match for logging late nights at the office, I couldn't help noticing we also share the same gym schedule, too. You're also there nearly every night of the week. What do you say you let me take you to dinner after the gym this week?"

His forwardness took her aback.

Who was this guy who, until today, has never uttered a single word to me? We've worked in the same office, about ten feet apart, for this long and now he wants to take me to dinner?

It may have taken him that long to ask, but it took a whole five seconds for her to accept.

"That sounds great," she said, giving casual flirtation her best shot.

"Shall we say this Friday? Why don't we promise to leave the office a little early and workout first? We can grab a bite afterward?"

Jess excitedly agreed and prayed this guy might actually let her order dinner.

***

"So," Jess began as Megan tied her hair back in a ponytail. By some miracle, Jess was able to leave the office early enough to meet for an impromptu trail run after work. "Shit epically hit the fan this week." The girls took off, heading down the cool, shaded trail.

Jess loved how much Megan pushed her during their runs. Standing well over a foot taller than Jess, Megan's legs went on for days, making every run look effortless. As she hopped over fallen branches and swiftly ran up the steepest hills, Jess felt an adrenaline rush pushing herself to maintain Megan's speed. Especially on stressful days like today, the pressure in her lungs felt cathartic.

"You told me about Greg," Megan called from a few paces ahead. "Let's be real, after that first date when you had to make the Uber take you to the Chick Fil A drive-thru after dinner, we knew that would never last."

She had a point. Who takes a girl to dinner on a first date and lets them leave without eating? But that was all water under the bridge now.

"No, I'm talking about work. Shit hit the fan at the office this week. Have you heard from Lea?"

Jess was fairly certain of Megan's answer but asked anyway. Jess knew she was the centrifugal force connecting her girlfriends and enjoyed knowing she brought together such beautiful ladies who might've otherwise never met. After Megan responded with a quick "no, why?" Jess brought her up to speed on the unexpected layoffs.

"Oh shit!" Megan yelled as she hopped over a fallen tree branch. Her speech was slightly labored as they made their way up the steep trail. "So now what? Are you scared you'll get fired too?"

Jess shared the conversation nasty Natalie had with her, and that she felt relatively confident she'd be kept around — for now. She waited until they hit a stretch of relatively flat ground to share some other latest news.

"So, there's a new guy."

"Wait!" Megan turned around, jogging in place. "Another guy? We just got rid of Greg. When the heck did you find the time to meet someone new?"

"It's not a big deal," Jess began, yelling so Megan could hear as they took off downhill. "We met at the office, of all places. And the guy is *hot*. Like Mark Wahlberg hot. Only in this case, Mark is a corporate accountant. And has a southern accent. He asked me on this pseudo-date, and I'm sort of excited. We're going to the gym and for dinner on Friday after work."

"Any man that takes you to the gym on a first date knows you well!" Megan yelled.

"That's the thing," Jess said. "I've barely spoken to him but more than three times! All I know about him is what Facebook, Google, and LinkedIn told me. And my flamboyant coworker who I believe has a crush on him."

"Forgive me for asking the obvious," Megan said as she rested her hands on her knees. They always took a break at this lookout to soak up the expansive views. "But why are you accepting a date with this guy if you just realized that you're not ready to date?"

"Because he's hot," Jess said, shrugging her shoulders with an easy smile. "And because I feel like getting laid."

The girls shared a laugh and turned on their heels to continue. They had another five miles to go and were losing daylight quickly.

***

By the time Friday evening rolled around, Jess could hardly contain her jitters. After a week of nearly killing herself to keep the marketing department up and running by her lonesome, she needed to cut loose and burn off some frustration. Arriving promptly at 6 o'clock, Erik reached Jess' cubicle and greeted her with a grin.

The two left the office together yet drove to the gym separately. Noticing his shiny new Jaguar as it was the only car left other than hers, she deduced that finance must pay better than marketing.

Unconventional to say the least, she enjoyed their first date. The time together felt more visceral, which she preferred over swapping awkward laughs over mini-golf, or whatever cheesy first dates most guys kept in their back pockets.

I forgot a change of clothes," he told her while they quickly stretched in a quiet corner of the busy gym after their workout concluded. "I'm going to head to dinner like this, if that's okay?"

He wants to go to dinner, all sweaty, flushed and makeup-free? Now, this is my kind of guy!

"I'm starving! Mind if I ride with you?"

Judging by the smile on his face, Jess' proposal was just fine with him. Chalk it up to endorphins, or tense sexual attraction, but their mutual interest in working out and staying in shape turned her on. She likely missed a few reps of their workout due to the distraction of watching him effortlessly hoist 100-pound dumbbells in the air.

But is there more to this guy than just a hot body?

If Greg taught her nothing else, it was that a guy so obsessed with his physique was not nearly as attractive as it initially seemed.

There needs to be more, she told herself as she rode shotgun in his brand-new Jag.

Over dinner, he shared that beyond being a Finance Manager for the past fifteen years, he was raised in the deep South and came from a large family.

"What do you do for fun?" Jess inquired, sipping her ice water.

"Outside of work? I'm a huge University of Georgia football fan. And I love to travel - if there's a mountain to snowboard anywhere in the world, I've probably been there once or twice." He smiled back at her as the server placed their entrees in front of them. Much to Jess' delight, he ordered a ten-ounce filet and a baked potato. And ate both.

Thank goodness, she sighed a sense of relief.

She learned that Erik lived alone in a brand-new townhome that he had professionally decorated by one of Atlanta's top interior designers. And despite rounding the curve on 40 years old and never having a single serious relationship under his belt, he claimed he truly did want to settle down – with *the right woman.* He seemed willing to share information, including his sister who married a man covered in tattoos – much to their mother's horror – and his younger brother who followed in their father's footsteps by graduating law school and joining the family practice.

After realizing he nervously floated from topic to topic, sharing details about himself without taking the time to ask about her, Jess couldn't help but feel an all too familiar feeling.

Is this just how guys date now?

After their entrees were cleared and dessert declined, the server brought the check, which Erik grabbed without hesitation. As he rifled through his wallet, Jess replayed their date. She loved their shared interest in living an active life, joint passion for furthering their careers, and appreciated that he went out of his way to explicitly state that despite never being married, he truly did want a family.

But are there fireworks?

Did this University of Georgia loving corporate accountant truly blow her hair back?

The jury was still out.

Once outside, she politely thanked him for dinner – something she now no longer took for granted on a first date. As he stepped forward, closing the distance between them, she felt his warm breath on her face. Taken aback by his sudden forwardness, he quietly mumbled "I just have to see what this feels like," and leaned in, taking the nape of her neck in his hand and with just the right amount of force, sending quivers down her spine. He pulled her in for a kiss that left them both slightly breathless.

His hands slid down, stopping only when they reached the small of her back – she didn't mind one bit. Groaning with delight as he gently bit her bottom lip, he whispered in her ear. "Let's get out of here."

She willingly obliged, and within minutes, Erik drove them well over the speed limit to his place.

Jess was always of the notion that you could learn a lot about someone based on the way their home was decorated. As she walked in the front door, she noticed just how pristine his house was. Not a single thing out of place, it seemed more like a model home than one belonging to a forty-year-old bachelor. Nothing appeared *lived-in,* and she marveled at the plethora of faux plants and lack of photos.

There isn't a single photo anywhere to be seen.

As the two made their way up the flight of stairs, Erik reached for her tank top, lifting it above her head as she held her arms up towards the ceiling. By the time they reached the second story landing, both had left a trail of sweaty clothing on the steps behind. He led her, with one arm wrapped around her naked waist, into his master bathroom. Turning the rain shower faucet on with his right hand, his left hand found its way to her ass, squeezing so hard it nearly took her breath away. They kissed with a passion that took Jess by surprise. After twenty glorifying gratifying minutes in the steamy shower, they lie in silence, sprawled across his bed. With pruney fingers and a pulsating heart, Jess stared up at the ecru-colored ceiling

Now that, she thought, *that was just what I needed.*

***

"I don't get it," Jess told Stef over the phone the following week. "This new guy from work I told you about. We've hung out a few times since our first date… but we sort of just hang out, watch TV, and have sex."

"Yeah," Stef said flatly, "sounds like you have a friend with benefits."

"Oh," Jess was surprised with the disappointed tone in her own voice.

"Does that bother you?" Stef asked.

Jess knew when she accepted that first date that she wasn't emotionally equipped to handle a 'real' relationship. After how things ended with Greg, she would have been kidding herself to think she was truly ready to start something serious. "I guess not," she began. "With this arrangement, I'm not distracted and can still focus on work. Did I tell you they asked me to go to the Manila office in a few months? The Philippines! Can you imagine? I suppose having a real relationship would be a professional liability at this point. I'll just keep things as they are."

"It's not like you to sound so… practical?" Stef replied. "Are you sure that's really how you feel?"

Jess didn't give her best friend enough credit. She saw through her bullshit.

What could I expect, she asked herself? If I'm not ready for a relationship, I either get to have casual sex or abstain from guys altogether. *You can't have your cake and eat it too,* she tried convincing herself.

***

By their third date, Jess spent the night. By their fifth date, he made them breakfast. It was only then, in the wee hours of the morning as Erik worked his way around the kitchen, did she observe a few of his obsessive tendencies. She noticed how he assigned her a set of towels so she wouldn't use his, and how he left a small stack of University of Georgia t-shirts on the nightstand for her to sleep in. As they got ready for bed, she'd watch in silence as he executed an impressive fifteen-minute application of a highly methodical nightly skincare regime.

Two weeks into their new normal – television, sex, sleep – Jess threw on a Georgia bulldogs t-shirt from her stack and walked downstairs. She loved the scent of freshly brewed coffee that she didn't have to brew. It was early Saturday morning as she climbed onto a stool at his impeccably clean countertop and watched as he prepared them breakfast.

Two bowls of cereal, two cups of coffee, and a single glass of orange juice for him to wash down his lineup of vitamins and supplements.

I wonder how many vitamins he'll take when he's really old?

For a man still in his prime, he sure did have geriatric tendencies.

She pulled the t-shirt well past her knees to conceal the fact that she had nothing else on, and as he tossed another capsule back

142

with a long, audible swig of orange juice he nodded his head towards her.

"Hey," he said in a casual tone, "You may want to watch out. That upholstered stool is custom."

Looking down, Jess searched around for signs of spilled coffee but saw nothing.

"Did I spill coffee or something?"

"No. You didn't," he said, cocking his head back to swallow another vitamin. "But you have your period and that's an expensive stool. I would just hate for you to ruin it."

Oh. Dear. God.

Frantically and intensely mortified, Jess jumped to her bare feet, feeling the wood planks beneath her as she ran as quickly as her legs would take her. Through the kitchen and down the hall to the powder room, she slammed the door shut behind her. Hosting his worn-out t-shirt underneath her chin, she peered between her legs.

Fuuuuuuuuuck.

Bright red blood dripped down her legs. She got her period, alright.

***

"I literally bled everywhere," Jess confessed to Stef later that day over a FaceTime call. "To say I was mortified would be a big, big understatement."

The look on Stef's face showed just how horrified she was, too. "What the heck did he do?"

"Well, after I came out of the bathroom, I had to run upstairs to grab my clothes. Of course, I didn't have any tampons with me – I wasn't supposed to get my period for two weeks! As I sort of shimmied myself by, I could see him from the corner of my eye with a spray bottle of bleach and a rag. By the time I came back downstairs with all my things, he barely even looked up from the stool he was scrubbing."

Stef pursed her lips and frowned. Jess couldn't help noticing the deep lines that took up residence on her friend's forehead. Stef must've caught the glance because she immediately responded. "Chill. I have an appointment for Botox next week. I managed to find the only medical spa within a fifty-mile radius of this god-forsaken town. But enough about my face – back to this asshole. I feel like that was damn insensitive of him. I mean all women get their periods. What's the big deal?" She shrugged her shoulders and Jess couldn't help but agree.

What hurt the most was his blatant lack of empathy. Clearly, she was embarrassed. It wasn't her intent to have this happen. The least he could've done was not make her feel like such a terrible inconvenience.

She left his house before noon and vowed that whether he called or not, a 'friends with benefits' arrangement with a guy who wasn't even a friend was no arrangement at all. Completely content to let things fizzle, she didn't call and neither did he.

"You're completely right," Jess agreed. If I want different outcomes, I need to make different decisions. And the first decision I'm going to make is to stop repeating the same damn patterns."

One-sided relationships. Men who only managed to take an interest in themselves. Negative inner dialogue. Allowing herself to fall victim to the losses and pain of her past. Jess finally felt ready to turn the page and change the narrative.

"I like this you," Stef told her, with a softness that warmed Jess' heart.

"I'm not even entirely sure who I am anymore," Jess confessed. "But whoever I'm becoming, I'm going to promise to love the ever-living shit out of her."

Chapter Ten

A spontaneous trip to ring in the New Year in Florida, surrounded by family, felt like the warm hug Jess needed. Her soul craved relaxing unapologetically in mismatched pajamas, eating all-you-can-eat sushi and frozen yogurt with her little cousins, and strapping on running shoes to lose herself underneath the warm Florida sun.

A few hours after landing in Fort Lauderdale and shortly after the last of the sushi rolls were eaten, Jess and her family returned to Aimee's house. Unapologetically sipping sleepy time tea in her baggy sweatpants, Jess observed Aimee fold her way through an endless mountain of laundry.

Nicknamed the 'Clorox Kid' and the oldest of twelve cousins, Aimee was a self-proclaimed *neurotic cleaner* and order-keeper of the family. She routinely used Windex on the inside of her car windows, notoriously bleached her toilet bowls before leaving on vacation, and used more cleaning supplies than some of the nation's busiest hospitals. As she stood at the foot of her king-sized bed, folding a tiny pair of Wonder Woman underwear, she yelled out to her daughters.

"Girls get your pajamas on! Brush your teeth! Bedtime in ten!" Turning towards Jess, who sat cross-legged on the carpeted floor, "So, cookie, how are things?"

"I'm fine," Jess nervously reached for a nearby sweater to fold. The unexpected pressures from work, coupled with her fallout with Erik – proved to weigh heavily on her. Topping it off, the woman in the cubicle behind her just announced her pregnancy via a sappy poster she printed and hung in the breakroom. It stung more than Jess expected.

I'm managing or *I'm fine* were never acceptable answers to Aimee. This family always talked things out. This family supported each other. Jess knew her lackluster response wouldn't cut it in her cousin's eyes, but that didn't stop her from giving it her most valiant attempt.

Aimee shot her a quick side-eye. "Talk to me. What's going on?"

Truth be told, she had no idea how to respond. *Where the hell to begin? Do I start with the fact that I'm suddenly jealous of the woman sitting behind me for being married and pregnant? Or the fact that I feel like I'm going to combust if I eat another cold dinner over my keyboard at the office? What about the fact that I feel like I'm simply existing?*

The two sat in dead silence just long enough for Jess to feel Aimee's eyes burning a hole in the back of her head. Ultimately, Jess opened her mouth and her raw, unfiltered words poured out.

"I'm scared my chances of becoming a mom are gone," she blurted. Having that salient sentence take precedence over the sea of thoughts swirling through her head took Jess aback.

The expression on Aimee's face appeared to be a mix of sadness and concern. "Oh Jess," she muttered.

"It's been six months since the divorce," Jess began. "I get that Chris wasn't the guy to give me the family I wanted. And I know Greg wasn't either. But I'm just feeling like the hope is gone. I've been trying to start over – whatever the hell that means – but I feel like I'm just falling flat on my face. And it's beginning to scare me." She tugged on her tattered pajama pantleg. The artificial smell of freshly laundered clothing consumed the bedroom. She felt a lump form in the back of her throat as tears welled in her eyes.

"I just feel lost," she continued, in a near whisper. "Who am I, now that I'm no longer someone's wife? Now that my dreams of becoming a mom are gone. Some days the sadness doesn't feel so palpable. I'll have a particularly productive day at the office, a feel-good session with Dr. Green, or laugh at a joke so hard I damn near pee my pants. But then, seemingly out of nowhere, a coworker announces her pregnancy and the sadness engulfs me. Joyous life events that I used to wish for people somehow become a reminder of the dreams I've lost."

The sheer admission felt painful to Jess. She was regarded as the *strong one* of the family. Known to everyone as the independent, driven and successful one. She wasn't the one to cry into a pile of girl's Frozen underwear.

Aimee joined her on the floor.

"Come here," she opened her arms wide. At five feet tall, Aimee was constantly mistaken for a student at her daughter's middle school. Her petite frame and tiny hands were the smallest Jess had ever seen. "It's going to be OK, cookie, I promise. You *will* find love again. And trust me, you will become a mother. If there was ever a woman deserving of bringing life into this world, it's you. I know it feels like those dreams are in a far off, distance place right now, but life has a miraculous way of working itself out."

It could've been five minutes or twenty, but there on the floor, time felt as though it stood still. As Jess finally released Aimee's embrace to reach for a tissue, she noticed Samantha standing quietly at the doorway.

"Can I come in Mommy?" she asked in a whisper.

"Sure," Aimee said with a smile.

Having Samantha beside her sent Jess down memory lane. She vividly recalled suggesting the name 'Samantha' to Aimee and Mike when they discussed baby names after Aimee announced her pregnancy. She remembered skipping high school baseball games and nights out with her friends to come read baby books to Aimee's blossoming belly. She met her cousin at the gigantic big box store to pick out furniture for the baby's nursery. She even spent her entire minimum wage paycheck on adorable pink outfits months before the baby came and slipping handcrafted babysitting coupons for post-baby date nights in the corresponding card.

Jess loved that little girl before she ever laid eyes on her.

And there she was, eleven years later, feeling Samantha's little arms wrapped around her. She let the tears cascade down her already damp cheeks. In that moment, despite the overwhelming sea of sadness, Jess grasped how truly blessed she was for the first time in a long time. Her marital status faded into the background as she felt just how much love remained.

She just had to be open to receiving it.

The three women kissed one another goodnight and headed to bed. With abundant gratitude, Jess knew no matter how bumpy the road ahead may be, she always had the love of her family to keep her safe.

***

Fewer feelings pumped Jess with endorphins like the feeling of running on fresh legs. The miles rolled beneath her feet with ease the next morning, and her lungs felt clear despite the thick Florida humidity. Mid-stride, her cell vibrated from the armband strapped to her bicep. Only two miles from Aimee's house, Jess let the call go to voicemail.

Later, as she closed in on the distance between herself and the end of her run, her cell rang again. Running in place on the balmy Florida sidewalk, Jess contorted her arm, reaching into the pocket to retrieve her phone. It was Lea.

That's odd, Jess thought. In all their years of friendship, she never knew Lea to be a serial caller. Her dad? Sure. Her mother? Absolutely. But Lea never double dialed. Jess took a sharp inhale, preparing herself for whatever Lea had to say.

Through sobs, Lea's voice was nearly unrecognizable. The always even-mannered friend, Jess had never heard her friend this unhinged.

"Jess, it's me," she said. "My dad. It's my dad… He died."

Her words felt like a million daggers straight to the heart. Jess felt a piece of her heart crumble right there on the sidewalk.

When Lea decided to attend school in the U.S. and stay for good, she managed to make an annual trip home every summer to visit her parents and younger sister. She had a trip planned in just six months, never her dad wouldn't be there for it.

"I never got to say goodbye…" Lea managed to say between the sobs.

"Oh babe. I'm so sorry." Wishing she could reach through the phone and envelop her, Jess felt helpless.

It's strange, Jess considered, *how lately it felt as though it takes a monumental loss or traumatic experience to bring loved ones closer together.*

Up until recently in their friendship, Jess was the vulnerable one. She got a divorce. She had the failed relationship and emotions that wreaked havoc. Yet now, Lea suffered insurmountable loss. First her job, now this.

"I'm flying back to Croatia tomorrow," Lea told her. "The funeral will be next week. And then I need to fly back. My new job is trying to be supportive, but my manager informed me that I only have so many days available to take."

"What can I do?" Jess asked. "Anything. I'm here for you."

Turns out, the friend who rarely opened up wanted nothing more than to bring Jess for a walk down memory lane. Jess walked back to Aimee's as she listened to her friend recount childhood stories of how Lea's dad held four jobs simultaneously to support a family of three women. She shared stories of how she and her little sister would vie for their father's attention, and how growing up in war-stricken Croatia brought their family back to love when the rest of the world seemed so full of hate.

"I'm so sorry I can't see you before you leave," Jess spoke again, "But I'll be there just as soon as you get back. We'll get through this together – I promise."

Even though she could not comprehend the feeling of such a devastating loss, Jess was committed to giving her friend whatever love and support she needed.

Before she could say anything more, Lea whispered, "I love you," and the line went dead.

***

The next day, while surfing the internet to educate herself on Croatian funeral customs, Jess' phone vibrated.

Hey. It's me. I know this is totally out of the blue, but you've been on my mind lately. I miss you. How are things?

Her heart sank instantly. *Nooooo,* she thought. *Anyone but him.*

She aggressively pressed her fingertips into her temples until they throbbed. She knew there'd be a day when she'd hear from Chris again, but in no way was she prepared for today to be that day.

She read and reread his text, feeling new emotions bubble up to the surface with each read.

Who the hell does he think he is, reaching out like this? All those months of silence. Of unreturned calls. Never replied to text messages. And now? Now he's ready?

Anger, fueled by pain, surged through every single one of her veins. And just as quickly, emotions overcame her, bringing her on a trip down memory lane.

South Florida was where their relationship began. She easily remembered the day they met as if it were yesterday.

She and her mother had just moved to Florida from New York,

precisely two months after her stepfather passed away from a brief battle with brain cancer. She was brand new, smack dab in the middle of high school, and terrified to leave behind everything she knew – including her dad, her friends, her surroundings - and start anew.

In stark contrast to Jess' chaotic upbringing in Queens, Chris was raised in a predictable suburban family of four – complete with a schoolteacher mother, corporate executive father, and an inquisitive younger brother. Jess and Chris became quick friends, and he'd often invite her over for pool parties, movie nights in their indoor movie theater, and Sunday family dinners. Jess grew so close to their family that she was attending their beach vacations before long.

She recalled the night he proposed. Taking her completely by surprise by preparing a four-course meal, Jess managed to make it through her entrée without suspecting a single thing. She was utterly confused when Chris disappeared upstairs after she ate her last bite of broccoli. Just as she stood to clear the dishes from the table, Chris reappeared, wearing his only suit and carrying a bouquet of long-stemmed red roses.

He dropped to one knee and held out a small black box.

"Jess, I love you. Always have, always will. Please, will you marry me?"

He was crying, and so was she. She nodded through the tears as he slipped a solitaire diamond ring on her left hand.

She recalled their honeymoon to the Grecian islands, where they sipped poolside cocktails until the sunset and gratuitously called each other *my husband* and *my wife* for two, blissful weeks.

There was a time, she recounted *when he showed his best self. When he overused the words, I love you.*

Yet it was much too easy to let those memories disintegrate once the divorce proceedings began.

Don't respond, she told herself. Aimee and Mike were at work, and the girls were with friends in the backyard. Jess stood from the kitchen counter and made herself a cup of coffee. She let the warmth of the mug distract her hands from picking up her phone and typing a reply.

This will only end in tears, and you know it.

Yet her fingers seemed to have a mind of their own, plugging vigorously away at her phone's keyboard.

Hi. What a coincidence. I'm here in South Florida. I heard from the grapevine that you left Atlanta and moved back here before the holidays. How are you?

She stared at the phone, hands trembling as she waited for his response. The silence felt deafening as she remembered spotting him across the long high school hallway for the first time all those years ago. Even though so much pain transpired since then, the butterflies felt the same.

You're here? I want to see you.

It was like him to skip the pleasantries. To skip over small talk and simply say what was on his mind. Chris knew what he wanted and made no qualms about asking for it. It was one of the things Jess fell in love with yet grew to become a double-edged sword. The stronger his convictions became, the less hers seemed to matter.

I can't right now, I'm watching over the girls at Aimee's. But tonight, after she and Mike come back from work, I can probably slip out for a bit. Can I call you later?

He replied immediately.

That's fine, I'll be here waiting. I'd love to see you, Jess. Let's have dinner tonight. Rosarios at seven o'clock?

It was like him to deliberately pick their favorite restaurant. The place where they'd sip Cadillac margaritas while discussing the flower arrangements and ceremony music for their wedding. The restaurant where they'd share a plate of fajitas, sitting next to one another in the booth in the back, just so they could have some privacy.

I'll be there, she responded with a smile that he couldn't see.

Isn't it ironic, she considered, *how she'd spent the past six months trying not to think about him? How she tried with all her might to leave the past in the past and move on. And yet with one simple message, she could throw her arms in the air and saying, 'Fuck it' to the universe?*

***

The angst Jess felt while staring at the clock and waiting for Aimee and Mike to return home from work that evening was killing her slowly. She knew how disapproving they'd be of her newfound dinner plans and decided not to divulge the news.

What the heck would I tell them? Oh, remember the ex-husband who I was crying about last night? Well, I'm going to meet him now for some fajitas. Totally normal, right?

Aimee would look at her like she had a few screws loose. She felt like she had a few loose, if she were being honest. She knew damn well that she was playing with fire accepting his dinner invitation. And yet she did it anyway.

This is beyond irresponsible, she considered as she walked through the front door of the restaurant. The place still smelled of fried oil and melted cheese. Not much had changed after all these years, Jess observed. Arriving a few minutes early, the hostess sat her at the booth in the back – per Jess' request.

As the server brought a bowl of chips and salsa and a glass of water, Jess shifted her weight anxiously in the red leather booth. She ordered another water for Chris and two Cadillac margaritas – one with salt, for him, and another without salt, for her.

She glanced around the dimly lit restaurant to see if she recognized any familiar faces. Their drinks arrived and before she took a sip, she pulled her phone out of her purse.

No missed calls. No text messages.

He's fifteen minutes late, she thought.

She let the salt of the freshly fried tortilla chip hit her lips as her eyes fixated on the front door.

Another fifteen minutes passed, and she reached for her phone yet again.

Was everything okay? Did he get into a car accident on the drive over? Gosh, I hope he was alright! Her mind raced with worst-case scenarios before sending a text message to check-in.

Hey, I'm here at Rosario's and it's almost eight o'clock. Is everything okay?

She stared at the screen as she unknowingly drained her cocktail.

What was taking him so long?

Three little circles appeared, and then magically disappeared.

Again. And again. He was typing a response that he clearly didn't feel comfortable sending.

Finally, after what felt like an eternity, his reply came through.

Hey Jess. Listen, there's no easy way to say this. I'm sorry I'm not there – but I had time to think about it this afternoon… and I just don't think it's a good idea for us to see each other. We really should leave the past in the past. I want the best for you, and I hope you find it.

Jess stared at the phone screen long enough for it to go black. That was it. He wasn't coming.

She contemplated ordering another margarita, but when Eduardo came back around, she paid the check and drove back to Aimee's in silence.

The man who was once her partner in crime, her best friend, was now an utter stranger. Feeling humiliated, betrayed, and completely moronic, shame washed over her, suffocating her like a warm, wet blanket.

That night, as she lay on the pullout sofa in Aimee's living room, Jess pulled the covers high up under her chin as she stared up into the darkness.

***

"Hi, Darling," Sarah's voice blared through the telephone early the next morning. "I'm so sorry I didn't get to see you on this trip. You know how it is, there's always something going on!"

Depending upon the man in her life – aka the 'flavor of the month' – Jess' mom could be anywhere in the world. Currently ringing in the new year in Johannesburg with a gentleman she met while walking her Maltese around the neighborhood last year, Sarah had a zest for life and made no qualms about it.

Did it disappoint Jess each time she came to visit, and her mother was either traveling the world with her new 'companion' or home feeling sorry for herself when there was a shortage of men around? Sure. But she learned over the years that it was easier to accept her mother for who she was, rather than fight to change her.

"So, what's going on with you?" Sarah asked. "I spoke to Aimee this morning and she said you came home quite upset last night. Is there something you want to tell us?"

When the heck did the two of them even have a chance to talk about me, Jess wondered? Nothing got by these women – *nothing.*

"Everything's fine, mom," Jess told her. "I'm just feeling a little… down and out? Not exactly how I envisioned starting off the year – waking up on a pull-out sofa all alone."

"Well it's like I always tell you, dear," her mom began. "There's always a choice to make. You can start acting like your own best friend and take care of yourself - or you can choose to be your own worst enemy. I think it's time you stop questioning why everything you had fell apart. I think it's been long enough that you lean in – let yourself feel whatever you need to feel – and then move on. Once and for all, it's time to come to terms with this new normal of yours. Maybe once you do, you'll realize it's not half bad."

Jess knew she was romanticizing the past, putting her marriage on a pedestal that it never really deserved to be on in the first place. Turns out, Chris was quite the asshole after all.

"Listen, I need to run. We're off to do a wine tasting and have dinner 'al fresco.' Do me a favor and just be appreciative for the life you've been given. None of us know what tomorrow brings, so just be grateful for today, okay?"

"You got it, mom," Jess replied. "Have fun. I love you."

As she hung up the phone and packed for her flight back to Atlanta, Jess had no idea where the road ahead would lead, but at least she now knew, with absolute certainty, forward was the only way she was willing to go.

Chapter Eleven

" **I** 'd like to discuss my position here," she managed to say in her strongest, most confident voice that Monday morning. The smell of brewed coffee floated through the air as Jess sat face to face in her CEO's in his corner office. Despite dressing the part in freshly pressed, black slacks and a silk button-down shirt that tied around her neckline, she was just a wee bit terrified. This conversation had been on her mind for quite some time, but that surely didn't make this sit down she requested any easier.

When she initially accepted the role slightly below fair market value, her options had been limited. She and Chris were eager to move out of New York City, and she didn't have much experience to bear. But now? Everything was different. After kicking butt and taking names, willingly taking on more responsibility, and keeping an entire department afloat, a raise — and promotion — seemed only fair.

"I'm sorry," Mark said, leaning back as he crossed his arms in front of his narrow chest. "It's not that you don't deserve it, but a raise is just not something we can offer at this time."

Her prior pillow talks with Erik indicated otherwise. During one of their last late-night, pillow-talk chats, Erik told Jess of his recent pay increase. And as a result of the post-sex dopamine that flowed through him, his confession didn't stop there. He shared his new salary – which happened to be *three times* what Jess earned.

"I respect your position," Jess lied, re-crossing her legs underneath the mahogany desk for the umpteenth time, "but as you can see, I've given one hundred and ten percent since my first day here. To me, this is not just a *job*, it's *who I am*. And I believe my work – especially over the past few months - proves that I am deserving of more."

The other night, while lying sleeplessly in bed, Jess began to run the numbers. She imagined, with a fair amount of certainty, that Kellye and John's salaries had to have equaled been at least two to three times hers alone. Then she factored in Lea's previous salary – all of which were now costing the company nothing since they loaded all of the work, and subsequent pressure, onto Jess' petite shoulders. She was working herself into the ground, finding herself googling terms such as 'career burnout in your 20's – it is too soon?' and 'work-life balance, is it possible?'

Why couldn't at least a portion of that money be reallocated to her?

She was wired this way since childhood – to work hard, and hustle. Ever since the age of thirteen, Jess had a job. Whether she was selling churros at a local amusement park in middle school or bartending her way through college. If Mark was willing to work her into the ground without adequate and fair compensation, she was determined to find another company willing to pay her what she deserved.

After an unproductive conversation, they reached a stalemate. She thanked him for his time, although as she walked down the quiet corridor, she reached the conclusion that it was now time to pull back, look out for herself, and start searching for a better opportunity. She promised herself she'd leave the office earlier. To stop checking emails in the middle of the night. To truly disconnect on the weekends. After being left to feel unappreciated and undervalued, Jess now had two goals on her mind:

Make more time for me. And find a new job.

***

"You really didn't have to do this," Lea choked back tears as she hugged Jess hello for the first time in weeks. Jess held her tight, resting her cheek against Lea's wool sweater, lingering in their embrace for just a few more moments. It had been three weeks since Lea's dad passed away, and when she returned to the States, Jess did all she could to ensure she was met with the warmest of welcomes home.

Lea's father, according to the stories Jess heard, was an avid bocce ballplayer. A founding member on a lifelong league, he played with the same group of men for nearly four decades – and so it only seemed appropriate that upon her return, Jess got the girls together for a tribute to Lea's dad.

"I'm so sorry," Raquel leaned in for a hug while Megan squeezed Lea's shoulders. The most emotional of the group, Raquel could always be counted on to shed a few tears, which were already falling down her cheeks.

It was an unseasonably warm day in Atlanta despite being the middle of January, which worked in their favor as the only bocce ball court in all of Atlanta happened to be outdoors.

With pristine, crushed granite courts and an unobstructed view of the city, the girls spent the entire afternoon laughing, creating their own rules to the unfamiliar game. Just after knocking the 'pallina' – as Lea referred to the small marker ball - off bounds, Jess' phone rang loud. Stepping out of the sunken in court, she quickly answered before taking note of who was calling.

"Hey, Jess." His voice surprised her. Outside of a few touch base conversations, they hadn't spoken recently. In all their years of working together, she could never recall a time when John called her over the weekend. "Listen, I'm so sorry to bother you, but I have something I wanted to ask you. Do you have a second?"

"Sure," Jess gestured towards the girls, mouthing 'I'll be right back' before finding a quiet place to chat. "It's great to hear from you! What's going on?"

"Well," he said. "Remember last year after we wrapped up that rebranding project - I told you then that if I ever needed someone to run a marketing team one day I'd call?" Jess stood a bit taller. "Consider today that day."

Run my own team? Her curiosity peaked. While she worked for John, Jess secured him hundreds of media interviews. They traveled extensively together and the two built a rapport unlike any Jess developed before. She knew John's wife and four children by name and respected him far more than any other executive she'd worked for.

"Tell me what you have in mind," attempting to sound as nonchalant possible despite her sudden excitement.

"Well, I joined a healthcare technology company… And they've never had a proper marketing team. They need the full Monty. Someone to come in and raise brand awareness, help the sales team generate leads with some of the top insurance companies, garner press coverage in the big players like *The New York Times and The Washington Post,* and develop a fresh, new look and feel. I've been wracking my brain and all roads come back to you. You're the only person I'd trust enough to get the job done," he finished.

Oh shit. He trusts me to run an entire department.

To say she felt flattered would be a grave understatement. Her brain ran at a million miles a minute. But then, reality came crashing down.

I have zero healthcare experience.

He continued to tell her all about the role and suggested that if she were interested, to let him schedule an interview with the company's CEO, an executive who John described as 'tough as nails.'

The idea of a fresh start sent chills throughout her entire body. She was ready for the next chapter and ready to take on a new challenge. By the time he stopped talking, she had just one question.

"When can I come in?"

When Jess returned, the girls had finished their last game and were slowly walking towards the parking lot.

"Well, this new job opportunity sounds so fab," Lea spoke up after Jess gave them all the download. "I say go for it! What do you have to lose?"

What did she have to lose?

Taking on a larger role, in a field she had zero experience in, sounded scary. Jess silently ran through worst-case scenarios but realized if nothing else, she was getting increasingly more comfortable living in ambiguity. Not that long ago, the life she lived changed drastically – and guess what? She was still here. Still living. *Thriving, as a matter of fact.*

"I'm not going to have a fucking clue what I'm doing," Jess said flatly.

"Oh, calm down, it won't be that bad," Megan said as she took the last swig of her beer before tossing the plastic cup in the garbage. "You're smart, you'll figure it out!"

Jess was wildly accustomed to feeling out of her comfort zone in her personal life. From the divorce to stumbling from one bad date to the next, she was becoming good at navigating ambiguity. But work? Work was her safe place. She could handle a demanding CEO and tight deadlines with invariable ease. She was the queen of multitasking, had zero qualms with presenting in front of hundreds of people, and always knew how to handle even the most arduous of tasks. Yet a new position, at a new company, in a new industry, was so far beyond the bounds of her comfort zone.

"Let's hope so," she mumbled. "I mean how hard could the world of healthcare be?"

"You think I know anything about the world of fashion?" Lea alluded to her recent career change. After the unexpected layoff, she was quickly able to mobilize her network and reconnect with a former boss who happened to lead Marketing for one of the most notable women's shapewear brands. Coincidentally based in Atlanta, their headquarters were a quick hop, skip and jump from Lea's house and within two weeks, she was running their direct-to-consumer digital marketing efforts. The only thing she knew about shapewear was that she liked the way they smoothed out her 'extra bits.'

"In all seriousness," Lea continued, "You'll do great. Just give yourself some time to get your feet underneath you. I'm sure you'll learn a ton. Just start. The first step in anything is just to get going."

"I'm sure you're scared," Megan interjected, placing a perfectly manicured hand on Jess' forearm. "But here's the thing about fear. We all feel it — but the way to conquer it is to lean right into that shit and just push through it."

Jess smiled. Megan was notorious for listening to the latest introspective podcasts. Never one to miss an episode of Oprah's Super Soul Conversations, she was the friend who could always be counted on to impart wisdom and convince someone in the value of self-reflection.

"What's the worst that could happen?" Lea asked. Jess noticed how she was smiling again. It made her feel so great knowing that while she couldn't magically take away the pain of losing her dad, the girls were able to interject humor, love, and laughter into Lea's life at such an unjustly painful time.

What's the worst that could happen? Jess asked herself again. *I fall on my face. I fail. My ego gets bruised. I get let go.* Once Jess laid out the potential downfalls, none seemed all that scary. She had faced real loss before. As had the ones she loved. If absolutely nothing in life was guaranteed, why not jump and let the net appear?

***

By Tuesday morning, Jess called in sick to make the 45-minute drive north to John's office in Alpharetta, an Atlanta suburb known for sprawling homes and prestigious golf courses.

Michael, the CEO who began Evolution Healthcare out of his garage nearly ten years ago, was approachable yet curt. Quick-witted and surprisingly welcoming, their ninety-minute conversation flowed effortlessly and before Jess realized, he stood, thanking her for her time and instructing her to take a seat outside for a few moments. Smoothing out the front of her skirt suit, Jess sat on the black leather sofa beside his assistant's desk. She crossed her legs at the ankles, reached for the latest issue of *Modern Healthcare*, and from her peripheral vision, spotted John walking into Michael's office. He shot a quick smile her way before closing the door behind him.

"Well," John said as he re-appeared not even ten minutes later, "let me walk you out." As they rode the all-glass elevator down to the lobby, Jess was dying to know the outcome. "Michael and I just debriefed." He let his words linger in the air just long enough for Jess to feel scantly anxious. "He said if I don't hire you, I'm an idiot." His smile spread effortlessly from cheek to cheek. "When can you start?"

Jess said yes before reaching the parking lot.

They shook on a verbal offer that nearly doubled her current salary, and he gave her a start date of exactly two weeks from now. In that very moment, Jess realized that perhaps the key to success is not always knowing it all but having just one person who believes you're capable of figuring it out.

"You wouldn't believe it, Dad," Jess gushed later that evening. "I got the job!"

"Of course, you got the job." Her father always knew just what to say to make her feel like a million bucks.

"I'm going to get my own office and an expense account. And they have offices all over the globe, so I'll be traveling internationally, now!" Her mind raced as she drained a can of hearts of palm and dumped them into her salad.

The idea of traveling around the world, on someone else's dime energized and excited her. In her new role, she'd be reporting directly to John this time – a promotion that came with a hefty raise and annual performance bonus. Her first order of business was to hire and manage a team and put together a multi-million-dollar marketing budget.

When she shared her resignation with Mark, he offered her a measly ten percent pay increase, but it was too late. Once her mind was made up, there was no turning back.

I gave him his chance, and he blew it. The walk into Natalie's office to formally submit her resignation gave her a level of gratification she hadn't felt in a long time.

"Well I have some more good news," Jess told her dad as she brought her finished salad to the couch. "I'll be doing a few days of training up in Boston in two weeks!"

In the four years her dad lived there, Jess hadn't made it to Beantown once.

"Well, that's fantastic news, sweetheart! I can't wait to see you and celebrate what a success you've become. I am just so proud of you," he gushed.

There was something, even still, that gave Jess such happiness when she heard the words 'I'm proud of you' from her parents. It didn't matter how old she was. What her relationship status was. It didn't matter how much she made. There was still something about those four little words that always made her heart sing.

***

"So how are you doing, sweet pea?" Adam asked over his martini glass. This was probably the third time in her entire life she saw her father have a drink outside of his annual glass of Manischewitz at Passover. "And I mean really doing, you don't have to sugar coat anything for me."

Her dad aged a bit since she last saw him. His eyebrows were a bit bushier, and his hair was now completely grey. He had a few more deep creases around his eyes, but he was still the same handsome, loving dad Jess adored. She loved how each time he saw her, he made a concerted effort to wear something Jess had previously given him over the years. Tonight, it was the pair of Ralph Lauren khakis and a turquoise Izod collared shirt from last Father's Day. When she hugged him, she picked up the scent of the cologne she gifted him last year on his birthday.

"I'm good," Jess began as she poked through the breadbasket in search of a pretzel roll. "It's been a time of adjustment, that's for sure. But I'm getting there."

"You know you're my number one daughter, right?" Adam said with an easy smile. That was his favorite line, considering Jess was his only daughter - *and* only child. After her parents' divorce when she was two, her dad didn't rush into another relationship. He stayed single for nearly two decades before throwing his hat in the ring one last time. After that second marriage ended in divorce less than a year later, he resolved to Jess that some weren't the 'marrying kind,' and to Jess' knowledge, hasn't dated since. "I wished for a better outcome in your marriage than I had for myself, but sometimes this is the way the chips fall. I'm not just saying this because I'm your old man, but you deserve someone who will put you on a pedestal. Don't forget it, okay?"

Although they may not have seen each other as much as Jess would've liked in recent years, her dad always knew the right things to say to let her know how much he cared for her.

They dined on buttery lobster rolls and crisp salads, catching up on the NY Jets, work, and life lately. Before long, three hours flew by.

"Well Dad, I better get to bed," Jess said with a yawn. "The conference starts early in the morning and I need to be on my A-game. I had such an amazing time tonight. I know we don't get to see each other often enough. I'll do better, I promise."

"I'm sorry I haven't visited more either," her told her. "I'll make it a priority this year, too Sweetheart. I promise."

They walked along Boston's Long Wharf, flanked by hundreds of boats and illuminated by twinkling lights.

As Jess re-entered the sleek lobby of her hotel, sounds of men cheering reverberated from the sports bar. Intrigued, Jess peeked her head around the corner to see that the NFL playoffs were in full swing. While she couldn't care less about football per se, the assortment of handsome men corralled around big-screen televisions was somewhat appealing.

I should go to bed. I've already had two martinis. I have a long day tomorrow — you cannot be hungover!

She knew better. She wanted to do better. Yet reason and responsibility lost out to curiosity and intrigue as she found herself bellying up to the packed bar.

"Make room for the lady," one man yelled as he slid an empty barstool Jess' way. When she ordered a tequila soda, the guy sipping his Heineken signaled to the bartender, "put it on my tab."

"Oh, thank you," Jess said, waving her hand. "That's not necessary. I'll get it."

"It's my pleasure, really," he said. "Think of it as an advanced apology for me screaming in your ear for the rest of the game." He stretched out his hand. "I'm Alex, nice to meet you." His eyes were the deepest color of emerald that she'd ever seen.

The New England Patriots were crushing their opposition and after her second tequila soda, Jess knew it was time to call it a night.

Holy shit, how is it one in the morning? Time to get myself to bed.

"Well Alex," she said, standing to her feet. "It was so nice to meet you! Thanks again for the drinks and teaching me the difference between a running back and a fullback. I'm off to bed." She turned on her heels and before she managed to take a step, Alex gently grabbed her arm.

"Let me walk you to your room," he offered. As he stood, Jess realized she didn't fight him on it. Had she been of lucid and sound judgment, she likely would've declined his offer, but her judgment left two drinks ago. They followed the black marble hallway into the first elevator bank and he promptly pushed the 4th floor.

"Oh, I'm on the 7th floor," Jess said.

"I thought we'd go to my room," he smirked.

"Holy shit," Jess screamed as her alarm blared in her ear. *Where the hell am I?!*

Jumping out of the pillow bed, she noticed Alex fast asleep beside her. *Shit. Shit. Shit. Running frantically* through his hotel room, she grabbed her jeans off the door, eying her heels that were partially hidden underneath the windowsill.

Now, where the hell is my bra?

Draped over the desk chair, she spotted her black lace bra along with her silk blouse. As quickly as her hangover allowed, she dressed.

Stirring from bed, he didn't look quite as handsome as he did after too many cocktails. Jess surmised he had to be about ten years her senior, at least. His skin looked a bit leathered and his hairline looked significantly thinner in daylight.

"Good morning, beautiful," he muttered.

Just the sound of his unfamiliar voice made her queasy. Her meeting was set to start in an hour and being late was not an option.

"Stay," Alex pleaded. He reached his arm out for her and the sheets fell past his naked waist. "I'll order breakfast."

I'm going to hurl, she thought. She wanted to get out of there and get out of there fast.

"I have to go," she coldly said. Reaching for her clutch on the nearby nightstand, she noticed a small gold band sitting on the hotel notepad.

Oh. My. God. Please tell me I'm hallucinating. Please don't let that be a wedding ring.

Standing there, frozen in disbelief, she screamed, "You're fucking married?"

She shut her eyes tight as last night's memories came flooding back. The stubble of his facial hair tickling her inner thighs as her eyes rolled into the back of her head.

"Oh," he stammered. "Listen, it's a complicated situation…"

How on earth did she not notice the ring on his finger last night?

He stood up from the bed, completely naked, and grabbed her hips in his hands. "Let me explain," he began to beg.

"I said I have to go," she demanded, breaking out of his grasp and heading for the door. She couldn't escape that room and get away from him fast enough.

Jess grabbed a seat in the first row less than an hour later, full of black coffee and self-loathing. Orientation was due to run until 5 o'clock, and she prayed for the strength – and energy – to make it through. Soon she'd be home, where the images of last night would hopefully become a distant memory.

At the moment the clock struck 9 a.m., three Evolution Healthcare executives appeared at the front of the room.

"Good morning, everyone" the tallest of the them said with a deep, commanding voice. "Welcome to Evolution Healthcare.

My name is Alex and I'm Senior Vice President, Global Sales. Behind me, I'd like to introduce my leadership team…"

I'm going to be sick again.

He didn't have to have a Heineken in his hand or be naked for her to recognize him instantly. It was him.

***#

"Hey, cookie!" Aimee cheerfully answered Jess' call later that week. "How was Boston?"

"It was fine," Jess said flatly.

"Oh no. What happened?"

She was dying to tell *someone,* even if she feared how her cousin would respond. Aimee had been happily married for fifteen years – how the hell would she feel if another woman slept with her husband?

"I slept with someone's husband," Jess blurted. Just spitting the words out somehow wafted relief over her. As if the deep, dirty secret was no longer just hers to bear.

"Say what?" Aimee retorted.

"Genuinely, I have no idea how the hell it happened," Jess began. What had started as an innocent dinner out with her Dad turned into a night of drunken regret.

Like a moth to a flame when it came to a juicy story, Aimee wholeheartedly enjoyed living vicariously through Jess.

"Did you not see a ring on his finger?" she asked.

"Honestly, I can't remember." Jess racked her brain, but the martini-induced haze made it nearly impossible. "We flirted at the bar for hours, and then when he asked me to go up to his room, he was just so… charming. He kissed me in the elevator, and I wanted to say no – trust me I did - but before I could, I heard myself uttering the word 'yes.' Next thing I knew, we were in bed and my legs were wrapped around his head."

"Oh my god!" Aimee whispered. "And then what?"

"Well, it gets worse," Jess said flatly as she pulled her duvet up around her chin. The safety of her bed tonight felt better than she ever imaged.

"Don't tell me he had a small penis?" Aimee laughed.

"Ha, I wish that were it." Jess massaged her temples. This might go on record as her longest-lasting hangover of all time. "I'm afraid it's even worse. Turns out, he works at my new company. He's a Senior Vice President. He led my orientation the next day."

"Well, cookie…" For the first time possibly ever, her cousin sounded at a loss for words. "Well, this is quite a sticky situation. Did you talk to him again?"

"Definitely not," Jess responded. Thankfully she was one of forty new employees in attendance and between presentations and breakout sessions, there was no opportunity to speak with him again. The guilt and shame consumed her, making it nearly impossible to stay engaged in the information presented.

"We didn't speak again, but when I came back to my seat after an afternoon break, a folded-up piece of paper was slipped inside my laptop."

"'Let's keep this between us, please' it said. I still feel sick about it."

"Well," Aimee said. "Mistakes happen. Don't be so hard on yourself. I mean, it's obviously not your best decision ever made, but it's done. So, forgive yourself and make better decisions going forward. And next time, before you bang a guy, make sure you check for a wedding ring!"

Aimee's humor made Jess temporarily smile. "You wouldn't kill a woman for sleeping with your husband?!" Jess asked.

"Oh, let's be real. I'd run them both over. And then throw the car in reverse for good measure. But it's not my husband you slept with," Aimee laughed. "Okay, the girls are fighting, and it sounds like they're out for blood. Gotta run! I love you."

"I love you, too," Jess said.

"Oh, Jess! One last thing," Aimee yelled. "Promise me you won't let this eat you alive? Shit happens. Don't punish yourself, okay?"

Jess smiled. Aimee knew how her brain operated. Of course, she knew she'd lose sleep tonight, obsessively replaying her indiscretion. "I'll try," she mustered.

As she tossed and turned in bed that evening, Jess decided to heed Aimee's advice and extend herself a little bit of grace.

This isn't the first time you've fucked up, and let's be real - it surely won't be the last. Go easy on yourself. I know you feel like you're falling on your face, but you're doing the best you can.

Chapter Twelve

*W*hat is this teaching me?

Of all the lessons Green instilled upon Jess, this was perhaps the one that resonated most. 'Failure is essential to learning,' he'd tell her each time she felt as though she just face-planted on her quest towards self-improvement. Tired of feeling as if we were in a perpetual state of taking two steps forward and five steps back, Jess became determined to make a name for herself at work - for all the right reasons. Harnessing the energy and effort previously spent overanalyzing her screwups and missteps, she now focused on doing great work. Plain and simple.

In the spirit of learning from past mistakes, Jess no longer let the days' work consume her. She was running more. Lifting more. Learning to relax more. Reading more. Spending more time with her girlfriends. Finally, she felt as though she were closing the gap between her personal and professional lives. Fully anticipating news of what happened in Boston to spread like wildfire around the office, Jess felt ungodly relieved to discover it went nowhere.

"You know this is not your fault, right?" Lea asked her over the phone once Jess mustered the energy to tell her what transpired while she was gone. "You're not the married one."

"True," Jess knew. "But I slept with a married man. Whom I work with. Just because I'm not married doesn't make me feel any less guilty about what happened." Truth be told, she knew the weight that seniority and the 'good 'ole boys club' had in corporate America. If Alex wanted her gone, she'd likely be gone. Jess woke every day with a pit in her stomach, fearing each day would be the day she got canned.

But I'm still here, she considered. And after two months rolled by and she was still gainfully employed, she thanked her lucky stars, approaching the entire situation as a chance to learn, grow and to move the hell on.

You're better than this, became her new mantra.

Just two months later, Jess found herself in her CEO's office after he personally requested that she and she alone manage a highly visible Request for Proposal from one of the U.S.'s largest insurance companies. She was being praised left, right, and center for her dedication since joining the team. So much so, that she was promised an expanded role if all went off without a hitch.

"Good work breeds more good work," Michael told her that afternoon. Five years after embarking upon her career and finally – finally – her hard work felt validated. With a salary nearly double her last, an office with her name emblazoned on the door, and a talented team at the top of their game. Jess felt immensely proud.

The countless hours she spent preparing, fine-tuning her presentation and cross-referencing her stats, felt manageable with Tiffany in tow. When Jess received the rather progressive email from Human Resources stating the office was now pet-friendly, Jess didn't hesitate to bring in her sweet pup - who took to her role as office mascot quite well. The Pomeranian gladly served as a greeting committee whenever a colleague entered Jess' office. Ed, the China Garden delivery man, became a rather close acquaintance, bringing steamed chicken and broccoli five nights-a-week. Until the wee hours of the morning, Jess plugged away, ensuring the presentation didn't only blow her executives away, but that it packed the punch needed to seal the deal with the prospective client.

After all, $20M was on the line.

When presentation day arrived, she and Tiffany left the office somewhere around 3 a.m. to head home, get a shower in, and change before returning to the office by six the next morning. The boardroom was reserved, although she was the only one in town – everyone else would dial in virtually. A firm believer in dressing the part, Jess chose a tailored, charcoal Theory suit for the big day. She attempted her best blow out, applied minimal makeup, and sipped on an extra-large cup of coffee.

Jess set up the boardroom to her exact specifications, methodically and purposefully. She tested the internet connection, the video conferencing system, and ensured the presentation material was free of typos and in its final format. As she double-checked the notes she scribbled onto her notepad, folks began dialing in.

At 8 o'clock sharp, Jess' CEO and CFO dialed in. Not long afterward, the Chief Solutions Officer and a handful of other prominent leaders from the insurance company all joined the conference call.

"Thank you, everyone, for joining us today," Jess kicked things off in her most jovial tone. "We at Evolution Healthcare thank you again for considering our solutions and we hope that you find the next few hours valuable and informative. Should you have any questions as we go through the material, please do not hesitate to ask. And with that, I'll turn things over to our Chief Executive Officer. Michael, the floor is yours."

"Thank you, Jessica. In the essence of time and the ground we must cover today, let's get right into it. As I understand it to be, you all are concerned most with being able to micro-segment your most at-risk patient populations. As you know, our advanced analytics platform allows you to stratify your risk at the individual patient level, drilling as deep with geospatial mapping to quickly identify where your sickest patients live. But I realize me telling you isn't nearly as impactful as me showing you. Jessica, please pass me control of the presentation so I may show our colleagues here our online portal."

Just as she rehearsed countless times leading up to this fateful moment, Jess used her mouse to pass presentation rights over.

"The floor is yours, Michael," she said, giving him control of her screen.

"Thank you, Jessica. So, one of the greatest differentiators to our portal is it's easily accessible from any internet browser. As you'll see here, I am simply going to open up Chrome and…"

Oh, holy shit.

Prepping for today consumed so much of Jess' time lately that personal time simply didn't exist as of late. So, when a photographer friend called a few weeks ago asking if she'd be a model for her budding new boudoir business, Jess obliged knowing she'd have no time to purchase a piece of special lingerie for the shoot.

One night while burning the midnight oil, as she ate steamed chicken and broccoli over her keyboard, Jess browsed lingerie options on HankyPanky.com. She added a black, lace one-piece – complete with thigh-high stockings – to her cart.

So right there, on a conference call with top executives from her company and one of the U.S.'s most prominent insurance companies, where the average attendee's age was north of 60 years old, where the stakes were north of $20M, Jess' latest lingerie shopping extravaganza displayed front and center for everyone to see.

The "oh my" and "dear god" comments could be heard straight away. The tension on the line was palpable. Jess froze, horrified beyond words.

"We'll just go ahead and end this session right here," Michael said, thinking on his feet as he frantically exited out of the screen. "The wonderful thing about our technology is it's adaptable for any browser. Did I already say that? Let's go ahead and open Internet Explorer and try this again."

Jess realized she was holding her breath. Taking a deep and audible exhale, she sunk low in her chair and prayed somehow, someway, this presentation didn't just seal her fate. She thanked her lucky stars to be the only one in the boardroom – she would've never been able to look Michael or John in the eyes after this.

Two hours and lots of tech speak later, the call concluded.

"Well, thank you, everyone," a gentleman on the other end of the call said. "This was impressive. A bit unconventional to say the least, but impressive, nonetheless. I think the last step in the process is flying out to see your Manila operations."

We might've just won the freakin' business, Jess thought. All those late nights in the office, countless versions of her presentation, all of it became worth it at that very moment. She knew the visit to the Philippines office would blow them away, and the nearly $20 million-dollar deal would be done, thanks in part to her hard work.

After she closed the meeting, Jess smiled. Sure, she just mortified herself in front of all her executives and a potential client, but the client loved the presentation. She grabbed her coffee mug off the conference table and walked towards the kitchen.

What the hell is going to happen now? She knew the presentation's success was due largely in part to her efforts, but the lingerie detour was entirely her fault.

Would Michael and John give me a free pass?

When she returned to her office, her phone rang.

Shit. Shit, shit, shit.

"Hello, Jess here," she answered with feigned confidence.

"Well," John said. "All in all, that call was a success, wouldn't you say?

Thank goodness.

"Absolutely," Jess said, perhaps a bit too eagerly. "John, I'm just so sorry about the snafu earlier. I swear I did not intend for that to happen. I'm mortified, to be honest, ready for whatever you called to tell me." Jess braced herself for what was to come.

"That was not what any of us expected to see, but I must say, it was a bit of comedic relief in an otherwise intense conversation. I know your work ethic and I know how hard you're probably beating up on yourself. I reassured Michael that something like this will ever happen again." He paused for effect, ensuring his message resonated.

"Of course not," Jess assured him. She silently sighed with the biggest breath of relief. "I will never let something like this happen again."

John continued. "That's what I knew you'd say. So, with that, I want you to see this through. I want you to meet the prospect out in Manila next month and win that business."

And just like that, Jess was given the biggest break of her entire career.

***

It was a chilly March morning and she could hear the sounds of wind tapping against her office window as she powered through her mountain of email before her day of back to back meetings began. It was no easy feat, teaching herself about the intricacies of healthcare, especially while learning an entirely new vocabulary of terms like Medicare, Medicaid, the Affordable

Healthcare Act, to name a few. Jess often came into the office early just to read up on the latest trending topics, so she'd have something valuable to contribute during the team's daily huddle meetings. During her first few weeks on the job, she'd turn beet red when Michael would turn to ask, 'So Jess, what do you think?' and she'd have nothing noteworthy to contribute.

When the need for a quick mental escape arose, Jess pivoted towards her personal emails, allowing herself a chunk of time to get lost reading about which celebrity slept with whom, and which of her favorite retailers was offering the best Spring sales. Somewhere between an email for a daily Flash Sale at Sakes Fifth Avenue and a Double Points Rewards Day at The Container Store, one email out of hundreds captured her attention.

LivingSocial Deal of the Day: 50% off introductory CrossFit classes

Years ago, Jess would've never given something like CrossFit a passing thought. The idea would've seemed too extreme, too beyond her capabilities. Yet here she was – a full-on fitness enthusiast. Now she found enjoyment jumping on the latest workout craze bandwagon, convincing her girlfriends to try out a new spin studio, kickboxing gym, or yoga studio around town on the regular. When no one was willing or able, she'd go alone quite happily. Not only was she loving how much better her clothes fit her petite frame, but she relished in the body confidence and positivity that came along with it.

Just one year ago, as she attempted to navigate her divorce and hopefully the darkest of days she'd ever see, she barely huffed and puffed herself through a one-mile run. Yet here she was, running 5ks, 15ks and trail runs through the Georgia

Mountains. Admittedly addicted to the rush of endorphins and newfound muscle mass, the sadness of the past was now fleeting, she regularly slept with ease, and finally felt content with the reflection staring back at her.

With her big project mostly in the rear-view mirror, Jess was back to logging less hours and with no dates intentionally on the horizon, she found time for *more*. More introspection, more mindfulness, and more time discovering the woman she was becoming. For the first time in her entire adult life, she felt empowered to mindfully create a life she deemed worth living.

Taking careful inventory of the people she surrounded herself with and the mistakes she made along the way, Jess was completely devoted to discovering what brought the 'new' her joy, and there was no denying that the entire process challenged every fiber of her being. It required time, patience, financial resources – Dr. Green wasn't free! - and a tremendous amount of grace. She wasn't perfect every day, and sometimes it was easier to default to bad habits and criticize herself, but with every passing day, she felt herself grow a little bit stronger. Her unsteady childhood, the failed marriage, and missteps along the way, all felt like memories from a long time ago that no longer had power to elicit a visceral, emotional response from her. They seemingly no longer had any real power over her.

Taking a sip of her morning coffee, Jess forwarded the email to Megan with a note included: Let's do it. I'm signing up tonight. You in?!

Just like that, thanks to a LivingSocial promotional email, Jess embarked upon a newfound hobby, starting small and attending a few classes each week as she familiarized herself with new, fundamental movements including squats, deadlifts, and pushups. CrossFit was nothing like the weightlifting she was used to. There was no lemongrass scented towel waiting at the door, and no one seemed concerned with wearing the cutest, most fashionable outfits. At CrossFit, there were copious amounts of sweat, tons of grunts and groans, and zero frills. It was totally different than anything she had ever done before.

She was hooked.

Sometimes she felt like a deer in headlights as she stumbled her way through the new movements, but she didn't mind much. Megan, a natural athlete, knocked out pushups and pulls in such an effortless fashion that it was tough for Jess not to compare herself with her friend.

"It's a process," her instructor told her one Saturday morning as Jess struggled and failed to hoist herself up for a single pullup. "Don't worry, you'll get there!"

The community CrossFit offered was friendlier and more supportive than Jess anticipated. Not only were she and Megan making new friends, but the tangible, physical results were undeniable. By her third month, in front of a packed gym cheering her on, Jess knocked out fifteen consecutive pushups! The more time she invested, the stronger – mentally and physically - she became. She was hooked.

Thanks to her newfound love, time flew by. So much so, that it was finally time for her first trip to the other side of the globe. The night before she left for Manila, Jess tossed a few handfuls of workout clothes into her suitcase. Rather than prepping for her upcoming meetings, she was googling CrossFit gyms in the Philippines.

***

As she peered out the airplane window, watching the distance grow between her and Atlanta, Jess sipped a crisp, bubbly glass of champagne. Thanks to Evolution's generous travel policy, she booked her on a first-class ticket to the Philippines.

Her seat unfolded into a bed that was bigger than the one she slept on in college. Kim – her lovely flight attendant – handed her a robust menu to order from, complete with sushi, sashimi, and butter-poached lobster tails. As Jess perused the menu, Kim laid a crisp, white, linen cloth across Jess' tray, topping it with a warm bowl of cashews and roasted almonds to accompany the glass of Dom Perignon. Kim wheeled over a silver cart, artfully displaying an impressive platter of fresh fruit and fine cheeses.

This is heaven, Jess thought.

After a nearly twenty-hour voyage, the foreign city of Manila appeared outside Jess' window. The excitement and anticipation of getting to her hotel and seeing the sights before her long week of meetings began consumed her. Walking off the jetway, a thick layer of humidity smacked her clear across the face. Eager to snap some photos to document her trip, Jess switched on her phone – noticing an alarming number of missed calls from Stef, followed by one single text.

Anthony dumped me.

Oh, no, Jess mumbled, as she navigated through the busy customs line.

Last year after an emotional cancer diagnosis, Stef moved back home to Oklahoma to care for her mom. Despite an optimistic prognosis, she passed after just two months. Stef couldn't bring herself to leave and lived in her mom's house ever since. Anthony, as Jess understood from the brief stories Stef shared, was the playboy of their tribe, making his way through most of the women in their small town.

The thought of anyone breaking her best friend's resilient heart made her livid and Jess had a zany, yet completely feasible cure for Stef's heartache.

She replied as soon as the Wi-Fi kicked in.

Listen, I know this is crazy, but I just landed in Manila. I'm here for two weeks. Why don't you book a ticket and join me?

Thanks sweetie, but you know I can't afford that.

My company paid for my flight. Let me pay for yours. What are friends for? Just book your ticket and let me know how much it is.

Stef was always, for as long as Jess could remember, the caretaker. The responsible one. The friend everyone called when they needed support. Or encouragement. Or a sober driver after too many drinks and a long night out. She deserved this and Jess felt honored to be able to help make it happen.

Fine. But I'm paying you back at some point. Let me see what I can find, and I'll let you know.

Jess smiled ear to ear. During her ride to the Shangri La Hotel in downtown Manila, she remembered their first trip together. It was Jess' twenty-first birthday and they spent a long weekend in Las Vegas, sipping cocktails in a cabana at the Palms Hotel and Casino. When Stef stood up to jump in the water, Jess noticed a small butterfly tattoo on her hip.

"What's the story behind that?" she asked, pointing towards her friend.

"It's a Native American thing," Stef told her. "We believe butterflies are messengers from loved ones who passed away, so in a sense, it's as if the ones we've lost are always with us along the way."

And just like that, on a busy street in the Philippines, a large purple butterfly landed on her window. Jess blinked her eyes and did a double take. When she arrived at her hotel and connected to Wi-Fi, Stef had sent a single email. Her flight arrived in four days.

***

After four exhausting days of meetings, Jess was losing her fight against jet lag. Somewhere between discussing how the company would scale up to meet the new client's needs and how many additional staff members they'd need to hire as a result, her phone beeped.

I'm at the hotel! Stef said. At least I think I am. Damn, everyone out here is so tiny! Each one of my boobs is bigger than the ladies checking me in at the reception desk.

I'm so happy you're here! Jess replied. I'm stuck here at the office for a few more hours. Why don't you get settled in? I'll be back around 6 o'clock and then we can go out for dinner. I say we go somewhere local and authentic. I'll ask my coworkers for a recommendation.

That's fine. But I still don't eat fish so let's make sure we go somewhere with chicken. And like, actual chicken. I've heard they cook up dog here and call it chicken.

You're crazy, Jess replied.

Thirty minutes later, Jess rushed to finish out the workday, another text appeared.

I couldn't handle the silence of our hotel room. Came to the bar. Hot Australian dude with big shoulders and a thick frame sitting next to me. Have fun at work sucker. See you soon. Xoxo.

With hip to waist proportions that brought most men to their knees, Stef exuded a level of confidence Jess always admired. On the heels of her breakup, Stef was on the prowl, and Jess could only imagine the conversation being had between her best friend and the beefy Australian beside her.

***

"Thanks again for today, Patricia," Jess called out as she walked towards the office's elevator bank. "I'm heading back to the hotel but please call if anything comes up tonight." Waiting for her outside was Christian, her driver for the duration of her time in Manila.

"Good evening, ma'am," he said, taking her briefcase as he opened the door to his all-black Mercedes. "Returning to the Shangri La?"

"Yes, please," Jess replied, with a tinge of exhaustion. Between the jet lag, humidity that rivaled Miami on its worst day, and the long workdays logged since touching down in the Philippines, she was beat. She spent the next twenty minutes rubbing her throbbing temples. Adjusting to the twelve-hour time change proved to be far more difficult than she initially anticipated, but the notion of seeing Stef tonight energized her.

Stepping into the opulent lobby, where fresh, massive floral bouquets were changed out daily, Jess inhaled the scent of lemongrass.

She rode the glass-enclosed elevator fifteen floors up, to room 1512. She held the room key against the sensor and waited for the green light to appear. With a quick turn of the handle, Jess walked in.

"Oh, holy shit," Stef screamed.

In their decade of friendship, Jess saw her friend in every way. Early morning plates of pancakes at Denny's after a late night at the college bars. Snot dripping down her nose when she cried after a bouncer called her fat. Laughing so hard that she'd let a fart slip out. But never, not once in their ten years of friendship, had Jess seen this side of Stef.

Her naked backside.

In the air. On top of an unrecognizable man.

"Oh my god," Jess screamed. Turning on a dime, she ran out from the direction in which she came. Seeking respite in the hallway, she did her best to un-see what she just saw, but it was too late.

Burned forever in her memory will be the image of her best friend riding a strange man like an amusement park ride in their brightly lit hotel room.

"I'm so sorry," the man mumbled to Jess as he fled the room. Shoes and shirt in hand, she couldn't help but laugh inside.

Finally, she thought. *A man doing the walk of shame!*

"Okay, come back!" Stef yelled from inside.

"Are you kidding me right now?" Jess asked her half-naked

friend as she tossed her bag down.

Despite her best effort of covering up, the towel Stef reached for covered half of one of her large breasts, neither of her nipples and none of her downstairs lady parts.

Holding up her hand, Stef simply said: "I don't want to talk about it."

And rather than argue, the duo did what they always did. Laughed until it hurt.

"Let me go get some clothes on so we can get dinner," Stef said. With a coy smile, she continued, "I've worked up quite the appetite."

Chapter Thirteen

L ess than a week after traipsing around the Philippines with her best friend, Jess missed Stef's company so much it hurt. The deep belly laughs when Stef tipped their Tuk Tuk over to their trip to the local, high-fashion mall where even Jess' American size 2 petite self couldn't wrestle herself into an Asian size 12 equivalent, Jess felt as though she'd said goodbye to her soulmate the day that they departed home.

Yet knowing the best way to adjust back to a sense of normalcy was to get right back into routine. At her usual 6 o'clock CrossFit class, Jess – alongside the rest of the after-work crowd - circled around a large whiteboard in the center of the no-frills gym to get a sneak peek at the workout of the day. It was then, as she stood around waiting for class to begin, that she saw him. Around six feet tall, he appeared to be in his mid-30s, with sandy brown hair that looked to be peppered gray, he sported black workout shorts which he paired with a bright red, fitted t-shirt with the word COACH emblazoned across the chest. Jess watched as he approached the group, noticing that he was nearly as wide as he was tall, with thick, muscular shoulders and a strong, broad chest. He looked like he could fling her over his shoulder one-handed.

"Alright, alright! Let's get it started!" he cheered, clapping his hands together with impressive enthusiasm considering it was the end of a full workday. "Tonight's workout is going to be a killer. We have ten rounds of deadlifts, squats, pull-ups, and sit-ups." As he spoke, the entire class seemed captivated by his genuine smile and contagious energy. "But before we begin, it's Monday and I always like to start the week off with a highlight from the weekend. I'll get us started! My name is Seth – for those of you I haven't yet met. I joined as a coach here two weeks ago, although I've been coaching CrossFit for four years now. This past weekend, I went out with some buddies to see Yacht Rock Revue. Anyone familiar?" He paused to take a pulse of the crowd. No one responded. "They do a mash-up of the best songs from the 80s, a total throwback to my childhood. Anyway, it was awesome. Okay – how about you?" He nodded in her direction. "Give us a highlight from your weekend, girl in the flashy neon shorts!"

Jess looked down. He was right. Her super short shorts could stop traffic. "Well," she began, now acutely aware of just how short and bright her shorts were. "My weekend consisted of lots of sleep. I'm still jet-lagged from spending two weeks in the Philippines."

He smiled from ear to ear and she saw him shift his weight towards the tips of his toes. "Get out!" he nearly shouted. "I travel to Manila every quarter for business. It's amazing out there, isn't it?"

Considering she had to Google Manila just to see where the hell it was, Jess was impressed to hear of someone so familiar with that side of the world. In the essence of time, the weekend highlight reel kept moving, but each time Jess glanced in Seth's direction, she felt his eyes on her.

The man didn't lie – the workout was a killer. An hour later, Jess found herself sprawled out in a pile of her own sweat on the padded gym floor, heart pounding and blood pumping. Slipping her hand between the sweaty mat and her left shoulder blade, Jess massaged the painful lump she'd been ignoring for weeks with her fingertips.

The first time she noticed it was as she sat down to board her flight to Manila. By the time she landed in the Philippines, it ached underneath her bra strap as she quietly moaned in agony. Tonight, with every sit up hitting her back against the padded mat, a painful sensation radiated through her. She didn't want to admit it, but the lump felt significantly larger than it did just two short weeks ago.

"Nice work today," Seth called out, leaning over Jess to give her a celebratory high five. She raised a limp arm in the air, slapping his hand in exasperation. While it felt cathartic to leave everything behind on that sweaty gym floor, Jess couldn't help but feel anxious about the mystery lump. Suddenly, she wished she would've asked Stef to take a look at it while they were together – but talking about it made it feel too real.

Before standing to her feet, she made a mental note.

Try and get a glimpse of this thing tonight.

In the process of tossing some grilled chicken into a salad bowl that evening, Jess' phone buzzed.

"Have you been able to poop since you got back from the trip?" Stef never wasted time with pleasantries.

"Well hi there," Jess responded. "Yes, I have as a matter of fact. I'm assuming you've been so busy with your constipation that's why you haven't returned my calls all week?"

"Ugh sorry babe," Stef said. "Work has been driving me bat shit crazy. They switched my facility after our trip and I swear, I'm never home. And to top it all off, Anthony was waiting at my doorstep when I got home. Can you believe that? Talk about pathetic."

"So, I assume your relationship is done and gone?" Jess asked, feeling the need to confirm.

"Let's just say my hour with the hunky Australian was enough to make me realize Anthony was coming up a bit… short. If you know what I mean. And besides that, work is literally my life right now. These kids are about to drive me damn near crazy. Soon I'll be locked up with them."

For some, career paths are determined early on. Jess knew from day one that she wanted to study Journalism. Stef, however, graduated with a degree in Political Science and not a single bit of clarity around what she planned to do with her degree. For a brief moment she toyed with the idea of becoming a lawyer but balked at the idea of Law School. 'I'm not paying that money to become a lifelong test taker' she'd tell Jess.

She put her best foot forward and tried her hand at various careers – a college admissions counselor to restaurant manager at a local Indian casino – but never found her groove. After moving back to Oklahoma, she began working for a children's drug and alcohol rehabilitation center on a local reservation.

It was hard for Jess to imagine how her friend slept at night, given the horror stories she shared, including the ten-year-old boy addicted to cocaine and the countless teenagers polishing off liters of tequila before middle school. Stef did some truly selfless work and Jess admired her for it. "How's everything else been by you?" Stef asked.

"Everything's fine. Work is crazy too. Just trying to play catch up since being out. The highlight of my day, as sad as this sounds, was this hot new eye candy at CrossFit." Jess tossed in a can of chickpeas, drizzled some balsamic vinegar and sat down at her four-top kitchen table to scarf down the simple dinner.

"Oh yeah? You haven't mentioned a guy in so long I started to wonder if you switched teams and didn't tell me."

"Ha! Well," Jess said, "there's nothing much to say. He coached my class tonight. That's literally the entire story. Sorry to disappoint you."

"Hey, everything starts somewhere!" Stef's excitement was enough for the both of them. "What's his story? What does he do? How old is he? Are we sure he's single?"

"I know none of those answers," Jess replied. Taking a long chug of ice water, she realized her insatiable hunger wasn't patient enough to have this conversation now. "Listen, I'm starving. Let me finish my dinner and we'll chat later this week. I love you!"

"Promise me you'll go friend this guy on Facebook and let me know what happens?" Stef yelled out before Jess could hang up.

"I promise," Jess responded, eyeing her MacBook on the counter. She polished off the last bites of her salad, poured herself some team, and began conducting a full sleuth-like search to discover who Seth — her new mystery man candy was.

She sat at the kitchen table until her ass fell asleep and learned that Seth, very similarly to herself, attended college on the west coast. Turns out coaching CrossFit was a hobby — he seemingly had a successful corporate career, judging by the copious photos of him at tradeshows, shaking hands with countless old men in custom-looking suits. From the hundreds of public photos on his page, Jess also learned of his passion for travel — scrolling through endless pictures of him in faraway places including Ireland and England to Thailand and India. There were also quite a few pictures of him smiling next to a woman who appeared to be his mother.

How nice, Jess thought. *A guy who's close to his mom.*

She stared at his profile picture for a few moments, noticing the kind smile looking back at her yet again. Before she managed to talk herself out of it, her fingers went to work.

An innate skill, Jess had a way with words. Whether explaining the intricacies of clinical chart retrieval for Medicare Advantage members by day or firing off a cute and casual message to Seth by night, words always came freely to her.

She reviewed the quick, three-line message and pleased with the draft, confidently hit send.

Slapping her laptop shut, Jess retreated to the bathroom to wash off the sweaty workout and attempt to get her eyes on the pesky lump pulsating on her back.

***

A twinge of disappointment came over her the following evening when she arrived for class and realized Seth wasn't coaching. She purposefully wore another pair of short shorts and a somewhat coordinating tank top that accentuated her budding muscles in a way that made her feel oh so good. Not long behind her, Megan walked in with five minutes to spare before class began, wrapping her arms completely around Jess for the first time in weeks. Just as soon as she pulled Jess in, Megan pushed her away.

"Turn around," she said twisting Jess by the shoulders. "Omg!" she squealed, with her hand at Jess' bra line. "What is this? Do you feel this?" She pressed gently on the bulge.

"Ouch!" Jess winced. "Yeah, I can feel that. What the hell is it?" She contorted her head around to no avail. "I tried to get a look last night, but my body doesn't turn that way. It's been bugging me for weeks. What do you see?"

"I see a big lump. You need to have a doctor take a look," Megan said, making no attempt at hiding her concern. "It's really big."

Her Dermatologist wasn't available until the following week, and thanks to the sheer discomfort of her mystery lump, Jess called it and took a temporary hiatus from exercising until she sorted this out. Finally, appointment day arrived and as Jess sat in the crowded waiting room anxiously anticipating her name to be called, she killed time by scrolling mindlessly on her phone.

"Jessica Klein? We're ready for you." A nurse called out from the corner of the waiting room, with what Jess presumed to be her medical chart propped against the nurse's hip.

Lisa, as her name tag read, led Jess to a small, sterile room down the long, stark white hallway.

"Please put this on, with the opening in the back," she instructed, handing Jess the small cotton gown. She sat, legs swinging, on the paper-lined bed waiting for her doctor to come in. Twenty minutes and two Parade Magazines later, Jess' phone beeped from inside her purse. Gingerly walking while strategically grasping her meager paper wardrobe, Jess glanced at the screen.

'New Message' appeared – and when she clicked on the alert, a note from Seth appeared.

Hey Jess!! I hope this isn't too weird – me finding you on Facebook and all. Anyway, how are you? I haven't seen you at the gym all week! Not sure if this is going too far, but I'd love to hang out together - outside of the gym – if you're interested! Anyway, hope you're great. Just let me know. No hard feelings either way!!

Boy, the guy uses a lot of exclamation marks.

His exuberance managed to jump off the screen as Jess re-read his message. As she opened a draft to reply, the doctor walked in. Instructing her to lie face down – 'put your face in the hole' – Jess did as she was told, realizing a few moments into the examination that her gown opened, and her full ass was totally exposed. A few moments of deafening silence later, he spoke.

"You can sit up, Jessica," he said, audibly removing his plastic gloves and tossing them into the nearby garbage bin. "We're going to need to remove this mass as soon as possible," Dr. Wuang said.

"I'm sorry, what?" Her eyes suddenly felt as though they were about to bulge out of their sockets. Walking into today's appointment, she didn't know what to expect, but surgery surely was not an immediate consideration.

"There's no need for concern just yet," he went on judging by her reaction. "But I'm not confident it's not malignant. I'd like to get it out immediately and send it off to pathology."

Jess hated people who used double negatives but stopped listening entirely after she heard the word *pathology*.

This cannot be happening, she thought. Life finally seemed to feel... normal? Ten minutes ago, her biggest worry was catching up on a sea of work-related emails and being asked out by a cute guy at the gym. Now, buck naked under the stark white lights of Dr. Wuang's office, she was listening to talk of *surgery, a mass,* and *pathology*.

This is why I ignored this for so many weeks, she irrationally thought. *Technically, if you don't know you have a problem, you don't have to face it.*

"Our front desk will help you with scheduling. You'll want to have someone bring you on surgery day," he told her as he collected his chart and turned the doorknob to give her privacy to redress.

"Can I not drive myself?" she asked.

He looked at her as if she were out of her mind crazy. "No, Jessica. No, you cannot. You'll be under anesthesia and unable to operate heavy machinery for at least a day or two."

"Well then, how am I supposed to drive my tractor?" she smirked, with a heavy dose of sarcasm intended to bring some much-needed levity to the situation.

He didn't laugh and now neither was she.

Just like that, Jess was having surgery.

The word malignant terrified the ever-living shit out of her. Perhaps it was her Jewish heritage that predisposed her to have anxiety flow freely through her veins, but she now found herself worried beyond measure. As a young child, whenever Jess came down with the slightest cold, Sarah would rush out to the small corner bodega to gather the needed ingredients for a pot of matzoh ball soup. Her mom would proceed to Clorox their entire apartment and quarantine Jess to her room. Hell hath no fury as a Jewish mother concerned for her child. For this reason, and the fact that Jess herself was terrified, she made the conscious decision to omit the latest health-related news from conversations with her parents. How could she get them all worked up and worried? What if it ended up being nothing? And alternatively, what if were actually something? Neither option seemed particularly appealing, so she proceeded to bury her head in the sand and pretend that everything was going to be alright. It had to be.

It has to be, she told herself as she drove home that afternoon. *Please*, she pleaded as she drove home. *Please don't let everything come to an end just as everything is starting to begin.*

***

Six days later, she arrived early on surgery day thanks to the skilled maneuvering of Max, her Uber driver. Much to her amazement, Jess managed to keep the surgery a secret from friends and family alike. As a result, she had no one to take her. Instead, she opted for the less chaotic yet extremely isolating approach – she chose to handle it alone.

If I don't talk about it, if I don't involve anyone, it doesn't feel as real, she rationalized.

The sun hadn't yet rose as Jess took a seat in the quiet waiting room of the outpatient surgical center. Opting for comfortable and loose clothing, Jess tucked her feet underneath her and silently waited for her name to be called.

A nurse in lilac scrubs appeared.

"Jessica Klein?" making eye contact was easy as Jess was the only patient in the entire waiting room. "We're ready for you." Walking hesitantly into the tiny procedure room, Jess felt intimidated by the bright lights and the overwhelming smell of sterile cleaner. "I'm going to have you take off all your clothes," the nurse instructed, handing her a paper gown. "You're going to put this on, with the opening in the back. Please tie back your hair and place this cap over your head. We'll be back in just a few moments."

She felt so scared and vulnerable under those bright, white lights. As she striped off her sweatpants, letting them fall to her ankles, she took a few deep breaths – in through the nose, out through the mouth.

Never a good patient, Jess feared needles and doctors for as long as she could remember. In fact, her mother loved to share the story of when Jess was five years old and proceeded to lock herself in the bathroom at the pediatrician's office on a day when she overhead her mother and doctor discussing 'shots.' Refusing to come out, the office's staff had to pick the lock and pull Jess out kicking and screaming. She got the shots anyway, and oddly enough, never overcame her fear of needles.

The nurse returned, this time with Dr. Wuang beside her. "Please lie down on the table, face up," she instructed Jess.

She did her best to discretely climb onto the table and failed. Yet again, she found herself flashing everyone as the paper gown opened rather ungracefully.

"Countdown to 10, please," the nurse instructed as she placed a small, plastic mask over Jess' nose and mouth.

God, I hope they give me enough drugs...

"One... Two..."

She never made it past three.

"Ms. Klein, your surgery is complete. You've been in recovery for four hours now. We will be able to discharge you anytime – you'll just need to have a successful bowel movement."

With drool running down her chin, Jess blinked her eyes a few times to see clearly. What does a successful bowel movement entail?

Within the hour - and a 'successful' movement later, the staff allowed Jess to be discharged. She got herself dressed in surprising ease and ordered herself an Uber.

I feel funny, she thought, climbing into the car. But the good news, she considered, is that her back was still entirely numb. No pain!

"Hey there," Jess slightly slurred to the driver. "One stop on the way. Do you mind swinging by the drugstore? I have some medicine I need to pick up."

"No problem," he said. "My name is Edward, by the way.

Happy to take you - just let me know where we're going."

"Right here, Edward," Jess said as she leaned herself so forward her head nearly rested on his shoulder. "That's right, the CVS up ahead. Just pull into the drive-thru."

Edward, a retired "My-wife-said-I-need-a-hobby" IT manager in his 60s obliged, pulling up to the drive-thru window as Jess requested. With the remaining drugs still pumping through her, Jess rolled down the back window and barked out to the Pharmacist, "Hey! My good man! Here's the prescription I need," handing over a small slip of paper. "Oh, and let's go ahead and throw in a big bag of Twizzlers!" She noticed some drool slipping down her cheek. Wiping it with the back of her hand, she added, "And hey, Edward, you get something special, too!"

Am I slurring?

"I'm going to need your identification and some proof of insurance, ma'am," the Pharmacist asked through the window. Edward sat silently, likely praying this ride would come to an end soon.

Fumbling through her purse, Jess struggled to locate her insurance card. "Ah, here that darn thing is! Right between my frozen yogurt membership and a gift card to Bed Bath and Beyond. Hey Edward, do you like Bed Bath and Beyond? I always get so many coupons from them!"

"I believe he's waiting on your card," Edward nodded towards the frustrated pharmacists.

She reached through the car window and accidentally dropped the cards between Edward's seat and the driver's side door.

Springing into action, Jess crouched down as Edward opened

the door. "Here, use your fingers like this," she instructed, motioning her fingers together like a scissor.

After fighting with the tiny cards, Edward came out successful, handing them over. Within moments, Jess had her antibiotics, pain medication, and they were on their way.

"Edward," she asked, still slurring. "Are you hungry? That guy didn't give me my Twizzlers. I know a great sushi place right around the corner from here. Let's go, my treat!"

Did I just sound like my mother?

"Oh ma'am, that's ok," he cautiously replied. "Let's just get you home."

Suit yourself, she thought, shrugging her shoulders as she leaned back into the stiff leather seat.

"Edward, this is an awfully nice car to drive around for Uber," she slurred as she repeatedly rubbed the leather with her hands. "What is this? An Escalade?"

"It's a Toyota Sienna, Ma'am."

***

Hours felt like days, and days felt like months while Jess awaited her biopsy results. In her best attempt to deflect and distract that week, she filled her time saying 'yes' to major initiatives at the office. 'Yes' to Lea, Raquel, and Megan's happy hour invites. It felt uncharacteristic and deceitful to keep such a secret but uttering the word 'tumor' simply terrified the shit out of her.

If I talk about it, it feels too real. So instead she silently carried the weight of her secret with her, as if it were neatly folded away in her Prada satchel.

About to wrap up at the office and meet the girls, Jess' phone rang at 4 p.m. on Friday. She glanced at the screen – it was finally Dr. Wuang's office. Praying for good news, she was ready to put the week-long wait behind her.

"The tumor is benign," was all she heard the nurse say.

Suddenly, the weight of her worries and fear dissipated. She wanted to jump through the phone and hug whichever nurse it was delivering the great news. Big, crocodile tears of gratitude welled up in her eyes as she silently thanked her lucky stars for the clean bill of health.

Her Grandmother Lillian was notorious for saying 'so long as you have your health, you'll have it all' and in this exact moment, Jess heard her Grandmother's familiar voice once again. Somehow during the excruciating wait for the 'cancer or no cancer' call, nothing in life seemed to matter much. Her relationship status, office politics, rapidly approaching deadlines at the office… they all fell by the wayside while she waited in angst to learn of her fate.

And now – with the clean bill of health – Jess felt invigorated. Blessed beyond measure, she was given a clean slate. A second lease on life, perhaps. Standing over the sink, Jess splashed cool water on her face as she stared back at her reflection.

I'm ready, she told herself as she stared back into her own dark brown eyes. Still craving the predictability, stability, and dependability of a family, she couldn't ignore the gaping hole in her heart. A void that long hours in the office, promotions galore, all the friends in the world, nor exotic vacations could give her.

She was ready to become a mom.

Few things in life are as empowering and invigorating as receiving a clean bill of health. The very night she received the call putting the c-word to bed, Jess laid in bed and couldn't fall asleep. Her mind raced as she resolved to hold herself accountable for living her life just a bit more... open. Staying open to new beginnings. To new friendships and relationships. Open to uncovering happiness in the mundane moments that she routinely overlooked.

Dr. Green had a small quote framed on his desk that she noticed every session, and it had become somewhat ingrained in her mind. Life is better when you're happy. When she first saw it, she rolled her eyes. Of course, it's easy to be happy when you're not getting divorced. Or when you're not stressed out about work. Or when you're not fumbling from one shitty date to the next. Happiness is meant for people who are married. Not for twenty-something divorcees like me.

But now? Now she realized happiness shouldn't be just for those who seem to have it all together. Happiness shouldn't be predicated by your marital status. If she wanted to be happy right here, right now, who was to stop her?

No one, she realized.

"I was beginning to wonder if I scared you off!" Seth said with a smile as Jess walked into the gym that Monday evening.

She hadn't spoken to him since he sent her the Facebook message asking her out, and she hadn't seen him in weeks. Finally healed from the tumor removal, she was excited to get back into the gym, but more so anxiously awaiting seeing Seth.

"I'm so sorry I've been missing in action," she started, as she stretched her legs out in a wide V-shape before class began. "Life has been a little… chaotic… lately. Anyway, I did want to let you that I'd love to take you up on your offer to go out sometime. That is if the offer still stands." She couldn't help but notice the big grin across his face.

"I'd love that," he told her. Something about the way he stood, with his impressively broad shoulders and thick, muscular build, had Jess feeling butterflies for the first time in a long while. "Let me know your favorite restaurant, and that's where we'll go." He spoke to her with such an air of confidence and assertiveness that she found herself becoming more attracted to him with every conversation. Fellow gym-goers flooded the small CrossFit gym, and before their date was finalized, his class began.

She felt his eyes on her for the next hour and was sure to run a little faster, lift a little heavier, and smile just a little more.

***

"Do you love it?" Jess asked Lea as she turned on her toes, showing off the new cocktail dress she bought for the upcoming occasion?

"It's so freakin' cute," Lea replied, bringing a glass of chilled Rose to her lips. "I love that he insisted on picking you up tonight, too. How chivalrous!"

There were quite a few things that Seth seemed to get right –

including letting Jess pick the restaurant, insisting on picking her up, and sending a 'Good morning, I can't wait for our date tonight' text to build anticipation for the night ahead.

"Thanks for coming by to keep me company while I get ready. After the way your date with Everett went last month, I'm hoping you've inadvertently brought some good dating juju with you."

Everett, a forty-two-year-old recruiter from Georgia – the country, not the state – was a guy Lea met on a Europeans-only dating website the month prior. Her first date in five years, she was rusty and skeptical at best, but after nonstop harassment from Jess, Lea reluctantly accepted an invitation for coffee on a dreary Sunday afternoon and has been smitten ever since.

For the first time in all the years she's known Lea, Jess swore her girlfriend finally looked content.

Chapter Fourteen

"Y ou look beautiful," Seth said, presenting her with a bursting bouquet of beautiful and bright sunflowers. He wore perfectly tailored navy dress pants with a crisp, white button-down shirt that hugged his muscular chest just right. Jess couldn't help but notice how his Hermes belt accentuated his narrow waist. Until this moment, she'd only seen him with beads of sweat dripping down his face in a musky gym. The clean shaven, well-groomed and refined version left her a bit speechless.

As he promised, he took her to dinner at her favorite restaurant – a quaint Middle Eastern spot near her house with a distinctly swanky buzz. They lingered over shared plates of lamb slides, grilled filet mignon and roasted vegetables, and a bottle of wine. Utterly lost in conversation, it wasn't until the attentive manager came by their table to thank them and let them know the restaurant was closing. She noticed Seth glance at his watch for the first time that night. She followed suit - 11 p.m.!

Over the last three and a half hours, she learned details of his parents' divorce that happened when he was seventeen, his troubled relationship with his dad – 'it's hard to respect a man who abandoned his family' he said with a tinge of animosity.

If my father left me, I'd probably hold a grudge, too, she thought.

Seth shared details of his many semesters spent abroad, studying international business in Singapore and Hong Kong, asking Jess how she enjoyed her Journalism studies in London. 'Europe is just so intoxicating, is it not?' he said with such conviction. Seeing twenty-five countries over the course of two years, they came to find out that both lived in the West End of London during the same time about ten years ago.

Like herself, Seth was an only child and fiercely independent. He was the youngest guy at the office by at least a decade, bought his first home at the age of twenty-three, and seemed to love his mother more than anyone in the world.

He let Jess order the entrée of her choosing, but insisted they share small plates – 'food is so much better when shared' he exclaimed after reviewing the menu. When the sommelier came to advise them on a wine pairing, Seth let her choose the varietal of wine she liked best. The way he conducted himself – with an unspoken level of confidence – impressed her. He managed, on their very first date, to strike the fine balance between letting her make decisions while taking control as he saw fit.

By the time they left the now empty restaurant, she was surprisingly enamored. When he kissed her at her doorstep twenty minutes later, the feeling of his strong embrace left her yearning for more. He pulled back, looking her in her deep brown eyes, and simply said, "I can't wait to see you again."

After placing her sunflowers in a crystal vase, she slipped her dress off and stepped into a steaming shower. Running her hands through her wet hair, she let her hands trace the tips of her nipples, imagining what it would feel like to have Seth's strong hands cascade across her naked body.

**

It didn't take long for them to become an item. Their chemistry was palpable, and she found it so easy to have fun with him. Ever since coming into her life, Seth managed to introduce a level of adventure into Jess' otherwise somewhat cautious world. She found herself with a newfound curiosity – from their daily CrossFit workouts where she'd suddenly push her limits, to hiking alongside him in the Georgia mountains, frequenting new speakeasies and trying fancy craft cocktails, and spontaneously booking weekend getaways to unforeseen places, Jess felt herself truly letting down her well-constructed walls for the first time in a very, very long time.

After only two months of dating, she met his mother. A sweet, exuberant Southern woman from Alabama, she spoke with a deep Southern accent and drank Kentucky bourbon straight. At the same time, Jess willingly began introducing Seth to her friends. Initially a foreign feeling, she settled into the feeling of wanting to assimilate him into her life. With summer in full swing, there were no shortage of barbeques and city festivals to attend and having him escort her felt comforting. Her girlfriends took to him right away and Jess couldn't have been happier.

It helped that her girlfriends took to Seth so quickly, as his friends were far more reluctant to welcome her. It was a rather large handful of guys in their mid 30s, all single, who had trouble saying no. No to another cocktail, no to heading to another bar. No to ordering a pizza at 2 a.m.

Around the three-month mark of dating, and as summer was coming to a close, Seth proposed an idea that Jess met with dread. As they sipped coffee on his couch one Sunday morning. "I'm thinking of having an end of summer pool party here at my place. You know, invite all the guys over and just hang out. What do you think?"

"That sounds fun," Jess lied.

Truth be told, she couldn't stand when he drank with his buddies. One evening, just two weeks prior, the guys were over for an ordinary Saturday night. Seth cooked up a dozen delicious pizzas, and after tons of cocktails and a few bottles of wine, Jess couldn't fight the exhaustion and decidedly called it a night. 'Have fun babe,' she whispered in Seth's ear before excusing herself and retreating to his bedroom for the rest of the evening.

She couldn't have been sure as to when exactly they left, but somewhere around one in the morning, Seth decided the pizzas from earlier in the evening were no longer enough. Drunk dialing the local 24-hour pizza place loud enough for Jess to hear, he ordered himself an extra-large pepperoni pizza, garlic knots, and side of chicken wings. Too exhausted to argue with him, Jess laid in bed as he stumbled into the shower and paced throughout his condo in a bath towel as he anxiously awaited the delivery. Not too long after, the doorbell rang and Seth answered, reaching for the pizza box as his strategically wrapped towel cascaded to the floor, exposing all of himself to the innocent kid just looking to drop off a pizza.

That's how many of their nights ended when spent with his

friends – Jess rolling her eyes, shoving him into the back seat of an Uber as he slurred profanities, upset that she was dragging him home only when the party was 'just getting good.' The days of drinking until she passed out and saying things she couldn't remember – or take back – where long behind her, and Jess preferred it that way.

When he wasn't intoxicated beyond belief, he was a pleasure to be around. Yet her patience playing the role of supportive girlfriend waned in moments such as these. Alcohol – and the friends he chose to surround himself with - inserted a new, complicated dynamic to their relationship, and although she knew all too well that this end of summer party would only end with one outcome, she offered to help.

"I'll send out the evites and make the food," she offered, silently dreading the day to arrive.

***

The party kicked off with Seth's first guests arriving at 10 a.m., sharp. "I wanted everyone to come early so we can maximize the day!" he said that morning, eager as ever to get the day started.

Watching Seth and his friends funnel beers poolside as they blared house music at his rooftop pool annoyed Jess from the onset, yet she engaged in conversation and did her best to enjoy herself. Neither a big drinker nor a big partier, she preferred more intimate settings for get-togethers – she also much preferred the company of her friends rather than Seth's drunken buddies. Two of them brought girls with them but judging by the way they each performed keg stands in their scantily clad bikinis, Jess assumed there was little to no common ground for them to discuss, and mostly avoided them throughout the day.

After the beers came shots. After the shots came the first wave of obnoxious comments from his drunken friends about how much more fun Seth was when he was single. Then there was more beer.

Jess secretly wished the guys would leave once the sun set. But rather, they simply moved the party from the pool to the adjacent hot tub. Coincidentally, some of Seth's neighbors were wrapping up all-day seafood boil on the rooftop and generously brought over uneaten trays of steamed shrimp, clams, and mussels for the group to enjoy.

"Anyone hungry?" Seth asked his buddies, holding out the large, filled to the brim, tray. One of the drunk girls aggressively reached her chlorine-covered hands into the pile of boiled shrimps and proceeded to eat them all at once – tails, shells, and all. Blissfully unaware that they were intended to be *peel and eat* not *shove it in your mouth and eat*, she started violently choking. Her date, who appeared to be quite intoxicated himself, slapped her on the back so hard that it sent one of the shrimps flying so fast out of her mouth it landed about a foot in front of her, in the bubbling water.

Then there was more beer. And more shots. The other drunk girl accidentally dropped a handful of shrimps into the hot tub, sending her and another girl into a visceral cackle that made Jess wish she were temporarily deaf. And then, much to her dismay, Jess watched the girl plummet her entire face into the cesspool of dirty, chemical-laden, hot water in search of her shrimp.

This, Jess, thought to herself, *this will forever be known as the time I witnessed a girl get completely wasted and bob for shrimp in a cesspool of bacteria-infested water.*

Seth and his friends sat back, laughing and drinking, completely unfazed by the travesty occurring before their eyes.

Too sober to pretend to be social any longer, and too tired to care what Seth thought of her for bowing out early, Jess stood up and excused herself for the sweet respite of Seth's quiet condo. It was late, and they had an early flight the following morning. At his suggestion just a month ago, the two were headed for a weekend in South Florida, where Seth could finally meet Jess' family. Introducing him to Sarah and the entire cast of characters was a big move, yet once he booked a room at the Waldorf Astoria in Boca Raton, Jess didn't put up a fight.

About an hour after she showered and slipped into his lush king-sized bed, Seth stumbled in. *How nice,* she initially thought. *He came to join me for bed.*

Yet rather than be met, in bed, by her boyfriend, she heard from yelling from the front door. "What are you doing? Everyone else is still in the hot tub," he slurred, sliding himself against the wall, making his way towards the nearby master bedroom.

He reeks of alcohol. She could smell him all the way from the bed.

"I needed to come up and feed Tiffany," Jess said. "Also, I started to feel a bit queasy after watching that whole bobbing for shrimp situation. I think I'll just stay up here for the rest of the night if it's all the same to you. We've been at the pool for nine hours now. You go back down, I'm exhausted and want to get some rest for our early flight in the morning." Sure, she was happy to be upstairs, in the air-conditioned peace and quiet. But was she cool with her boyfriend leaving her alone just so he could continue the party with his buddies? She wasn't, yet she found herself ignoring the situation just to appease him.

Why can't he be content just to call it a night with me right now? She wondered, but never said aloud, in fear of starting a fight with him in his already compromised state.

"I want to break up," he slurred.

Jess, froze in place underneath his crisp white sheets, stared at him in disbelief. "I'm sorry, say that again?!" She was utterly shocked at the words coming out of his mouth.

He pressed himself up against the doorway for balance.

Are his eyes even open? He's not going to remember this in the morning.

"Why are you being like this?" he yelled. "Everyone else is up there having fun. And where is my girlfriend when I want her to be with me?" He began to slide down the door frame. Slowly sinking to the floor, he continued with his dramatic outburst. "Where is my girlfriend, you ask? She's upstairs in bed… with her dog!" He gestured his arms in the air in the most exasperated fashion. "You're just… just… such a Grandma."

Oh, fuck this. Jess tossed the comforter aside and leaped to her feet. She tightly squinted her eyes with fury as she stared at him. Beads of sweat dripped down his forehead and she knew nothing she said would register, nor would he remember it by morning, but she couldn't bite her tongue any longer.

"You bet your sweet ass I'm upstairs! I have been nothing but a wonderful girlfriend to you today. I helped you prep and plan this party. I've been at the pool since the ass crack of dawn. I drank with everyone. I talked to everyone. I endured and ignored all the obnoxious comments from your 'friends' — including how your ex-girlfriend was taller and more well-traveled than I am. How your mom loved her and is on the fence about me. I took it all in stride while you were where? Doing keg stands like this is some sort of frat house and we're twenty years old again?"

She felt her hands ball into fists by her sides. She slowly walked towards him, with the bottom of her ass slightly exposed underneath his baggy t-shirt. Her voice increased a few decibels with every step. "I've done nothing but play the role of supportive girlfriend. I think nine hours, too many cocktails, and a shit ton of patience is enough for one day!" She silently watched him, waiting for a reaction. When none came, she continued. "Last time I checked, I was a grown-ass woman willing and able to make my own decisions. If I feel tired, or have simply reached my threshold for drunken idiocrasy, am I not allowed to call an audible and go to bed?"

By the time she finished speaking her mind, he was sheepishly slumped on the floor, his head propped up in both hands. Topping the scale at just over two hundred pounds, he was far too bulky to be sitting Indian style in the narrow doorway.

After what felt like excruciating silence, he finally spoke. "Forget it, Jess," he stammered as he clumsily rose to his feet. "I don't want a girlfriend who acts like she's eighty years old. Get your dog, get your stuff and just go."

***

"I'm sorry, he said WHAT?!" her mother exclaimed the following morning when she picked Jess up from the Fort

Lauderdale Airport. Expecting to see her daughter and her new beau, Sarah's poker face was nowhere to be found.

"Yeah mom, you heard me," Jess said as she proceeded to explain the happenings from the day prior. "He called me a grandma, told me to get my stuff and leave."

"Jess, I don't understand." Sarah pressed on. "You two have been a hot and heavy item for months. He seemed completely smitten, from what you've explained to me. How could that all go up in flames overnight?"

Jess has spent the entire morning asking herself the same question. She surprised herself when agreeing to bring Seth home to meet her family, which indicated to her – and the rest of them – just how much he meant to her.

She considered their many similarities. *Perhaps we're too similar,* Jess deduced. They each possessed a strong desire to achieve professional success, no matter the cost. They both overworked themselves, had next to no patience and were so competitive that they often fought just to be right. They weren't the yin to each other's yang. They often brought out the best - and worst - in one another. When she sat back and compared, he reminded her of Chris in a lot of alarming ways.

"We pushed each other to be better, which was nice," she told her mother, "but we also pushed each other's buttons. Sort of like Chris and I, we had lots of great highs, but the lows – like last night – were pretty damn low."

The car was filled with unexpected silence as they made their way to the hotel. "Are you sure you don't just want to stay at my house?" her mother asked as they pulled into the valet line at the esteemed Waldorf Astoria. With tall palm trees and a full staff in all-white uniforms awaiting their arrival, Jess was adamant about enjoying the weekend despite her newfound relationship status.

"Absolutely not," she retorted. "Stay with me and let's try to have a fun girl's weekend." Within two hours, Aimee and Michelle joined them poolside, the first round of lychee martinis in hand.

Am I just continually repeating the same freakin' mistakes? Jess asked herself as they all lounged by the crystal-clear pool. *I saw the red flags each time we were around his friends – the partying as if we were still in college, the drinking until he threw up, the way he became angry after too many cocktails – yet I stayed around, convincing myself he wasn't the guy he was proving himself to me.*

"Have you ever considered freezing your eggs?" Michelle blurted out as if she had just asked Jess what the time was.

"Huh?" Jess asked as she swirled a lychee fruit around in her no-longer chilled martini glass. "What would make you ask me that?"

Her cousin, five years her junior was single with no suitors on the horizon and as it turns out, had been contemplating the same idea herself. "I don't know, I was just wondering if you've considered having a baby on your own. I just made an appointment with a doctor here to discuss having my eggs frozen and I figured maybe you should too?"

Jess stared out into the cloudless blue sky. *Freezing my eggs?* Truth be told, she hadn't considered it much – but that didn't mean she shouldn't.

"I think that's a great idea!" Sarah chimed in.

"So do I!" Aimee added. "Who said you need a man to have a family these days? You could even move down here – we'd all help you!"

A few of the reasons Jess yearned for a family of her own was because she craved the predictability, stability, and dependability of a family life she never had. But could she have that if she embarked upon becoming a single mother?

"I want a family," she told them, "but I'm not sure I want it like that."

"Like what? I've never told you, girls, this before," Sarah began, "But I considered adopting when Jess was eight years old. She handled the divorce so well but would always ask if I could get her a little brother. Not a sister – a brother. I started the process but never went through with it. My mom talked me out of it, telling me two kids as a single mother would be too much. This was the 80s, let's remember. Anyway, Jess I'm telling you this because I want you to know that your dad and I support you no matter what you decide. I think you'd be a great mom." She looked at Jess with a smile.

"Back to this Seth guy," Aimee chimed in. "Do you love him?"

Jess let the question sink in. Did she love him? At one point, she thought her love for him was growing. But was she in love with him? *No.* And now, being humiliated by him the night before he's set to meet her family, she realized that she is just unwilling to settle for anything less than she deserves. She did that once before. *And look where it led me.*

"No," Jess said aloud. "Outside of his drinking, we had a great time together. Life with him would have been full of adventures, and I know he would've worked his ass off to give me the family I want. But no, I wasn't truly in love with him."

"That's okay, honey." Her mother said reassuringly. "If there is one thing I've learned over the years – and through my marriages – it's that sometimes love takes time to grow. Don't always expect fireworks and rainbow-shitting unicorns from the start. Those stories are saved for fairytales. This is real life, sweet pea. Heck, I couldn't say I was in love with your father until a few years into our marriage. By the time I realized how in love I was with him, it was too late. All I'm saying is just have fun and stop putting so much pressure on yourself. Heck, I wouldn't even see the problem with giving him a second chance. Maybe last night was a fluke. Everyone makes mistakes, yourself included. None of us are perfect. I say just have fun. Nothing needs to be serious until there's a ring on your finger."

Jess considered her mother's advice. For a woman married three times herself, Jess consciously took the words of wisdom with a grain of salt.

"Let's get lunch, I'm starving," Michelle grumbled, polishing off the last of her lychee martini. Just as Jess stood to grab her pool bag, her phone buzzed for the umpteenth time. She reached inside and stared at the screen.

Seven missed calls. Twenty unread text messages. The last of which read, Jess, please. I screwed up. Call me. I'm so sorry. I love you.

The weekend with her family felt like a big pot of matzo ball soup on a cold winter day. Jess left feeling loved, safe, and content. She agreed to consider making an appointment to discuss freezing her eggs and placated her mom by agreeing to let Seth explain himself for the recent outburst.

After ignoring his endless calls and incessant text messages, Jess realized she'd have to face Seth at some point, and that time might as well be now.

What do you want? was about all she cared to text as she soaked in a steaming bath that Sunday evening, complete with flickering candles and lavender Epsom salt. Before having the chance to set her phone down on the rim of the bathtub, he replied.

Gosh, Jess. I have been dying to hear from you. I'm so sorry for everything. I want to talk. Please. Have lunch with me tomorrow? You deserve dinner, but after the shit I pulled, I don't want to wait that long.

She ran her toes along the warm bath spout and reluctantly agreed to meet for a midweek lunch to hear what he had to say. *Would it matter? Probably not.*

But perhaps her mom was right. Perhaps everyone does deserve a second chance. She'd be lying if she didn't admit she was the least bit curious as to what he had to say for himself. None of it made sense, really. They may have only dated for a few months, but their relationship deserved more than an abrupt ending over shrimp floating around in a hot tub.

That much Jess was certain of.

***

Arriving just a few minutes early, the young hostess promptly sat her at a small table underneath a bright, airy window. The sun was shining, and Jess wore a bright yellow and white striped sundress she bought while in Florida this past weekend. The server dropped off two glasses of water and once he left, Jess nervously polished off her glass in a single gulp. As she wiped her mouth with the white linen napkin lying in her lap, Seth walked in.

The type of man who garnered an audience when he walked into a room, he wore what Jess only assumed to be a custom-tailored Armani suit and looked elated to see her. He sported a fresh haircut and as he approached the table, she noticed his freshly polished Prada loafers.

"It's so good to see you," he whispered into her ear as he leaned down to kiss her cheek. He wanted her back — she could see it all over his face. And he was a man who stopped at nothing to get what he wanted. That was another thing she found so sexy about him. The man was persistent. A real man's man, he was always eager to seize control and make things happen.

He spent the next hour making excuses for himself, telling her how sorry he was, how he truly didn't realize how out of control the drinking got that day. He went as far as to make excuses for his friends, saying that they were just jealous of someone new coming into his life, and tended to be overprotective of him, but Jess shut that down.

"Your friends should be happy when you're happy, plain and simple. This is not a competition of me against them."

"And you're right," he resigned. "I'm sorry they can be such assholes. And I'm sorry I can be, too." He opened his mouth to continue just as their server came by to clear their plates. Once the table was emptied and no one was around, he took her hands in his, leaning in towards her. "Let's go ring shopping this weekend."

He has to be kidding. She stared at him, silently, for what felt like an eternity. He never broke eye contact, and judging from the expression on his face, he was in fact *not kidding*.

"You can't possibly be serious," said Jess. it was a good thing he waited until their lunch was finished because if she was still eating, she surely would've spat her lamb kebab and sent it flying across the table. "You don't think we should start with dinner and a movie? Maybe give it a few weeks of being back together. You want to go right for an engagement?" She was stunned.

He wasn't just going for it; he was fucking *going for it*.

"I want you back, Jess. And I want you, your family and the rest of the damn world to know how serious I am. You are my person. Ever since our stupid argument, I've been telling myself that if I ever got you back, I'd commit to forever. I didn't act like I was ready then, but I am. I'm ready for our future to start now."

Ever since our argument? That was three days ago! What is he talking about? Her mind began racing at rapid speed, and just as she opened her mouth to respond, she started hallucinating. She had to be hallucinating. Because if not, he was getting down on one knee.

What the ever-living fuck is happening!

"Jessica Klein," he spoke softly, holding her hand as she tensely sat in her seat, ignoring the fact that the entire restaurant was now staring at them. "I love you. I know this is quite non-traditional, and I honestly had no idea this is how this lunch was going to go, but I want to marry you. I'd do it today, if you'd let me." He was kneeling beside her, staring up into her eyes. For the first time since knowing him, she saw his hazel eyes well with tears.

Her hands felt as slimy as a platter of clam's casino at an Italian wedding buffet. *Did the heat just kick on in here?* she fanned the bottom of her sundress and reached for her water. "You can't. We definitely can't. It's WAY too soon." She heard her voice shake but couldn't control it.

"I just know this is it, Jess," he spoke with confidence. "Not a single day has gone by where I haven't missed you. I'm ready to start a life with you. I want to have children with you. I know what I did really hurt, but I promise to never hurt you again." He stared at her with such an intensity in his eyes that it was no surprise he was so successful in business. The man may be lacking in a multitude of ways, but he oozed confidence. "Listen," he continued, "I'm ready to give you everything you want and deserve. I know I can't pressure you into something you're not sure of but make no mistake Jessica Klein – I want you to be my wife."

Feeling as if she were split seconds away from a heart attack, Jess quickly pulled her hands away from his. "I can't do this," she frantically said. Technically she *could* do it, she just didn't *want* to do it. Nothing about this felt right, and that much she was certain of. Being away from him – even briefly for a weekend – made her see that this was not right. She didn't have the energy to vie for his attention, coming in third or fourth in line, after work, and his friends, and his partying lifestyle. He was too driven. Too stubborn.

Too much like me, she thought.

If all of her time with Dr. Green taught her nothing else, it was that life, relationships in particular, should not be such hard work that they become taxing and burdensome. That's not to say that things worth having don't require a level of effort, but that effort and sacrifice should come easier than they did with Seth. Being with him actually felt like *work*, and Jess decided that, despite her mother's advice, she was done forcing things. She was done letting herself be treated as anything less than she deserved. And she sure as shit did not deserve to be humiliated and dumped over an argument about shrimp and hot tubs. If she wanted to break the cycle of relationships that left her feeling like shit, she'd have to break the cycle herself. Once and for all.

"I'm sorry," she muttered, quickly rising to her feet. "I just can't do this."

Before he could offer a convincing rebuttal, or stand up himself, she was gone.

***

She gave it two days. Two whole days of hibernating at home, in relative silence, before calling someone to spill the beans. "I need to talk. Meet at the trail this afternoon? Say 2 o'clock?"

Without hesitation, Lea acquiesced.

"Hey!" Jess flagged her down from the opposite side of the unpaved parking lot where they'd met so many times before. Pulling her in for a hug, Jess couldn't help but notice that her friend was… glowing? "What's up with you?"

"Who me?" Lea asked, saucily. Without skipping a beat, she continued, "Everett asked me to meet his parents!" The pure joy beaming from her face. "We leave for Georgia next month. And after we meet his family, he's taking me on holiday to the Amalfi Coast!"

"Oh, my goodness!" Jess squealed. "This is fantastic!" Selfishly caught up in her own stuff, Jess hadn't realized just how wonderfully things were progressing for her girlfriend. Truth be told, she couldn't think of someone more deserving of love and happiness.

The two set out on the dirt trail like they did hundreds of Sundays before this one as Lea gushed about her upcoming trip. "Okay," Lea paused a mile and a half in, "I haven't even let you get a word in edgewise. Enough with me. What's going on with you? You told me you wanted to talk. The floor," she said, motioning towards the dirt trail before them, "is all yours."

"Seth proposed at lunch the other day." Jess shut her lips and stared at Lea, waiting for a response.

"I'm sorry, what?" Completely dumbfounded, Lea stopped dead in her tracks, rapidly blinking her eyes as if she had something stuck inside them. "You're going to have to say that again."

It sounded ridiculous because it was. Who on earth proposes less than a week after breaking up with someone? Jess realized how asinine the entire thing sounded. Frankly, she was exhausted from the roller coaster of emotions.

"You heard me," she said. "It's ridiculous, is what it is. I don't know if he seriously thought that was the right way to win me back or what… either way, it was an epic failure. But I'm grateful that in happened, because it actually taught me one hell of a lesson."

Lea stared at her in disbelief. "And what on earth is that?"

"That I'd rather be alone and my own than be with the wrong person."

Hearing the words come out of her mouth made Jess grin like a kid in a candy store. She never knew something to be so true before, and judging by the look on Lea's face, her friend couldn't agree more.

***

Later that week, Jess found herself back on Green's sunken in sofa for an overdue 'check-in.' Over the last six months, their check-ins became less and less frequent. As she waited for him, she stared at the familiar sign that hung above his desk.

Sometimes what feels like the end is actually the beginning.

Throughout their time together, she cried countless tears, gone through too many tissues, shared career struggles, dating blunders, and a shitload of self-growth. Today, Jess felt like a new woman on that old couch.

"Hello!" Dr. Green greeted her with his usual excitement. "Where would you like to start?" he asked, settling into his seat across from her.

"We could start with the surprise proposal I had last week," she casually said, crossing her legs while placing a brown microfiber throw pillow on her lap.

Dr. Green, with his notorious poker face, set his mug down and the look of confusion and disbelief spread across his face. "By whom? I'm going to need you to elaborate."

Explaining Seth's proposal gone wrong somehow didn't get easier the more times Jess told the story. They hadn't spoken since, and she truthfully had no desire to speak to him again. In reflecting back on their brief yet intense relationship, Jess couldn't fathom how a surprise proposal, just a week after dumping her, made sense. The man was all over the place, and it was fair to say that life had been enough of an emotional roller coaster before him. She didn't need anyone to add to it.

"Do you plan to speak with him again? Reconcile? Start again slowly?" It was unusual for Green to ask this many successive questions, but then again, Jess had never been proposed to out of the blue before.

"Not if I can help it," she felt her voice trail off. "I'm just so tired of the cycle."

"That's fair," he acknowledged. "So, what's next?"

The million-dollar question.

"You know... I've been seeing you for how long now?" She asked even though she knew the answer.

He gave her a warm smile. "It's been a while."

"Well, for as long as I can remember, I feel like I've been running from goal to goal – from distraction to distraction. Promotions, new jobs, a new house, traveling to magical places..." She thought back to some of those tough decisions, the relationships strengthened, the memories made. Rather than squarely focusing on the divorce and the laundry list of mistakes that ensued thereafter, she was able to look beyond her tumultuous past and wholeheartedly believe in the future. "I've become healthy and strong – inside and out – and believe it or not, I'm good without a goal for now."

Dr. Green looked pleased. "Is that so?" he asked.

"It is! My new plan, for the first time, is to have no plan. I think I've exhausted myself creating a long list of goals and ambitions and accomplishments... even though I always seem to achieve what I set out to do, it's just a temporary distraction until the next goal. So now, I am on the no plan, plan."

Not too long ago, Jess was so uncomfortable being in her own company that she ran. Ran into the arms of the wrong men. Ran headfirst into her career. Ran around the world... She just... ran. Clutching the musty throw pillow for probably the hundredth time, she spoke again. "I think this is what happy feels like," she said with a smile. "I just feel... happy. Despite the recent crazy events, of course."

"I must say, Jess, this is what I've always wanted to hear from you," Dr. Green looked at her with... pride? Sitting across from the man who had become somewhat of a mentor, the man who helped her cope with the most difficult, painful time in her adult life, Jess realized that she had outgrown their time together. It's a lesson he taught her that may take her entire life to master, but she felt well on her way towards treating herself with grace, patience and unconditional kindness.

"Do me a favor," he began. "There are parts of you that are so wonderfully unique. Whenever you find yourself diminishing them or finding yourself feeling unappreciated, promise me you'll celebrate yourself – and do it often. You've put in the work, and you deserve happiness. Much of life cannot be promised, but I can promise you one thing."

"What's that?"

"Once you love yourself, I mean really, truly love yourself... Everything else will fall into place."

"But I do love myself," Jess interjected.

"Then it's time you start living like you do." Dr. Green rose to his feet as their time ran up. "Now go. I'll be here any time you need me. Oh, and accept my friend request - my son set up this thing called Facebook. Let's be friends!"

Jess stood and walked towards him for what likely would be the last time. "Thank you for everything," she spoke, embracing him with a rare hug. With his full head of white hair, oversized cardigan and worn-in loafers, he reminded her of her grandfather, who she lost nearly a decade ago. "I'm not sure I would've gotten through this time without you."

"You would've figured it out," he told her. "But I'm sure grateful to have been a part of your journey. I can't wait to see what you're going to do with this new chapter."

As she walked down the long corridor just like she did many times before, she knew something was different.

Today, she was finally ready to trust in the magic of new beginnings.

Chapter Fifteen

J ess loved weddings. Everything about them, from the tasty food down to the blaring music that lasted till the wee hours of the morning. The hand-written, heartfelt vows to the multi-tier, elaborate wedding cakes. She was a sucker for a good party, and the fact that tonight would be her first-time attending nuptials without a date surprisingly didn't faze her much.

'Should I just find a guy to take as my date?' she asked Lea the month prior. She didn't truly mind going stag, but she knew with this particular group of friends, she'd be the only one showing up without a *plus one*.

'Just go with your head held high!' Lea told her. 'You're not some sort of leper – you're just single for crying out loud. Go, dance, eat, and enjoy.'

Jess followed suit, declining the *plus one* on the invite and letting herself get excited for what was promised to be the wedding 'of the season.' Willow and James had only recently come into Jess' life – ironically, she met them through a Tinder date gone wrong. Tim was a forty-something, insurance salesman she met online one weekend when she couldn't bear the thought of staying home alone for another quiet Saturday night. Although their time together was short-lived, she hit it off with his friends and kept in contact with them long enough to receive an invitation to their over-the-top, black-tie wedding.

It was a Saturday night affair, being held at The Biltmore Hotel in Atlanta. The building was constructed in the 1920s and designed by the same architect who was behind other stunning resorts like The Breakers in Palm Beach and The Waldorf-Astoria in NYC. From her limited knowledge of the future bride and groom, Jess knew the duo to be notorious for throwing lavish, extravagant, over-the-top parties. Their wedding would undoubtedly be no exception. Rumor had it that the groom flew in his favorite Mezcal from Mexico. The bride shipped in her favorite peanut butter and jelly macarons from an exclusive bakery in Paris. And if details such as those weren't enough, the couple's beloved risotto chef arrived yesterday – straight from Italy - with a gigantic wheel of Parmesan in tow. Saliva puddled in the corners of Jess' mouth as she imagined the salty, gooey cheese and chewy bits of arborio rice that would hit her lips in just a few more hours.

Sitting in front of her bedroom vanity, Jess mentally prepared herself for the inevitable question she'd likely be asked tonight. 'So, Jess, how's dating life?'

Five simple words - yet such a loaded question. She prepped herself with an arsenal of carefully curated responses such as, 'He's out there somewhere!' and 'If you see him, let me know!' And the rather appropriate and accurate, 'I'm just having fun, I'm not looking to meet anyone right now!'

Because the truth was, she *wasn't* looking to meet anyone right now. After a plethora of underwhelming dates since Seth, keeping the wrong relationships afloat for the wrong reasons, and who could forget the recent surprise proposal, dating somewhere along the way stopped feeling fun. Like with most things in life - the more she tried, the less likely anything was to work out.

Instead, she began to consciously release her fears of the future and simply accept the present. It wasn't an overnight process, that's for sure, but she learned to try and *go with the flow*. To accept what is while still praying for what could be.

Standing before the mirror, she felt beautiful. Her new floral, floor-length gown accentuated her frame, highlighting the new muscle mass she worked so hard to achieve. She found herself staring at her newly sculpted shoulders, petite yet defined biceps, and appreciated that the last bit of fat had melted off her abdomen. Seth quit coaching at her CrossFit, and she was grateful to continue her workouts and maintain her community at the gym without the awkward distraction of seeing him there.

Still staring at her reflection in the floor-length mirror, she smoothed the front of her gown, grabbed her Kate Spade glittery clutch off the nearby vanity table, and jumped in an Uber to head downtown.

***

Met with opulence from the second her Louboutin's hit the marble floor of the hotel lobby, Jess was enchanted by the oversized crystal chandeliers that hung from above, each drenched in enough flowers to last a years' worth of wedding receptions. From across the exquisite lobby, she spotted Katie and Rob, friends of hers who moved to Atlanta from Orange

County a few years ago. Eight months pregnant with their first baby boy, Katie looked stunning in a navy bodycon dress that hugged her burgeoning bump in the most adorable way. Jess saw her shifting her weight uncomfortably between her high-heeled feet from across the way. She also spotted Chelsea and Michael, a couple from Alabama who ran in this same circle, ordering a round of champagne at one of the many pop-up bars.

"It's the Alabama UGA game tonight," Michael announced, passing out the filled flutes to his wife, Jess, Katie and Rob. A true guy's guy, nothing, not even this wedding, would keep Michael from watching his beloved college football game. Especially one in which his alma mater was favorited to win.

"Please do not embarrass me tonight," Chelsea groaned to her husband.

"I'm not embarrassing you," he said proudly. "I've got it right here," he said, tapping the phone in his tuxedo jacket pocket.

Jess felt the cold champagne hit her lips as she smirked. Perhaps one of the upsides to coming alone is there's no one to argue with, she told herself. Music signaled that the ceremony was about to begin, and the five of them proceeded to their seats. The ballroom was glowing, thanks to the soft, romantic light of crystal chandeliers hanging from the fabric-wrapped ceiling and tall, white pillar candles flanking all four walls. As three hundred guests were ushered to their seats, Jess and her friends opted for one of the far back rows.

As they settled into their seats, Jess noticed Katie fidgeting to her right. "How are you feeling?" Jess asked.

Katie let out a heavy sigh. "Pregnant. Very, very pregnant." She rubbed her bump as she leaned back in her chair, resting her feet on the seat in front of her.

"Well, you look gorgeous. And you're making this whole pregnancy thing look easy!" The ladies were quickly interrupted by dimming lights and the sounds of a harpist playing.

One by one, the groomsmen made their way down the aisle, followed by ten bridesmaids in blush colored gowns. As they made their way down the rose petal covered aisle, Jess noticed Michael silently watching the game on his phone, which he had strategically placed between his legs. With the bridal party lined up, and the priest and groom anxiously awaiting the bride's arrival, nearly twenty minutes passed without any action. The harpist continued to play, yet there was no bride. No nothing.

"I think my water is going to break before this girl makes it down the aisle," Katie huffed, rubbing her swollen belly as she discreetly slipped off her stiletto heels. "How long have we been sitting here?"

Rob checked his watch. "Almost thirty minutes now," he said flatly.

"Jesus," Michael muttered without taking his eyes off his phone.

The guests all began to whisper. The priest and groom no longer hid their looks of concern. Would the bride show at all? The crowd became restless, yet the harpist played on.

Finally, after another long fifteen minutes, Jess spotted commotion at the end of the aisle.

The music changed to Canon on D and the bride finally appeared in a full-length crystal-encrusted ball gown. Her gigantic, silicone-enhanced breasts exploded out the top and reminded Jess of childhood days when her mom let her knock the can of Pillsbury biscuits across the kitchen counter.

"Jesus Christ," Jess heard a man whisper a row behind. She saw his wife elbow him in the side as she whispered *shhhhh*.

Accompanied by her dad and stepfather, the bride appeared to be clutching both men rather desperately. As she made her way down the aisle, Jess noticed the bride swaying side to side, with her eyes appearing to roll back into her skull. Her face and décolleté were about as red as the bottom of Jess' heels.

There was no doubt about it. The bride was wasted.

Muted laughter and snickers broke out amongst the crowd as the bride attempted to gracefully make her way down the candle and floral-adorned aisle, her future husband anxiously awaiting her extremely belated arrival. This wedding was rumored to have cost over a million dollars, and it was par for the course with them that the bride didn't take even this day seriously to show up sober enough to walk down the aisle. The ceremony itself was rather uneventful outside of the overt display of intoxication - canned vows slurred by the bride, rehearsed vows repeated by the groom and a quick yet ironic and poignant speech about the power of forgiveness from the priest. Five minutes later, the groom supported his wife as she stumbled back down the aisle, making their first official walk as husband and wife.

As they disappeared behind the double doors at the end of the aisle, Steve Aoki began to blare through the sound system. The bass rumbled as an Elvis impersonator appeared quite unexpectedly in the ballroom.

"What in the fucknuts is that," Rob yelled.

"Omg, he told me he'd do this," Katie began.

"Told you he'd do what, exactly?" Jess asked, completely

perplexed.

"Last time I talked to John he said, 'be prepared.' Apparently, it's a game he loves to play with Willow – pissing her off with random, over the top surprises. He told me to 'expect the unexpected," Katie said. "I had no idea this is what he had in mind!"

"I'm going to need another glass of Champagne for this," Jess announced.

After a painfully long, completely gratuitous two-hour cocktail hour, complete with Cher and Elvis impersonators, Jess and her friends took their assigned seats at table twenty-one. Rob smacked his hands together and yelled so loudly that he managed to startle everyone despite Tiesto now blaring in the background.

"I got it! I have someone for her," Rob yelled, looking at his wife.

"For Jess? You do?" Katie asked with trepidation. "Who?"

"Kyle!" he screamed, arms in the air, vodka spilling over the side of his glass. The man loved to shout with conviction.

"Kyle? Are you, crazy? The guy doesn't even live here."

"So?" Rob asked.

"So? She has a career here. A whole life here. You think she's going to want to start dating some guy on the other side of the country?"

The way they discussed her as if she weren't sitting next to them made her feel uncomfortable.

"Who are we talking about?" Jess asked, reaching for a pretzel roll. She took a swipe of butter shaped like a swan from the china plate in the middle of the table.

"You tell her," Katie motioned towards her husband.

"Tell me what?"

"We have a guy I want you to meet," Rob said, draining his cocktail.

"Well that's nice of you, but I'm done dating. In fact, I've decided to get a cat."

Katie squinted her eyes from across the table. "But you hate cats," she said flatly.

"I know. Fine, I'm not getting a cat. But you know what else I'm not doing? I'm not dating. I literally cannot muster up the energy for another bad first date. You guys have no idea how exhausting it is."

"Well, good thing you won't have to," Rob told her.

"Let me get this straight. You're introducing me to this guy, but I'm not supposed to actually meet him? How does this work, exactly?" Color her confused.

"Easy," Rob said, holding his hands up. "He lives in California, so you won't be able to meet in person right away. Maybe you guys could just talk. Who knows? I just think you two would be really great for each other. You both love to travel. You both stay active. He wants a family, too. Just trust me on this one."

"So, I'm supposed to disregard the fact that we live on opposite coasts?" Jess rightfully asked. She may not have lived in New York for a few years now, but she was as New York as they came. She couldn't fathom the concept of dating someone who chose flip flops and board shorts over suits and loafers.

"Don't get all caught up in geography," Rob said in his typically dismissive way. "I'm telling you, just talk to him. I bet you guys hit it off."

"I need to know more," Jess pressed. "Tell me about him."

"Well, you guys are the same age. He's close to his family in the fun uncle kind of way, although I know he's definitely ready to settle down and have a family of his own. I've known him my entire life - our fathers have been working together long before we were born. And now Kyle and I work together, have for the past ten years. He's a super sharp guy."

"Interesting," Jess said with blatant reluctancy. It all sounded so farfetched.

"Oh, come on, just be open," Rob continued. "He's a really nice guy. He wants to settle down with the right girl. In fact, I keep telling him if he stays this picky, he'll be single forever."

I know the feeling, Jess thought to herself.

"So other than the fact that he lives in California, what's wrong with him?"

"What do you mean what's wrong with him? Is that a trick question?"

"Why is he still single?" Jess asked.

"I don't know. He hasn't met the right girl yet, I suppose." Rob shrugged.

"That's bullshit," Jess said. "The only guys still single in their 30s have something wrong with them." She spoke it as if it were an absolute truth.

"That's not true," Rob said.

"It's common knowledge. All the good ones are gone." Jess stuffed half the warm roll in her mouth. The words coming out of her mouth sounded pessimistic, she knew it. But she wholeheartedly believed them. After the past year of horrible dates and disappointing relationships, she felt as though the well had dried up. *The good ones truly are all gone.*

"Oh really?" Rob asked. "Well then, why are YOU still single?" He darted his eyes towards her.

With a mouthful of half-eaten pretzel bread, Jess acquiesced. "Well played. Give him my number."

Chapter Sixteen

The smell of Fall always reminded her of new beginnings.

For as many years as Jess could remember, she and her dad spent the weekends in Lake George, up in the Adirondacks of New York State, to pick apples and snap hundreds of photos as the leaves changed their color. She'd eat vanilla soft serve out of freshly baked cones, covered in multi-color sprinkles. Adam would laugh as the ice cream dripped down her chin as she cracked a big, gapped tooth smile.

New York City summers always felt too oppressive and the winters felt too cold. Fall just always seemed to feel… just right.

All these years later, despite living in the South, Jess still found something cathartic about the cool, crisp air as she watched the Georgia pines standing tall, like attentive soldiers on guard, from her living room window. With the flip of a switch, she fired up the gas fireplace, letting its ambient glow warm up her cozy, plush living room. She reached for the ivory cable knit throw her grandmother made years ago and pulled it up over her bare feet. After all this time, Jess never tired burying her face into the thick fabric, smelling the faintest scent of her grandmother that managed to withstand the test of time.

It was then, as she felt Tiffany press up against her on the white upholstered sofa, that Jess got to thinking about change. As she went from day to day, week to week, and month to month, it was hard to notice when things truly changed. Yet suddenly, on a brisk Sunday morning, everything seemed different somehow.

No longer scared to be alone, she found herself relishing in peaceful moments such as these – where she could quietly stare out of the single pane, floor to ceiling windows and just watch the colorful leaves gently fell to the ground. She let the gentle warmth from the whitewashed fireplace and steamy tea warm her cold hands. The solitude felt comforting, somehow. Like a long hug from a dear friend.

It was only mid-morning, but her eyes felt heavy and since she had nowhere else to be, she let herself to drift off to sleep.

***

Woken by the sound of her phone vibrating on the coffee table just arm's length away, Jess rubbed the sleep from her eyes, answering the call just a few seconds too late.

She didn't recognize the number, and before she could return the call, the number called again.

"Hello?" she sleepily answered.

"Hey! Is this Jess?" She didn't recognize his voice, but there was no mistaking that whoever it was, he sounded like he was smiling.

It can't be, she thought. *Rob just gave him my number last night.* A guy who called the next day. A year of awful dates and sour experiences left her skeptical, at best.

"Hi!" she returned his enthusiasm. "This is Jess. Is this Kyle?" Always one to pace while on the phone, she rose to her feet, slipping on a pair of nearby fuzzy slippers and as she typically did when talking nervously, paced around her condo in continuous circles.

"It is! It's so nice to meet you." He paused for a moment and continued, sounding about as nervous as she felt. "Well, I mean over the phone, that is." He let out a small laugh that left Jess feeling at ease. She imagined what he looked like from the other end of the phone, on the other end of the country. "So, Rob tells me you live in Atlanta?" he continued. "Is that where you're originally from?"

She was impressed the way he jumped right in. No awkward silence or small talk about himself, he jumped right into questions about her, and there was a distinct kindness about his voice that wasn't lost on Jess. Never one to willingly offer up information, the tables felt turned ever so slightly with him asking all the questions and her doing most of the answering from the get-go.

"I live in Atlanta now, but I'm originally from New York. I've sort of lived all over - I grew up in New York, went to college in Arizona, studied abroad in London, lived in South Florida, back to New York, and then down to Atlanta."

"And what brought you to Atlanta?" What she liked most, she considered, is that he asked and seemed genuinely interested in knowing the answer.

"My career," she told him, deciding to temporarily omit the superfluous details that didn't concern him just yet. Uttering the phrases 'ex-husband' or 'divorce' didn't seem like appropriate material for an initial conversation.

"And how about you?" she asked, decidedly changing the tables. "Rob and Katie tell me you live in Orange County? I've been to California so many times, but I've somehow always managed to skip over O.C. Do you love it?"

"I do!" His voice had an expected ease to it. "It's the only place I've ever lived, outside of the four years I went to college in LA. It's beautiful and laid back, and the perfect place to raise a family one day, so I've never really seen any reason to leave."

Given her somewhat nomadic lifestyle, Jess couldn't fathom the feeling of never leaving the city that raised you. She and her mom hopped apartments and cities every few years after her parents' divorce, and despite her mom's attempt at making them all feel comfortable, no place felt like home for long. And despite living nearly all over the world at one point or another, Jess couldn't wrap her head around what life in California truly entailed. If given the choice, she'd choose high heels and high-top sneakers over flip flops and surfboards any day. She preferred the bright lights of the city over sleepy beach towns and more than anything, pegged herself for being far, far too uptight to live that laid-back Cali cool lifestyle.

As he continued on, Jess could get a real sense of his bubbly personality. He bragged about his three-year-old nephew with pride, told her stories of how his parents emigrated to the United States three decades prior, and seemed to overuse the word *family* with a gentle ease. As her mind raced, Jess consciously reminded herself to stay in the moment. Just five minutes into their conversation and she had so many questions. *Be. Here. Now,* she reminded herself.

Once he took a pause, she followed up with another open-ended question. "So, what do you do for work?" Jess asked.

"Well, that's actually how I know Rob. We work together, developing and designing healthcare websites together."

She walked over to the kitchen and poured herself another cup of coffee from the carafe, settling back on the sofa as their conversation pivoted to travel, and Kyle shared with her details of his most recent, month-long trip to Thailand. As she listened to him talk with such enthusiasm about the idyllic blue ocean and the sweetest mangos he'd ever eaten, the strangest thing happened. She wasn't judging. She wasn't analyzing. She wasn't even planning what to say next. She was just... *listening.*

Somewhere between swapping their top ten must-see travel lists, to similar CrossFit Competition war stories, Jess glanced over at the clock hanging in her kitchen.

Somehow, three hours went by in the blink of an eye.

***

"Katie! He called!" Jess could hardly contain herself, screaming into the phone before allowing her girlfriend to utter a proper 'Hello.' Less than twenty-four hours after giving her friends the theoretical thumbs up to pass along her number, Kyle had called. And not only had they spoken, but it was quite possibly the best conversation she'd had with the opposite sex in as far back as she could recall. The type of conversation that left butterflies floating through your belly and sent tingles down to the tips of your fingers. Jess left no detail behind as she paced throughout the house while simultaneously gushing over the conversation still fresh on her mind.

Calm down, she tried to convince herself. *You don't even know the guy.* Yet something felt different. Perhaps it was the way he made her feel so at ease. Or the way she felt his smile through the telephone. Three hours felt closer to ten minutes as their conversation traversed topics including mundane items such as their favorite foods, to more interesting subject matter such as their favorite exotic travel destinations.

Turns out, Rob *was* right. The duo had a ton of commonalities, from their mutual love of working out to their burning desire to see the world many times over. It all seemed just a bit too easy. A bit too smooth.

"Is there a catch with this guy?" Jess playfully asked Katie.

"Well," Kate interjected. "There's just one thing…"

If only calories could be burnt from the exercise of jumping to conclusions, Jess would've dropped a few pounds right then and there.

"What? What is it?" Her mind began to race. "Does he have kids? Is he in some weird religious cult? What's happening?"

"Girl, calm down." Katie spoke. "He's single, childless, and no, not a member of a cult."

"I'm going to need you to get to the point faster, then." Like many women, telling a woman to calm down almost certainly guaranteed that she would in fact, not calm down.

"Oh, it's not that big of a deal," Katie placated her. "Just a detail

Rob and I may have left out. It's minor, really."

If she could reach through the phone and impatiently shake her dear friend, she would. "Spill it!"

"His last name. It's… it's seventeen letters."

"Seventeen!?!?!?"

Jessica Klein, the Jewish equivalent of John Smith, was about as easy of a moniker as they came. Easy to spell and easy to pronounce, no one flinched when she wrote it, no one poked fun when she made a dinner reservation or filled out a customs form. She couldn't fathom the idea of walking around with a name that sounded as though it belonged in the encyclopedia.

"Interesting. What is it?"

"Engchawadechasilp."

Oh hell no.

"You're going to have to repeat that again."

Jess replayed the earlier conversation back. Kyle hadn't had an accent, had he?

"It's actually not that intimidating if you break it up and say it phonetically. Here, I'll text it to you."

As Jess awaited the text to come through, she realized until now, she had a fairly distinct type. American, for starters. Caucasian. Suit and tie kind of guy. Suddenly, she realized Kyle might be different. It was undeniable she gravitated towards a certain 'type,' but where had it gotten her? Maybe someone new – completely new – would be just what she needed. She clicked the link to Kyle's Facebook profile via the Katie's text, and was shocked by what she saw.

"Umm, he's gorgeous!" Jess' mouth hung open as she stared at the bright white smile of an absurdly handsome man. Entranced, she rapidly began swiping through hundreds of photos.

Handstands at the Taj Mahal, CrossFit competitions in sunny California, grinning on a beach in Thailand, holding a newborn baby at a friend's christening. She scanned the comments on each photo, gave a quick read through his profile, sprinting down a rabbit hole in warp speed.

"You still there?" Katie asked.

"Oh right, sorry," Jess apologized. "I need to sleuth. Let me call you back."

In solace, Jess continued snooping through Kyle's profile, while simultaneously conducting a full-on Google search. She needed to know everything there was to know about this new man. As she sifted through the search results, she played back some of the sage advice Dr. Green imparted months back.

According to Einstein, the definition of insanity is doing the same thing over and over, expecting a different result. In her heart of hearts, she knew if a different outcome was what she wanted, then a new approach is what she needed. Perhaps geography shouldn't matter. *Who cares if this guy lived on the opposite end of the country?*

Would a long-distance relationship be the worst thing in the world? For a girl who used to cringe at the very thought of going for a coffee alone was now a ruthlessly independent woman. Going to a movie alone – shit, going on vacation alone – no longer phased her. She actually enjoyed her own company. Dating someone on the opposite end of the country might not be the worst thing in the world. Although as she considered long-term potential, her career is in Atlanta. Her friends are here. Her house is here. Her *life* is here. What would happen if things took off? They didn't seem geographically compatible.

Just stop, she told herself. Recognizing her feelings of wanting to plan, wanting to control, passed by like fleeting thoughts in front of her. *Maybe nothing will come from this. Maybe something will. Who knows and who cares? Just have fun! Be present,* she reminded herself. *Let yourself just enjoy this feeling, right here, right now.*

***

"Check this out," Jess slid her phone across the table as a tall bottle of hot sake was placed in front of them. "Katie and Rob introduced me to this guy at the wedding. Well, virtually, anyhow."

She squealed like a preteen gossiping about the new cute boy at school. "Jess! He's so cute! And tall. I need to know everything, leave no detail left behind." With her eyebrows raised, there was no hiding Lea's genuine shock of staring back at a photo of a tall, dark, and handsome Asian guy.

"Well," Jess filled their sake cups to the brim, "He works with Rob. He's single, obviously..."

"Well I'd hope so!" Lea threw her arms dramatically in the air. No stranger to dishing out dating advice cloaked in her ruthless opinion, Lea found it near impossible to hold back her thoughts on Jess' dating decisions. After a string of men over forty earlier in the year, Lea reminded Jess 'You do realize men over forty have all sorts of impotence and prostate problems. Erectile dysfunction. Low flow. You really feel like dealing with all that shit?' She took the tiniest bit of pleasure in poking fun at Jess' choices with every chance she got, and Jess couldn't blame her. She had a point.

"Anyway," Jess continued. "His name is Kyle. He actually called me this morning. We talked for three hours!" She felt her smile spread across her face as their bento boxes arrived.

"Well, this is exciting!" There was a genuine, lightheartedness to Lea's voice. "I'm so thrilled to hear you met someone worth getting to know..."

"What is it?" The way Lea's voice trailed off was clear that she had more to say on the matter.

"Don't kill me for being a Debbie downer, but do you think it's smart to start something up with someone clear across the country?"

"I know," Jess smoothed her napkin out in front of her. "I've obviously considered that. And I know it's a bit crazy, but so what? I haven't been interested in someone for a long time. And I'm not necessarily interested in this becoming the end all be all, but I'm definitely game to get to know him."

"Look at you!" Lea smiled. "I'm not even sure what to say. It's refreshing seeing you so excited about someone. Who is this laid-back lady and what have you done with my friend?"

"He's traveled the world twice over, seems super passionate about his career, and talked nonstop about his family," Jess shared as she took a bite of seaweed salad. "Can you believe he lives within a fifteen-minute drive from his parents, grandparents, brother, and nephew? I'm not sure if that's the sweetest or scariest thing I've ever heard."

"Oh gosh, could you imagine" Lea dipped a slice of salmon sashimi in some soy sauce. Considering it had been years since she lived in the same state as her parents, Jess literally could not imagine. Having a plane ride between her and Sarah was for the best, as far as she and her mother were concerned. "It sounds like his roots go deep in California. So, I assume that means he wouldn't consider moving to Atlanta?"

"I'm honestly not sure. Considering this was our very first conversation, I thought it would be premature to ask him if he was willing to move across the country for a girl he hasn't even met yet. Green once told me 'If you start right, you stay right' and I'm just at the point where I'm ready to start on the right foot. Go slow, get to know someone for who they are, and just see where it all takes me. No expectations, no pressure. And definitely no rush."

Their conversation pivoted towards Lea as she shared the latest happenings with Everett. Turns out, things were going swimmingly well, and Jess couldn't be more thrilled to see her dear friend this happy.

After their plates were cleared and the last of the sake drunk, Lea couldn't help herself. "So, when do you get to meet this guy in person?"

"I know this is going to sound crazy," Jess began.

"Oh god, this should be good…" Lea interrupted.

"He's coming to visit in two weeks!" Jess announced.

"Seriously? That soon?" Lea was shit at sugar coating.

"I know, but what is there to wait for? He was planning to come visit Rob and Katie at some point, or so he said. Honestly, I think we're both anxious to meet and see if this chemistry is real."

"I can't argue with that, I just want to be sure you're not throwing caution to the wind and losing control of sound judgment. Jumping on a cross-country flight after one phone conversation is a big commitment! And then what?"

Jess reached for Lea's hand and took it in hers. "Look, I know you're concerned, and I love you for that. But I've got this. He's been Rob's friend for twenty-five years. Just trust me to make a decent decision and let's have faith that it'll all work out. Whichever way it goes, that's the way it's intended to go. Okay?"

Lea sighed. "I just want you to be careful, that's all. I'm sure he's a great guy, but the reality is we just don't know him."

"Yet," Jess corrected her. "We don't know him, yet."

"Fair," Lea resigned. "It is quite refreshing to see you like this. I'm not sure I've ever seen you this… calm… before."

After Chris left, Jess willingly threw herself into work. Not only was one of the only things she could control, but without a partner meant there was no fallback plan. It was all on her. No one to call if the mortgage didn't get paid. No one to call if she was suddenly laid off and had no job prospects in sight. She became self-sufficient out of necessity. Her circumstances threw her headfirst into the deep end and she taught herself how to swim.

"I'm so glad things are working out with Everett," Jess changed the subject. Seeing her otherwise guarded, somewhat rigid, friend soften around the edges was an unexpected change.

"It feels really great," Lea smiled contently. "We're actually talking about moving in together after the holidays. I think after all these years of living alone, I'm ready to take the plunge. I told him yes, on the condition he handles all trash and all laundry."

"Oh, my goodness!" Jess squealed. "This is so exciting!" Lea never wanted children, but she was always vocal about her desire to get married one day.

"You know," Lea continued, "With how busy life has been lately, I haven't heard you talk a single word about having kids. Have you changed your mind?"

"I still want a family, but I took the pressure off myself. If it's ever going to happen, it needs to be under the right circumstances. I'm not going to rush to have a baby all on my own just to have one. That's not fair to a child or to me. I want a family, sure. I want the life I feel like I missed out on growing up. I want the Friday night pizza and a movie on the couch. Sunday cartoons with a short stack of pancakes. What I don't want is to give my kids a single mother who has to work her ass off just to provide."

Since shifting her mindset about what 'having a family' meant to her, Jess felt a whole lot less jealous seeing others and a whole lot more at peace with her own life. It's how she was able to see Katie at the wedding, round belly and all, and feel joy. It's how she was able to toss out the idea of adopting a baby on her own, despite her family's support and encouragement, and embrace where she was in life – right here, right now.

When she took having kids on her own off the table, she silently promised herself that if she ever did meet an amazing guy, a truly amazing guy, she'd commit to doing whatever it took. She vowed to let her guard down. To drop the unspoken rule book of what she should or shouldn't do. What she should or shouldn't say. She promised herself she'd do whatever it took for true love.

Often wondering if that day would ever come, she inadvertently came to terms with the fact that it might not. And that would be okay. *She would be okay.* The last year showed Jess that whatever she wanted - to visit the far corners of the world, grow her blossoming career, become a more engaged daughter and friend, take on new hobbies - she was capable of it all. Not because of a marriage certificate or a man to kiss goodnight, but because she was finally whole. *All on her own.*

It was only now that she began to appreciate the irony of it all. She spent so much time and energy giving it all her might trying to "make something happen" that she forced herself into accepting dates from men she didn't even like. She said yes when she meant no. She cried herself to sleep, wishing for someone to lie next to. Yet life taught her that letting things fall apart was necessary so that better things can come together.

And the overwhelming sense of failure she once felt? Turns out her worth was never measured by how many times she succeeded or failed. Her worth, she realized, was measured by her relentless dedication to pursuing the things that made her happy.

Maybe, Jess thought, just maybe… it's not about learning to rebuild our old lives but learning that the true power lies within our ability to create a new life. New hobbies. New friendships. Newfound confidence. Making happiness a how, not a when. Relying on the comfort of friends helped, depending upon close family helped, too. Even Dr. Green helped. Yet, unquestionably, the most valuable relationship Jess could credit for pulling herself out of the depths of her despair is the relationship she finally cultivated with herself.

"You know what's weird? It took me so long to comprehend the distinction between being alone and being lonely. I finally, somewhere along the way, forgave myself for all those shitty decisions that seemed like the end of the world. It was damn near impossible for me to just chill out and treat myself with the forgiveness I'd extend to you or anyone else I loved. Why?"

"The million-dollar question," Lea said. "I wish I knew the answer, but alas, I'm just as mystified as you are."

The girls paid their bill and Jess grabbed her purse.

"Okay love, this was amazing, but it's way past my bedtime."

They hugged before stepping outside into the cool, crisp evening air.

"Brrr," Jess shivered as she pulled her scarf around her neck. A breeze passed, sending a chill down her spine.

As she made her way home, driving underneath the dimly lit streetlights, she replayed the last year, remembering how she repeatedly sought out happiness in all the wrong places. In a never-ending stream of questionable decisions, she struggled to grasp any sparse shred of happiness – happiness, which felt like a distant, far-off place - always just outside her reach. The harder she grasped for it, the further off it felt.

If only I had known, she realized, *that happiness and acceptance were inside me the entire time.*

Chapter Seventeen

Running on adrenaline and copious amounts of caffeine, the anticipation consumed every fiber of her being as Jess drove well over the speed limit to the airport. She fidgeted in the driver's seat as she drove white-knuckled through Atlanta's horrendous rush-hour traffic. Creeping slowly behind the hundreds of cards in front of her, Jess' mind was the only thing raging at a million miles per minute.

Will meeting in person live up to the picture I've created in my mind? What if there's no physical chemistry? What if we run out of things to talk about?

She nervously switched the radio on, flipping mindlessly from station to station, ultimately opting for comforting silence. *Calm down,* she told herself. *It's going to be great.*

In what felt like hours of gridlock traffic and countless curse words muttered underneath her breath, Jess approached Delta's bustling terminal. As one of the busiest airports in the world, Atlanta Hartsfield was a place she loved to witness. Whether waiting for a visitor or a flight to depart, Jess easily entertained herself by merely observing the crowds and counting the number of hugs exchanged.

This is it. Will he look like I pictured him to be? Will he kiss me right away? Do I want him to kiss me right away? Her stomach did sequential summersaults as she dismissed the numerous 'no parking' signs, opting to pull up to the curb of the first set of revolving doors. As the doors parted, a group of passengers spilled out. A young family with a handful of suitcases and matching floral shirts appeared first. *Hawaiian vacation,* Jess assumed. An elderly couple lovingly holding hands walked towards the middle-aged woman awaiting their arrival. *Her daughter,* Jess assumed. Finally, a group of post-pubescent boys donning University of Georgia sweatshirts busted out with travel golf bags slung over their shoulders. *Golf tournament had to be.*

Her eyes darted back and forth, searching for any sight of Kyle. In her peripheral vision, Jess spotted a police officer approaching. As he blew his whistle, motioning his arms in a large circle, the words, "Hey Ma'am, you gotta drive around!" shouted towards her. As she took the split second to decide whether to loop around, Kyle appeared amidst the crowd.

He was even more handsome than his photos. Standing six feet tall with broad shoulders, golden skin and a thick head of jet-black hair, Jess watched in awe as he made his way through the crowd. His smile was like that of an old friend or close family member – warm and familiar, even if this was the first time that they ever laid eyes on each other. He walked towards her with a black duffle bag draped over one shoulder. Wearing black jeans and a black t-shirt, he donned the smile that she now had heard many times over the phone. She maneuvered her car a bit closer to the curb and before she could check her reflection in the rear-view mirror, he was sitting in the passenger seat.

"I can't believe it's you," he said, hugging her tightly. He smelled of fresh cologne and peppermint gum.

Sounds of the persistent police officer and cars driving by somehow faded into the background and time stood still as they shared their first embrace. Being in the arms of a near-stranger felt unusually familiar and Jess wanted to freeze this moment in time. He took her head in his hands and kissed her, sweetly yet with force. She let herself melt into him.

"It's so good to see you," she mustered. The next two and a half days together would be spent wine tasting, hiking the Georgia mountains, eating at a few of her local favorite spots — all in one of her favorite cities. Yet with a slightly packed agenda, all she wanted to do was freeze time and sit here, kissing him. As the police officer's whistle blew again, she broke their embrace and headed towards home.

As she looked forward, staring at the jammed highway, her heart fluttered. No matter how the weekend went, she was going in with no expectations — only an open mind and an open heart.

***

For nearly three, glorious days, their first visit went off without a hitch. The fall air felt crisp and cool, completely conducive for a day at some local wineries. They discovered a mutual love for dark, rich Syrah, buying a bottle to drink over Atlanta's finest BBQ. Their connect, visceral from the start, pleasantly surprised them both.

From the moment he kissed her at the airport, Jess was utterly smitten. His hand seemed to perfectly cup the small of her back as they walked, and his muscular body enveloped her with such each when they laid beside one another in bed.

"How do you take your coffee?" she asked him as he sleepily shuffled into the kitchen Saturday morning.

To her surprise, their conversations did much more than scratch the service. Despite being raised by two completely different cultures, it was a pleasant surprise to uncover how similar their parents were.

"She wasn't necessarily a tiger mom," Kyle described his mother that morning as he propped himself up at the kitchen island, "But she certainly emphasized the importance of a solid education. My dad didn't care as much about my grades, but he insisted I become an engineer, just like him."

"Wait, I'm confused," she interjected. "You've never mentioned engineering before."

"Well, technically I'm not an engineer. I graduated with the degree, but it was done really just to placate him. It was so ungodly boring. After my first job, I realized that was not the life for me. Just testing equipment, seeing what's broken, and trying to fix it. No thanks. But that's how I got into UX and UI design. Something about figuring out the way a website is broken and how to fix it really excites me..."

He could have been explaining how to make a bowl of cereal, or breaking down the most complex mathematics equation, it was irrelevant. She was fully entranced, regardless of the subject matter.

The rest of their time seemed to rush by. Her cheeks had hurt from laughing and by the time Sunday rolled around, she felt close to tears.

As she drove him to the airport that day, she reminded herself that it had been three days. Three! *Get it together,* she repeated on the drive.

Thankfully Kyle broke the temporary silence. "If it's possible, I miss you already. When can you come see me?"

Enter the cross-country conundrum. This wouldn't be as simple as scheduling another date. Long-haul flights needed to be purchased. Expensive flights, at that. The time needed to be taken off of work. She had to arrange for Tiffany to stay with a friend. Logistically, this was anything but convenient.

"Well," Jess said, "I could come out next month. Maybe make it every other month? And you could come to Atlanta on the months I don't visit?" She knew it sounded like a lot of work, but if this relationship stood a chance at taking off, mutual effort would be very necessary.

"I'm down for that," he said with a bright, white smile. "I know this isn't going to be easy, but I'm in. I am all in."

They knew one another for a month in totality, but she believed him. For the first time in a long time, she wasn't worried. About herself, about their budding relationship. About anything.

***

"So darling," Sarah asked later that Sunday evening. "Tell me. How was your visit?"

Replaying the last few days made her beam. "It was so great, Mom. I like him. We just had so much fun together. Everything felt... easy."

"You know, there's truth to that," Sarah began. "The Buddhists say if you meet somebody and your heart pounds, your hands shake, your knees go weak, then that person is not the one. When you meet your 'soul mate' you're supposed to feel calm. No anxiety, no agitation."

Calm. That's precisely what Jess felt waft over her. Calm. For the first time, she wasn't ruminating over the same tried and true questions. *Is he into me? Am I into him? Is he going to call? Will I want to answer?* She wasn't overanalyzing, planning for a future that didn't yet exist. She was happy to have him in her life and excited to see where things might go. They committed to alternating coasts through the holiday season to see how things progressed. If it ever felt like too much work, or if one person felt they were investing more energy and effort than the other, they vowed to communicate openly and honestly.

In the three weeks leading up to her first trip, Jess found herself completely gob smacked with how effortless becoming Kyle's girlfriend continued to be. He answered when she called. In fact, he called her so often, she rarely had a chance to dial him first. He took a genuine interest in her work. He remembered the names of her family members and asked her to tell stories of her childhood. In turn, he shared stories of his past in a way that made her feel comfortable and at ease. She felt as though she were sitting right next to him, despite nearly two thousand miles between them. With every story, every conversation, she fell deeper.

The night before she flew out, he called.

"Hi there," she warmly answered. The reality of seeing him in less than twenty-four hours hit her.

"I have something I want to talk to you about," he blurted.

Before she could count to three, a pit the size of a watermelon began taking share in the base of her belly. *Please don't let a shoe drop.*

After so many ups and downs, pseudo breakups, and letdowns, her mind reverted to the familiar place of self-doubt. Yet this felt different. At least she hoped it did.

"What's up?" she casually asked, holding her breath at the top of the question.

"I want you to meet my family when you visit this weekend." After a few moments of met silence, his question followed. "Will you meet my parents?" he laughed.

Holy shit! Meeting the parents was a monumental event in any relationship, no less one that has only just begun. The sheer idea thrilled her. Was it soon? Hell yes. Did that matter? Not really. It felt as natural as anything else about their relationship to date.

And this feeling right there – the feeling of ease and comfort – this is exactly what she had been waiting for her entire life.

Without hesitation, without questioning whether it was too soon, or whether she was ready – or whether they were ready -

her mouth opened, with the words flowing out as easily as the air she breathed. "Yes, sorry. Yes! I'd love to meet them."

***

"Start from the beginning and don't you dare leave a single detail behind," Raquel instructed as the girls gathered around Jess' kitchen island that evening. It had been six months since Jess' first trip out to California and the relationship felt as wonderful as it did the very first weekend they spent together.

"Well ladies, it's official!" Jess squealed over the top of her wine glass. "The move is happening."

There were smiles and squeals – and a plenty of wine-induced tears - but not a single look of confusion or doubt. The three women who knew Jess so well had not a single shadow of a doubt Jess would be moving, they just didn't know when.

Never one to shy away from practicalities, Lea was first to bring out the heavy questions. "What about work?"

"My boss is totally on board to let me work remotely," Jess happily explained. "Good news for you is I'll be traveling back here often. You can't get rid of me so easily, you know!"

"This is all happening so fast!" Raquel chimed in. "Don't get me wrong, we're so happy for you... It's just that it seems like I blinked and poof, you're moving clear across the country!"

Jess anticipated having to explain her rationale at some point. Afterall, it wasn't every day she did something appearing to be this risky. She had an established career. A home. A group of friends who now felt like family. She didn't make permanent decisions based on temporary emotions.

"Listen, I get that this seems quick, and maybe even a bit risky. I get it. But this feels right. It feels like the only option, really. I love him and he loves me. Is it too hard to believe that we're ready to start a life in the same time zone?"

She smirked, considering just how at peace she felt with her decision. Since she and Kyle discussed her moving to California, there hadn't been one singular doubt in her mind. Their relationship, even from thousands of miles apart, provided the balance, stability, and calmness that she had yearned for but never found. He's a great match to her wild and free personality – and everyone who knew them both knew it to be true.

Lea opened another bottle of prosecco and spoke in the loving tone that Jess grew to love. "To new adventures and to finding love in the most inconspicuous of places!"

"To love!" They all raised their glasses high in the air.

As the bubbles effervescently rose in their glasses, Jess looked around. These women were her tribe. In the darkest of hours, they were the ones to help her find all that she had lost. Her smile, her hope, her courage. All of it. And now, knowing that tonight would be the last night they'd all live in the same city, able to make plans without airlines and time changes involved, it all felt so bittersweet.

But that's the thing about friendships, she now knew. The strongest ones don't require daily conversation or interaction. They don't require constant togetherness or attention. So long as the friendship lived inside their hearts, they'd never truly be apart.

***

Where the hell is my wallet.

Jess darted frantically from room to room in what felt like a constant quest for her wallet.

"Ma'am, we're just about done in here!" she heard Walter's voice yell out. He and his crew had been a godsend. Showing up at seven o'clock on the dot, they packed every single item in her condo for a full eight hours, without so much as taking a single break. Only once she saw the entirety of her life packed into countless carboard boxes did she realize how much one person could accumulate over the years.

"Thank you, Walter, just give me a second!"

Rifling through her overstuffed purse for the wallet buried at the bottom, Jess searched for cash to tip the crew.

Shit, only twenty bucks.

Four men stood, dripping in sweat, in her now empty living room. Three, gigantic moving pods loaded outside, ready to be loaded onto a flatbed truck and head west for sunny California. Desperate to gift the men something for their hard-earned laborious day, Jess ran into the kitchen and surveyed the contents of her refrigerator. Four bottles of champagne from last night's debauchery remained.

This'll have to do.

With four bottles of champagne in tow, Jess joined the men in her living room, feeling the wood creek beneath her bare feet.

Memories suddenly flowed through her, as she recounted the first time she fell in love with this place. It was next to Raquel, where she stood on these very same hand-scraped floorboards that she fell in love the magic of new beginnings.

"Thank you all so much!" she exclaimed to Walter and his crew, handing each a bottle of Veuve Clicquot. In the absence of cash, it was the next best thing she could offer in appreciation for their day of grueling work.

Their blank expressions suggested the offer wasn't what they had hoped for.

"Err, sorry ma'am," one man said, staring down by his feet. "I don't drink. Do you have anything else?"

With her whole place packed and loaded, it was either these bottles of champagne or the lone $20 bill in her wallet. Somehow the idea of suggesting they split twenty bucks four ways made her feel even worse than handing champagne a man who didn't drink.

I should've planned this better.

"I'm so sorry guys. If you're good to hang here, I'd be happy to run to the ATM. I could be there and back in ten minutes, tops." As her eyes scanned the men, Walter stepped forward.

"Yo guys, this lovely lady is trying to give us a nice gift. Just give it to your wives. I bet this fancy stuff gets us all some nice brownie points. Okay?"

She smiled. *Thank you,* she mouthed.

The men tucked their respective bottles under their arm and were gone before she could thank them again. As she closed the door behind them, she took in how empty the condo had become. All the furniture - from the four-post bed to the beautifully impractical white sofa – were all gone. Every family photo, every knick knack from her travels, all wrapped and sealed in boxes.

The warm afternoon sun flooded through the windows as she took one last walk around.

This place was all mine. The very first home that I chose for myself, by myself. I bought it. I decorated it. Every single tile, every shade of paint, even the perfect shade of white grout. That was all by me, for me.

Unlike the homes she grew up in, or the one she shared with Chris, this place felt like hers. It felt like home. When she found it, she was lost in every sense of the word. Lost within herself, lost with her place in the world. And now? Now she felt like an entirely different woman. Confident, comfortable, and content.

Thank you, she said aloud as if the walls could somehow hear her. *Thank you for being my haven. For showing me what it means to have a clean slate and a fresh start. Thank you for bringing me hope and letting me discover self-love.*

Tears slowly trickled down her cheeks. She bought this condo because she needed somewhere to live. But as it turns out, this house gave her a gift more precious than she ever expected. For the first time in her entire life, she finally stopped dreaming about tomorrow and began living for today. The home provided a haven to embrace the hard times and appreciate the joy. It's where she learned to live alone. To be alone.

And now, with all of her belongings packed and an Uber on the way, Jess felt more ready than ever. As she flipped the lights off, her phone beeped from her back pocket.

You ready, baby? You take off in three hours! I can't wait to see you!! You better be on your way to the airport. I love you so much!

Meeting Kyle was like running into your best friend while

waiting in line to see an encore presentation of your favorite movie. No matter how many times you repeatedly watched the same scenes, with the same cast, it somehow felt as magical as the first time. From their very first call, to their first visit, his presence had a way of wafting peace over her, a feeling which only intensified the more time they spent together.

As she stood at the doorway, smiling at his text, she pulled out the note from her pocket. Neatly folded, the paper turned from yellow to beige over the years, but the words were clearer than ever.

'A Promise to Myself,' in Dr. Green's distinct cursive handwriting. She imagined his familiar voice telling her, 'Well, Jess? What are you waiting for? Take the risk or lose the chance!' She neatly placed the note back in her pocket and locked the door behind her.

As she walked out of her condo and embarked upon the next chapter of life, Jess realized that the biggest blessing, by a landslide, was having the ability to start again.

ABOUT THE AUTHOR

Jennifer Cohen is a coffee-drinking, exercise-loving author, wife, and mom. When she's not lost in a great novel, she's spending her days as a corporate marketing executive, helping craft strategies for businesses of all sizes. She studied Journalism and Strategic Media Relations at The Walter Cronkite School of Journalism at Arizona State University and began her career as a speech writer for General Norman Schwarzkopf and General Alexander Haig. Falling Forward was born during her own quest for self-love and acceptance and is her debut novel.